THE ZEN GAME

Also by Nancy Pristine

The Victory Dance:
Placing Yourself in the Winner's Circle in Sports and in Life (for adults)

Victory Dancing for Teens:
Smooth Moves for Getting to the Winner's Circle

THE ZEN GAME

HOW TO WIN AT THE GAME OF LIFE WITHOUT SELLING YOUR SOUL

NANCY PRISTINE

Illustrations by C.A. "Charlie" Aabø

HATHAWAY PRESS
Silver Spring, Maryland

The Zen Game: How to Win at the Game of Life Without Selling Your Soul copyright © 2011 by **Nancy Pristine.** All rights reserved. This book may not be copied or reproduced, in whole or in part, by any means, electronic, mechanical or otherwise without written permission from the publisher except by a reviewer who may quote brief passages in a review.

Interior design and typesetting by Manor Typesetting Services. www.ManorTypesetting.com

ISBN 978-1-45383-831-0

Visit the Author's Website
http://NancyPristine.com/

TO MY STEVEN
*forever, ever, and ever my husband,
soul mate, and very best friend*

♈

Ten percent of the proceeds of this book will be donated to
NAWS (National Animal Welfare Society of the U.S.)

Founded in 2007 in Mokena, Illinois, NAWS is a 501(C)3 nonprofit organization dedicated to ending euthanasia and suffering of companion animals. The NAWS team came together to take a different approach toward ending the enormous number of pets that are euthanized every day in our country due to a lack of good homes with responsible pet parents. The only way to end the problem is with *prevention*, which means we must:

- Spay/neuter all pets.
- Educate the public, especially children, about responsible pet care.
- Sponsor and support animal welfare legislation that regulates puppy mills and over breeding.

NAWS is also committed to caring for the pets that are already on this earth with us today. Through its Pet Rescue program, the organization is able to rescue homeless pets and help them to find loving, forever homes. In addition, NAWS recognizes that there are many pet parents that love their pet but simply cannot always afford to provide necessary veterinary care for them. To be sure that no pet needs to suffer because of the parent's financial situation, NAWS has created low-cost animal clinics and subsidized programs to allow pet parents the opportunity to provide proper veterinary care for their pets.

To learn more about NAWS, including ways you can help, please visit its website at www.NAWSUS.org.

~ *Acknowledgments* ~

Infinite heartfelt thanks to all the people who helped and supported me in the writing of this book. I would like to acknowledge and give loving appreciation to the following people:

Bill Cole, MS, MA, an internationally and nationally recognized authority on peak performance and coaching. He is founder and CEO of Procoach Systems, a consulting firm that helps organizations and professionals achieve more success in life, sports, and business. Bill's most recent books are *The Mental Game of Golf* and *The Mental Game of Tennis*. For more information, go to www.MentalGameCoach.com.

C.A. "Charlie" Aabø, illustrator of *The Zen Game*. Charlie is an American-trained Norwegian cartoonist and illustrator. His work has appeared in various media, including children's books, comic books, theater posters, and advertisements. He also created, wrote, illustrated, and produced the comic book *JON PAY, P.I.*, sold both in Norway and in the U.S. To learn more about Charlie's work, go to www.cobb-city.com/aabo.

Jimmy Mack, a theta, reconnective, and matrix energetics certified practitioner. Visit his website at www.advancedthetapractitioner.com.

CONTENTS

Foreword		xiii
Introduction		1
Chapter 1	It's a Social Game	7
Chapter 2	Rules, Codes, and Traditions	25
Chapter 3	More Traditions, Habits, and Isms	43
Chapter 4	All I Want Is a Little Respect... and to Pay It Forward	55
Chapter 5	Dress Not to...Be Naked (Among Other Things)	79
Chapter 6	We Are Family	95
Chapter 7	Partnerships	113
Chapter 8	Sports and the Sport of Life	141
Chapter 9	Role Models and Superkids	169
Chapter 10	Breaking Old Molds	181
And in Conclusion...		193

FOREWORD

Respect self. Respect others. Respect life. *The Zen Game* embodies these elegant, simple, yet profound and timeless truths. *The Zen Game* seamlessly moves between the ageless, enduring thirty-thousand-foot view and granular, day-to-day advice and tips for living a magnificent life.

The Zen Game is enduring wisdom blended with modern, practical strategies and guidelines for living a wonderful, meaningful life, leaving the planet the better for your having been here.

Nancy Pristine is a modern-day sage, one who has infused wisdom from the ages with nuggets of contemporary gold on how to live life more fully and more beautifully, with excellence and in the right way.

She speaks to you as a good friend would—honestly, frankly, and with concern, humor, and perspective. Nancy shows us timeless, universal insights and modern methods so we can stop struggling and find the blissful zone, the source of flow that enables our full potential to come forth.

At the heart of Nancy's writings is a deep compassion and caring for others and a profound respect for humanity and the world at large. Indeed, she says, "Life is not a zero-sum game, where in order for one person to do well another must do badly. If *you* have peace and happiness and *I* have peace and happiness, then there is a greater chance for universal peace and happiness." This is indeed wisdom personified, for each of us to live out on a daily basis.

I call this book "the wise person's guide to living in the universe."

In sports vernacular, the Zen Game teaches us how to play the game of life to win, not to avoid losing. As Nancy phrases it, "I want to win, but winning does not own me. I also am unafraid of losing, thus losing does not haunt me." This is the championship mindset, the winner's mantra that takes champions and winners past any inner obstacles and all outer challenges, launching them into their powerful potential fulfilled. This is the zone. This is Zen.

Reading this book made me a better person. Reading this book changed my outlook and life practices. Reading this book will be a treat for you and yours. Enjoy it. Practice its tenets. Live a wonderful life. Play the Zen Game.

Bill Cole
CEO of Procoach Systems, international peak performance consultant for business, sports, and life

INTRODUCTION

We've all heard references to the "game of life." But have you ever stopped to think about whether life is, indeed, like a game? As a life-long athlete, I appreciate the ideas behind this analogy: Human beings *are* competitive, we do want to "win" in our personal and professional lives, and it is very satisfying to achieve our goals.

But I also recognize the limitations in this philosophy. After all, life is not about me winning and you losing, me scoring more points than you, or me being right and you being wrong. It is about each of us living to the best of our ability, reaching for success while still playing by the rules—the "universal truths"—that promote honesty, fairness, and justice for everyone we encounter. Yes, we want to win at the game of life—but we want to do so without having to sell our soul. This balanced approach to life is what I call the Zen Game.

The Zen Game is a mindset that will help you to empower yourself, lift your consciousness, and live in a more harmonious way with others. It is a way to "play" the game of life without the win-at-all-costs attitude that leaves us feeling dissatisfied and lacking peace of mind. As tempting as it may be to focus only on the "good of me," the reality is that we are all on the same team and must work together for the "good of all." The Zen Game perspective will help you to do just that, and in the process, it will transform your life in positive ways. You will get along better with other people. You will honor the rules, codes, and traditions of society. You will give and receive more respect. You will enhance your family relationships and partnerships.

In my own life, the Zen Game has been a powerful tool in helping me to give and be my best self. It helps me to see life as a journey rather than a struggle. In my former career as a tennis pro, I learned that I could influence the attitude and behavior of my tennis students through my *own* attitude and behavior. When clients saw that I was truly happy to be there and enthusiastic about my work, their response to me was like a mirror image. Today, when I give motivational lectures, the Zen Game mindset helps me to present myself in a confident and sincere way. There is nothing greater than giving a speech in a positive environment where you feel that you are among friends and everyone wants to learn and grow from the experience. With the Zen Game perspective, you automatically feel connected to others in a positive, compassionate, and thoughtful way.

The Zen Game will teach you how to deal with people and get along better with others, but the best part is that it will give you personal satisfaction. People who are personally satisfied with their lives are usually happy just for the sake of it and have more fun in life. They have that certain zest for life that so many of us wish we could find.

So how can you embrace the Zen Game mindset and make it a part of your day-to-day life? Your best guide to this process is the "Noble Eightfold Path," a set of principles established thousands of years ago in the teachings of Siddhartha Gautama (the Buddha). The Eightfold Path is the core doctrine of Buddhism. The Buddha proclaimed this path to be "The Middle Way"—a life in which we do our best at all times and show respect and goodwill toward others.

The Buddha used the symbol of a wheel with eight spokes to represent his philosophy of the Noble Eightfold Path. Remember that all the spokes of a wheel are necessary for it to keep turning. This is why we must follow all the steps of the Noble Eightfold Path—the route to self-awakening and liberation. The Buddha believed it was the way to nirvana.

Both the practice of Zen—in which a person seeks enlightenment through introspection—and the Noble Eightfold Path require you to live life with a "mindful awareness." You must be truly aware of how you are living your life and how your words and actions affect other people. Do you really see others and want them to be happy and successful? Are you playing by the rules of society to avoid friction and trouble and get along with all the people you interact with each day?

Mindful awareness is an important part of the Buddha's Noble Eightfold Path. Let's take a closer look at this path, which consists of eight "pillars." I have interpreted these pillars in twenty-first century language while staying true to the basic principles behind them:

> **1. Right View.** Show compassion, forgiveness, and goodwill toward your fellow man. This point of view will help you to

achieve mental, physical, and spiritual balance. You will feel happy for no reason except that you are in the flow of all living things.

2. Right Intention. Give and be your best self. As the law of magnetism and attraction says, "What you give out you get back." Choose to see good in everyone and in every aspect of your life.

3. Right Speech. Refrain from harsh words. When you speak to other people with respect and kindness, you will be trusted and bring out the best in them.

4. Right Action. Be the bigger person when it comes to arguments. Do the right thing in life even when it bruises your ego. It's not about who is right and who is wrong. Through Right Action, you develop discipline, personal responsibility, and self-empowerment.

5. Right Livelihood. Do not live your life in a way or do work that does harm to others. True happiness is not achieved when we compromise our values and ignore our moral compass.

6. Right Effort. Do not waste time on things that do harm to you or to others. Always put effort toward giving and being your best self. This will help others and bring happiness and peace of mind to you.

7. Right Mindfulness. Be aware of your thoughts, words, and actions because they have a direct effect on your reality. You reap what you sow. Be understanding of other people's lack of understanding. No one is better than anyone else just because he or she is farther along the personal path to enlightenment.

8. Right Concentration. Focus on one thing at a time to maintain a quiet, peaceful mind. Notice how life becomes less confusing. Also, detach from other people's egos. Stay attached to your purpose and good intentions.

It is largely through the application of these eight pillars that we can find Zen's "Center Path"—the Middle Way—where we operate for the highest good of all. This is the point of perfect peace, where you no longer speak in terms of winning or losing but rather of being freed from the shackles of either. The Center Path can be described as follows: "I want to win, but winning does not own me. I also am unafraid of losing, thus losing does not haunt me." It is when you stop pushing, pulling, and competing that you calm your energies, release your worries, and open your heart and enjoy the journey. You live life with contentment and a peaceful dignity that become contagious to everyone around you.

I'm sure many of you have applied some of these eight pillars in your life. But have you engaged all of them, and are you conscious of doing so consistently? Take it from me. It is in your highest and best interest to do so. It's like anything else in life: If you do it halfway, you will only get half the results.

Whether I am giving a speech or going to the grocery store, I consciously want to set the stage for a positive atmosphere and a good experience by remembering my Zen Game. Yes, there are times that I do not get back the same positive energy that I am putting out. But when this happens, I don't want to push against this negative energy or allow it to affect my emotions and ego. Instead, I leave the world alone and focus on myself. Giving and being my best self is the best way for me to strengthen humanity.

By aligning your good intention with that of other people, you begin to see others as you see yourself. You see the world through the eyes of the Buddha and want to extend goodwill and kindness to others because you are sensitive to their importance to humanity. After all, life is not a zero-sum game, where in order for one person to do well another must do badly. If *you* have peace and happiness and *I* have peace and happiness, then there is a greater chance for universal peace and happiness. That is how the game of life is won. And what could be greater than that?

1
IT'S A SOCIAL GAME

Socialization lies at the very core of human nature. Although we may treasure our moments of solitude, we continually draw inspiration from the world around us. There is social interaction in all elements of life—our work, relationships, sports, and any activity that fuels our passion. The quality of these social interactions—and thus of our overall lives—can be greatly influenced by the Zen Game perspective. When we operate with this mindset, we seek to harness the power within to change ourselves and to embrace the world around us in a new and open way. Nowhere, in fact, is the Zen Game perspective more relevant than in how we deal with others.

When we care too much about "winning" in our interactions with others, we are focused on the destination, not on the journey, and even less on the work it takes to get where we want to go. If we had to be honest with ourselves, we would admit that the journey is equally, if not more, important. The journey encompasses all the small aspects of daily life—the things we do to show and receive respect, the growth we experience as we reach for the prize, and the people we encounter or touch along the way. If we fall flat on our faces while trying to talk to that adorable surfer guy on the beach, things may seem messy. But if we gain something from the attempt—learn a lesson, perhaps, or pick up a little self-confidence just because we tried—then isn't that a worthy goal as well?

When we use our Zen Game perspective and cut through all the "winning" and the "getting," we can find wisdom in the eight pillars of Zen: Right View, Right Intention, Right Speech, Right Action, Right Livelihood, Right Effort, Right Mindfulness, and Right Concentration. In a nutshell, we must consider the following question in all of our social interactions: What is the right thing to do in this situation? This is a very important question, one we must constantly ask ourselves—and one that we sometimes ignore, even unwittingly.

For example, when a goal begins to push the envelope of Right Intention—encroaching on the comfort and well-being of others—we are indeed treading on dangerous ground. Things can get mighty hairy. There's nothing worse than going to work, the gym, a restaurant, or a party and having the person next to you try to push his or her ego, attitude, beliefs, or agenda on you. Or how about when you are playing a game of tennis or basketball and see another player openly disrespect your opponent or team members so that the spotlight falls on him. That's when the "getting" part "gets" out of hand. But frequently, proper behavior—"Right" behavior—is an issue even when someone is not overtly trying to win or get something.

When we are around our fellow humans, the most relevant of the eight pillars of Zen are Right Intention and Right Action. The accepted mores of social interaction are passed on to us as children, and as we grow up, we either adopt these mores or reject them out of, perhaps, a sense of rebellion. How wonderful it would be if we could all go back to those basic teachings and relearn how to love ourselves and others through the tiniest of responsible deeds.

Let's consider some specific areas of social interaction, keeping in mind the Zen Game perspective and our desire to do Right by others.

COURTESY: They say that the right to swing your arm ends when it hits another person's nose. Nothing could be truer. Courtesy represents the limits we put on the swing of our arm, but it is also the thought we put into how to be kind to our fellow man.

The last time I checked, "please" and "thank you" were still part of the English language, and it never hurts to use them. Being courteous is always a good way to score points in any social situation. Opening the door for another person, helping someone cross the street, acknowledging a stranger with a smile or a "good morning" as you pass him in the hall—these and other acts of kindness will (and should) never go out of style. If they ever do, we should probably just pack up and move to an isolated island.

Consider dating. When you first go out with a person, courtesy is usually the order of the day. Regardless of gender, most people are on their very best behavior. For the most courteous among us, this deportment remains forever. But for others, it slowly disappears over time.

I believe that "first date" manners should be in place in all social situations. It doesn't matter if you're with someone toward whom you have no romantic inclinations. It's all about that attitude of performing at your most chivalrous. Also, I believe in equality and think it is good form for women to extend themselves in a chivalrous manner toward men as well. For example, if I am the first out of a taxicab, I offer a helping hand to my husband or whoever comes out of the car after me. Wordlessly, I make it known that each of us is looking out for the other, and this attitude sets the tone for the entire evening.

Here's another wonderful tidbit I've picked up: If you are out to dinner with someone who is nice to you but rude to the waiter, he or she is a rude person, period. Truly nice people are nice to everyone, while those who are trying to "get" something will be nice only to the people they want to impress. We should all try to impress *everyone* with our manners, all the time. I have found that the person serving me dinner at a restaurant may be one of the attendees at my motivational speech the next day. Imagine the embarrassment I'd feel if I had made an egomaniac fool of myself at the restaurant by completely disregarding the staff. Kindness never goes unpaid. I'm sure you've heard the old saying, "It's nice to be important, but more important to be nice!"

There is also the issue of that "swinging arm" I mentioned earlier. Consider the people who are not disabled but pull into a handicapped parking space "just for a minute." Or the people who sport a handicap sticker on their car when they're really healthier than a horse. It is a strange logic that would drive people to such lengths. The Darwin Awards, which are presented tongue in cheek to people who make the news by doing extremely stupid things, are perfect examples of the fallibility of the human mind at crucial moments. Stupid things happen and they happen often. Therefore, acts of selfishness often rule the day and to some are even a source of pride. I am suddenly reminded of my friend whose overweight aunt was allowed to go to the front of the line with her kids at an amusement park because she told the attendant she was pregnant. These actions are minor and, after the fact, deserve a good old-fashioned laugh. But as my father always says, "Why look for trouble?"

Here are just three examples of situations in which common courtesy can make a big difference—for you and those around you:

Respecting your environment. Lord Baden-Powell, the wonderful man who started the Boy Scouts (and Girl Scouts too, believe it or not), always said, "Leave your campsite better than you found it." It was a metaphor. He meant that we should leave every place we go in this life better than the way we found it.

How many times have you been to a public park or a place specifically marked "scenic view" and found that the beauty of Mother Nature was overshadowed by a litter of empty beer or soda cans, fast-food wrappers, and assorted garbage? Often, when my husband Steven and I go to these places, we not only clean up after ourselves but also clean up as much as we can in general and leave the place in better shape. I think it's something we should all get into the habit of doing every day.

There used to be a public service commercial, one of the first about pollution, which had a jingle that went, "We've got to pitch in to clean up America." The song was kind of corny, but sometimes I wish they would revive it.

We're not as bad today as we were when I was a child. Back then, some people—and I'm talking about adults, not kids—would actually dump trash out of their car windows as they sped along the highway. That's indefensible, and it's mind-boggling that they had to develop an entire ad campaign to get people to wise up to this issue. Even today, we could use a little cleaning up.

When you go to a fast-food restaurant, bus your own table. Sure, they may have staff to do it, but most of these places cannot afford to have a bunch of "minute men and women" to clean up the second you rise from the table. Do it yourself so that the place looks as nice as you found it and the next party won't have to wait for a clean table. If you use a public bathroom, act similarly. Treat it the way you would your own bathroom. Tidy up.

Also, particularly in fast-food restaurants, don't be a taker. Taking excessive numbers of napkins and packets of salt and ketchup for home is a no-no. I try to be practical when I use these freebies. I know they cost someone money, so if I take more than I end up needing, I put them back. It's such a waste to take more than you know you will use and then throw them out. I suppose if people had to pay for such items, they would be more conscious of not being wasteful. And if one day they do start charging for these things, I suppose it will be our own fault. It seems that everything is becoming à la carte these days. (This same kind of pilfering also happens at work when people take home office supplies such as Post-its, pens, and paper. You know who you are, and it's time to shed this naughty habit. Enough said.)

A final note about the environment: I like the idea that it has become chic in New York City to use your own tote bag when picking up dinner or a few groceries after work. I'm sure it saves the establishments lots of money, but more importantly it saves a lot of trees. I also think it is a step in the right direction that grocery stores are paying customers one cent for every plastic bag they bring back to the store.

Using cell phones. Don't get me started. They're great for emergencies and short, quiet conversations in appropriate places, but describing everything you see as you walk down the street is not an emergency. People with Bluetooth or cell phones pressed up against their ears all the time are not living in the moment. Wherever they are physically, they are somewhere else mentally. What's the point of that? None, I say, especially if it makes you more prone to stepping on toes, elbowing little old ladies who get in your way, drowning out other people's conversations within a quarter-mile radius, cutting off other cars in traffic, and in general being a nuisance to others.

Using baby carriages. Children are wonderful. Who can argue with that? But have you ever been slammed in the shin by another person's baby carriage and not received an apology? I won't rant here, but having a child does not exempt anyone from all the courtesies a person should exercise when interacting with others. The nicest parents I know are the ones who realize that having a young child around means having to be *twice* as courteous to others, not morphing from Dr. Jekyll into Mr. Hyde.

POLITICS AND RELIGION: A piece of advice given to me was, "Never discuss politics or religion." It's unfortunate, but it is often true that these topics are too sensitive for social situations. Although conversations about religion or politics can be some of the most thought-provoking in the world, few people have reached a high enough "Zen state" to accept constructive, insightful opinions that challenge their own. Religion is an issue of faith, and faith is defined as belief in that which cannot be completely proven. Here's a typical "debate" on this topic:

"My religion says that if I fulfill my purpose here on earth and have loved and served my fellow man properly, I will go on to better things when I die."

Immediately someone will riposte back to me, "Well, how do you know for sure? Have you ever been to 'heaven'? Have you ever met any flesh-and-blood person who has died, gone to heaven, or been reincarnated and come back later to tell you all about it?"

"No, but I have *faith*."

It can go on and on and on, each side trying to one-up the other—without resolution.

In the end, we either fume at each other or play it safe and delve into a different category of discourse altogether. Some people also take politics and certain political issues—such as abortion and guns—as immovable articles of faith. So it's best to stay away from such arguments. It's why they call them *hot-button* issues.

I know a staunch political conservative who is good friends with an ex-hippie who protested and was arrested countless times in the 1960s. The ultimate odd couple. They share coffee and a sandwich and have wonderful, rollicking, intellectual discussions about politics. They agree on nothing, but they cherish each other's company and perspective. These are people with probing minds, intellectual curiosity. They each possess a "faith," but that faith can stand up to scrutiny. I would suppose this is the true definition of faith, for who else gets all red in the face and angry but someone whose faith has been tested and found wanting? Open-minded faith, as well as beliefs that are open to intelligent questioning, is the essence of the Buddha's Center Path. My beliefs may be in flux and I may be searching for answers. Or, my faith is so strong that nothing you say can move it, and so *I am at peace and can intellectualize it, rather than emotionalize it.*

I would caution people not to begin a discussion on any hot-button issue with a total stranger. And, certainly, if such an issue comes up organically and the person becomes strident and angry, I would move quickly to change the subject. The truth is, as much as I hate to judge, I do not consider it a virtue when people cannot hold their anger on such topics. When I meet such people and find this to be the case, I end up avoiding them in general, and that speaks volumes.

I usually advise people not to proselytize. If your belief system requires you to do so, realize that this may turn some people off. It also may cause their ears to crumble and turn to ashes—which, in turn, can instill an impatient streak. Accept this potential response as the price to pay for such a philosophy.

Lighten up! Learn to be more tolerant of others' opinions. It is a wonderful thing when people who are willing to listen and learn can discuss these deeply probing topics less intensely. Always remember to cool it before you lose it, and if you encounter others who cannot take the heat, be sure to steer away from the fire.

PROFILING: I pray for the day when all the "isms" of the world are dead and buried, as long gone as corsets for women. But it seems that they merely change with the seasons. Historically, we have always had ethnic, racial, religious, or other groups defined by some sort of distinction. Such groups would be lumped together and treated badly by the majority. The new, trendy word used to describe this prejudgment is "profiling."

My motto: Take people as individuals, not as negative profiles. Be nice to everyone and hope for the same in return. When you attend any social event, open your mind and your heart to any new person you have the opportunity to meet. You may as well be in a straitjacket if you are going to walk around being cautious of everyone you meet, especially if he or she is different from you. When you open your heart and mind, you may be surprised to find you've made a wonderful new friend.

GOSSIP: Anyone who gossips *with* you will gossip *about* you. How does *that* make you feel? Gossip, after all, only exists on a two-way street.

So what qualifies as gossip? Tales that put someone who is not present in a bad light. Even if the stories turn out to be true, it is poor form to run around spreading them. Gossiping is no different from walking up to a person and kicking him or her. In fact, the kicking would be more honest. Ouch!

Bad things happen to all of us. If you lost the job of your dreams, would you want someone running around telling everyone, cackling at your despair? I say one thing: Karma is everywhere, and that which we plant will someday be harvested.

ALCOHOLIC BEVERAGES: They call alcohol a social lubricant and, in fact, it is. I once read a wine slogan that went something like, "The world is fine as seen through wine." Some people find that alcohol calms the nerves, allowing them to socialize more comfortably. And many nice leisure venues have a bar area where people can sit, chat with old friends, or make new ones and imbibe…something stiff and strong.

The issue here is one of volume. If we drink a bit too much, the telling redness on our faces may not be due entirely to the alcohol but also to pure embarrassment. Shena, the CEO's assistant, may not appreciate the comment that her new haircut makes her look just like the singer Prince. And a potential investor's face may become tinged with rage at your enthusiastic, "Hey Fred, look at that belly! So when's the baby due?" Indeed, the ancient

Romans said, "In wine, there is truth" (*in vino veritas*). And we all know what can happen when we're *too* truthful in a social situation.

Holding off on those five margaritas—and avoiding a state of full inebriation in favor of a manageable drink or two—can do a lot to save your behind, your job, and your social standing. If you're careful enough, people will still like you at the end of the party. Plus the dreaded day-after hangover won't be pounding on your door—or your muddy head—just before that important meeting or appointment. After all, people have all sorts of expectations of us. If we're three sheets to the wind when we need to be most clearheaded, there is no way we can play the game of life well. This is a surefire way to lose friends and allies—and infuriate enemies.

For those who choose not to drink at all, another kind of moderation may be needed—moderating one's judgmentalism. Those on a personal crusade to rid the world of ole devil alcohol are similar in ambition to the Food Fascists—the folks who feel they have discovered the world's secret to good nutrition and won't be satisfied until they have spread their new religion to everyone doomed to share a meal with them.

While it may be "right" to suggest to an obviously drunken associate that he or she should not drive home alone, to tell everyone hoisting a drink that they are doing a terrible, terrible thing is, well, inviting them to make us gag on our tirade. So perhaps the Middle Path is truly the safest route for everyone, no matter what side of the fence you happen to be on.

RESERVATIONS: Have you tried to make a restaurant reservation lately and had the maître d' ask you for a credit card number? These poor people have been burned too many times! Many people feel they have every right in the world to make a reservation—at restaurants, symposiums, RSVPs for parties, or function rooms—and then either forget about it or else change plans and book somewhere else without canceling the first reservation.

All it takes to avoid this problem is to employ Right Action. If you can't make your reserved time or have found alternate accommodations more to your liking, call and cancel. I've had parties where I was expecting seventy-five people and only fifty showed up, and I've had parties where I was expecting fifty people and seventy-five showed up. It's interesting to hear the wild, way-out excuses offered up the next time you run into people who said they were going to come but didn't. It will not ruin the event if you are unable to attend, and Martian rocks will not fall on your head if you pick up the phone to cancel. Someone else will be happy to have your share of food and wine, or the host may be glad to save a few pennies on the cost.

Either way, it's only fair to be grateful enough for the invitation to let the person know if you cannot attend. If, on the other hand, you want to bring grandma, your godchildren, the family dog, and fourteen cousins along, that would also demand a phone call to the host long before you show up with the posse. If the host knows that the people they have invited are bringing friends with them, they may even choose to have the party outside where there is more room. Also, be mindful of other people's dogs and kids. I've had parties where everyone is feeding my dogs the hors d'oeuvres. Of course, after everyone leaves I am left to clean up the mess from my angels' upset stomachs.

DISCRETION IN PUBLIC PLACES: Public demonstrations of affection are fine when they are limited to handholding, a friendly embrace, or a little kiss on the cheek or lips. But beyond that, whoa! Nobody likes to see Tarzan and Jane going at it jungle-style in public. There's a time and place for everything. You're making others around you uncomfortable—or perhaps *too* comfortable in a few cases. It's a distraction the world is not waiting for, trust me.

FLIRTING: What is it about the flirting game that makes the hormones rage? Put men and women together in a vibrant, engaging atmosphere, and the most outrageous behavior can erupt.

If you're single, yes, a club, an entertainment venue, or a gym can be a great place to meet new people who may become dating material. But don't let discretion fly away in the winds of passion. And for heaven's sake, it is not really a great idea to come on so strong that you drive people away screaming for the management or the police. Read the signals and take it slowly. Don't confuse "do not enter" with "full speed ahead."

Now if you're *not* single…sometimes it's tough in this world to be a friendly, demonstrative person and not be thought of as a flirt. I've found that the best strategy is to give equal attention (the *right* kind, of course) to both men and women. If I meet a couple who are friends of mine, I will douse both with an affectionate hug and greeting, not just the male. But no matter what, I try to always check the signals I am giving out so that no one takes me the wrong way. The same concept applies if you are single and spending time at a club or any public place with a married person. Be yourself—demonstrative or not—but make sure you are not being misinterpreted. If you think things are going down a bad path, abort, abort, abort! Be of Right Intention or some jealous spouse, justified or not, may be knocking down your door holding a bazooka.

BREAKING THE ICE: Back in the day, when I was playing on the women's tennis circuit, I used to travel a lot for tournaments. I would usually find some familiar faces, but sometimes I would be surrounded by strangers. From that experience, I know that being in a new place with new people can be as scary and uncomfortable as we choose to make it. If I enter a new environment and trip over a chair, for example, I can either crack a swift joke or break out a curse and a frown.

People perceive us as we present ourselves. Furthermore, everyone we see around us is a normal person with normal needs and wants. Superheroes are the stuff of fantasy, not reality, so it won't do to put others on a pedestal and pull ourselves into the surrounding pit. There is a well-known saying that a stranger is merely a friend we haven't met yet. He or she is certainly not a deity fallen from Mt. Olympus! If I say "hello" and flash a sincere smile at someone I am sharing an elevator with, standing next to in line, or almost bump into as I round a corner in a building, it lightens the mood for myself and the person with whom I've just made a connection.

No one can make us confident but ourselves. Often, the way to create confidence is to take charge of the space we are occupying and make it a pleasant place to be, where we can do and be our best. A smile or an upbeat, ice-breaking comment allows us to make ourselves comfortable. *When we are comfortable, we are confident. And when we are confident, we are winners.*

Many people have a fear of approaching strangers. I'm amazed that some people end up limiting the number of friendships they have simply because of this fear. If you are afraid to approach a person cold, consider using an intermediary—perhaps a mutual friend—whenever possible. And though I may seem to be stating the obvious, it makes sense to approach people when they seem most likely to be receptive. Try not to interrupt someone who appears to be engrossed in another conversation or doing something that requires a lot of concentration.

Now what do you do if you get the brush-off? Simple…you smile and show your grace and class.

It is interesting to note that people who are nice and are comfortable in their own skin not only can approach strangers with ease, but also are nice and comfortable when receiving the attention of strangers. I will repeat this idea throughout the book, but *confidence comes from within*. It may take some playacting to jump-start your inner confidence (also known as faking it), but once you've done it a few times, it should begin to take hold of your soul.

Incidentally, I recall when I was a young girl being on vacation and having a handsome older gentleman begin a brief but amicable conversation with me. He appeared to have no agenda—it was pure sociable neighborliness, and his smile made me feel good about our encounter. Other than the pleasant feeling it gave me, I thought no more about it until someone came up to me and asked, "Do you know who that guy was who was talking to you?"

"No," I replied.

"Ralph Lauren."

Here was a famous, successful man—a celebrity. I was just a young adult. It's obvious that Ralph Lauren is a man who is comfortable in his own skin. He's the sort of person who is nice to everyone, regardless of their station in life. That's what a Zen-like approach to life can give you. When you are trying to meet a new person, the Middle Path is to want to meet them but not have it become a goal you *must* attain. If they are not interested, then it was not meant to be and perhaps is for the best.

MIND YOUR OWN BUSINESS: People who are determined to know other people's private business often flabbergast me. I find these intrusions to be rude and very disrespectful. Many years ago in Maryland, I heard a lady in a department store ask a complete stranger, "Did you get a face-lift? May I ask you who did it?" I pretty much wanted the floor to swallow me whole. Good thing it wasn't me or my mother who was the victim of such rudeness, or I would have had some serious issues! I don't remember the other woman's response, but I do remember telling my mother about it and she was just as aghast as I was.

I like Cher's riposte to questions about plastic surgery. She said, "If I want to put my tits on my back it's nobody's business but my own!" It must be extremely frustrating for celebrities to be constantly bombarded with personal questions about their love lives and other private matters. It makes you wonder, when did the line in the sand get erased so that people think nothing of putting you on the spot with a question that is none of their business?

I have an aunt who has thick, beautiful hair. Complete strangers have come up to her and asked if it was her own hair or a wig. What if she were going through chemotherapy and wearing the wig because she had lost her hair? How embarrassing this encounter would be for both parties, and certainly an unnecessary embarrassment.

I have been asked, "Do you have kids?" I tell these curious people that I have three four-legged kids. Needless to say, this is not the answer they wanted to hear from me. Their next interrogating question is usually, "*Why don't you have kids?*"

Family and friends are also guilty of insatiable curiosity and gossiping. Just because you are related to someone does not mean you have any right to know his or her private business. If someone breaks up with his or her spouse and wants you to know the reason why, he or she will tell you whether you want to hear it or not. Don't go up and ask the person. Let this be your rule of thumb: If they want you to know, they will tell you!

Yes, there are certain types of questions you can ask of people you do not know. For example, if the person standing next to you in line is using crutches, I would not consider it out of place to ask how it happened. But if you can see he is uncomfortable in this situation, you can let him off the hook by telling him about how you broke your leg a few years earlier. Often, this is why we ask such questions, because we associate a situation with a similar experience we have had in the past. However, some people are not associating it with anything but their own perception. Too often, they think they are entitled to know everyone's business.

When we live with a Zen Game attitude, we choose not to give a knee-jerk response to such people and stoop to their level. Instead we apply Right Mindfulness and Right View and say something that will keep us centered and in control without giving away our power. An example: "What an odd thing to say…. Have a nice day!" Oh, and don't forget your sincere smile! Don't let people like this get the best of you, and have patience with them. That's where the smile comes in. Half of them really don't know any better, but somewhere along the line they were misguided into believing that this is acceptable behavior. As for the ones who do know better but do it anyway, bless their little hearts.

INTERROGATING OTHERS: People like to talk about themselves, and giving them the opportunity to do so is a great icebreaker. But everything is a matter of degree. Small talk—such as "What's your name? Are you from here? Oh, do you know so-and-so? She lives there too."—is all perfectly acceptable. As long as you're not jumping down the other person's throat when you ask these sorts of questions (always mind your physical space), you should be okay.

But sometimes we may go too far. Through my neuro-linguistic training, I have been coached to always watch for verbal and nonverbal signals in this area. If a person is giving tight-lipped, one-word answers, is very fidgety or is not looking in your direction, and appears to be preoccupied, it is fair to deduce that he or she is not interested in talking right then—or at least not about the topics at hand. If he appears evasive, as if he's looking for a door to rush out of, that's a definite sign too. This does not mean you should try even harder. Quite the opposite. Back off, go for a short stroll, and take the edge off.

What do you do if someone steps over the line and asks too many questions of you? The best you can hope for is that if you send out as many verbal and nonverbal signals as possible, the person will eventually get the hint. If you are asked a question you sincerely do not want to answer ("So, how much did you sell your house for last year?"), be dignified and caring, but also direct, with your feelings. "I'm sorry, I'm not comfortable sharing that information." A demure smile takes the edge off the confrontation. Hopefully, this will put an end to the interrogation. You could even crack a joke—"For more than you can imagine"—and wink. Then veer the conversation in another direction.

As this example suggests, you must use the etiquette inherent in your Zen Game when getting people to respect your boundaries. You have a right to your privacy. If that right is not respected, it is often because your desire for it is not understood by the other party. It is then your job to communicate your feelings, set boundaries, and stand by them. If you do so delicately and with aplomb, no one should get their feelings hurt.

A variation on this theme are the people who never ask *you* any questions. All they do is blather on about themselves. This is never good if you are trying to get to know someone, but it will probably help you decide that you may not wish to know him or her better after all. I know one gentleman who calls himself "spiritual" yet loves to rave about how good he is at cooking and reading people and other assorted things. He is invariably better than you at your own profession, and he has no qualms telling you about it. He'll spend an hour and a half talking about himself and never ask the question, "So tell me about you. How are you?" He obviously wants me to get to know *him*, but I have reached the point that I'm about as interested in deepening our acquaintance as I am in the craft of cross-stitching. (Not that there's anything wrong with cross-stitching; it's just not my thing.)

When I encounter this type of person, I don't want to walk away. I want to *run* away! In a perfect situation, you would make a pleasant introduction and then hope for a nice give-and-take. It's a lot like dancing—two people, both equal partners. If one person is hoofing up a storm and the other is standing still, it's ridiculous.

PEOPLE, NOT PROFESSIONS: Years ago, when I was teaching tennis in Palm Beach and would mention to new acquaintances that I was a tennis pro, they would get really excited. To some, it was a cool-sounding job. This interest may have led to a deeper discussion, and I felt the glare of positive attention on me. As long as such an experience stayed within reasonable boundaries, it was rather heady. On the other hand, some people were dismissive of me because of my profession. "Oh, she's just some jock. What does she know about anything?"

The fact is, I've had the privilege (and the misery) of meeting people of many, many professions, and I can tell you this: What they do for a living, who their parents are, where they went to school…mean nothing at all. Nothing. Some of the dumbest, dimmest people I have ever met have Ph.D.'s, and some of the sharpest, most perceptive, and intuitive people I have ever met are skilled laborers. Toss in any and all preconceptions you harbor about any profession, and I can probably say I've met the cliché as well as the exception: Caring funeral directors, rude and uncaring funeral directors. Inefficient government workers, highly efficient government workers. I find it amusing when people assume the person they are talking to is a genius because he or she is a doctor or an attorney.

Do not think you know a person simply because you know his or her profession. Yes, certain personality types and people of a certain level of education tend to be attracted to certain professions, but these generalities have multitudes of exceptions.

Open yourself up to what is right before your eyes. Take people as they come, not according to what is written on their business card.

MASS HYSTERIA: You're a nice, quiet, respectful sort, always mindful of others. You go out in public with another person and it's the same way—nice and civilized. You and your significant other go out with another couple and it's the same thing—you are properly behaved and comported.

But then you are invited out to celebrate Cynthia's birthday with twelve other people, and before you know it, you, Cynthia, and the assembled masses begin to look like the party scene in *Animal House*.

Is this cool? Well, if the party is at Cynthia's house, then it's her call to make. If you've rented a private room somewhere to whoop and holler, the same thing goes. But if you and your crew are in the middle of a restaurant where other people may be, oh, making a wedding proposal, consoling one another after a funeral, or simply having a nice, quiet evening, then you need to take a sedative. No, not an actual pill—a mental "chill pill."

Learn how to "feel the room." Some places you enter will already be as bubbly as the crater of a volcano on eruption day. If so, feel free to add to the ruckus. If, on the other hand, a string quartet is playing softly in the corner and people are asking one another to pass the Grey Poupon, this is not the time for slam dancing.

Being in crowds often leads to groupthink, and if that groupthink is out of line simply due to the power of large numbers, bad behavior can ensue. We are not exempt from being of Right Mindfulness just because we are in a group. This is never an excuse for inappropriate behavior. Our responsibility to those who surround us remains the same. Yes, it may dampen spirits a bit if you're the "wet blanket" who has to bear this in mind, but you will have every right to feel good about yourself when you do so.

2
RULES, CODES, AND TRADITIONS

Much of how we get along with others in the world is made simple by the rules of society. Rules are the directives we agree upon and codify to govern our behavior. At the most basic level, we have notions such as the Ten Commandments, which can be further simplified as "Do not kill, do not hurt others, do not steal, do not lie, and do not envy." But as a society, we can't leave things as simple as that, can we? Have you ever seen a copy of the Federal Tax Code? We *live* to make new rules, new laws, and new codes of behavior. Furthermore, these types of documents are merely that which is written. What about the rules and behavioral codes that are only stated and inferred? And then there are the "traditions" that tell us how to behave as well.

Every new activity we begin includes a whole new set of rules to learn. The same goes for any new environment we enter—a new club or organization, a new workplace…heck, even just meeting a new flame and beginning a relationship. No sooner do we enter a new situation than we are confronted with, "We do things *this* way here, don't you know?"

So what are we to think of the countless rules, codes, and traditions that we encounter in our personal and professionals lives? I believe that people who take the time to learn rules and follow them are showing Right View, Right Intention, Right Effort, and especially Right Action. Through Right Action, you are setting an example that will be respected by others and will help make the world more civilized. Most rules are based upon good sense and innate fairness to all. They may evolve over time as new conditions arise and society and technology progress, but courtesy and being a good world citizen will always be at the foundation of all good rules.

I'll never forget the trenchant comment made by fellow Ohio State athlete and Olympic Gold Medalist Jesse Owens in the documentary *The Jesse Owens Story*: "…Live by the rules of the game and by the rules of society; otherwise you don't have a good game and you don't have a good society." Jesse Owens lived his life with Zen Game and was an inspiration to the many people he touched both on and off the track.

In most situations, it is incumbent upon us to learn new rules, regulations, secret handshakes, and age-old traditions. Choosing not to do so may make us merely "colorful" in some cases—consider the person who orders pancakes for dinner and veal parmesan for breakfast. More often than not, though, adhering to reasonable protocol is, well, *reasonable*. We may not fully agree with a rule—what if I'd really *like* to wear white after Labor Day?—but if no one is hurt, then "going along to get along" isn't the world's worst idea, especially if it means we'll be surrounded by peace and harmony.

In the sports world, only a rank amateur would ever suggest violating the sanctity of the rules when playing a game competitively. Rules are the thread that holds a game together. They are like a universal language that binds us all in brotherhood and sisterhood. The same goes for society at large and the groups that inhabit it. All of life is a game bound by rules.

And yet, without necessarily suggesting that we reinvent the game, people often ask us to "bend" the rules, codes, and traditions for one reason or another. Often, it is to give them some sort of perceived or real advantage. This is wrong. In golf, players have handicaps that help "level the playing field" and allow competitors of varying skill levels to play together amicably. A golf handicap is something official and orderly. But if someone were to show up with a bazooka to shoot the ball from the tee box or a laser-guided ball to lead into the hole off the putting green, I'd say this violation of the rules would be too outlandish for anyone to find reasonable.

Let's consider some areas where rules, codes, and traditions can help guide our behavior, allowing us to better experience harmony with our fellow human beings.

FOLLOWING CODES AND TRADITIONS: Codes and traditions govern our conduct in specific situations, just as rules do. But they usually are not as accessible or readily available as rules. Codes are also more prone to vary from situation to situation, while rules are more akin to laws and therefore tend to remain the same no matter where you go. Some codes are completely unwritten, and certainly traditions are rarely written down anywhere, unless you look for a specialized book to accompany an official rule book (presuming a vocation or avocation has a rule book at all).

In business, the phrase "corporate culture" encompasses the unwritten traditions a company has adopted over time. Sometimes they are a little silly—"Casual Friday" comes to mind. If you took a job with a new firm and showed up on Friday in a suit and tie while everyone else paraded around in shorts and Hawaiian shirts, you might be the butt of some good-natured office humor, but no harm would be done. On the other hand, you would have learned a new corporate tradition for this place of employment, and I would bet that on the following Friday, you would ditch the suit for something more relaxed.

Listen. Ask questions. Yes, find books that accompany the official rule book for an activity and read them (employers often create "employee handbooks" for this very reason). All of these things will up your game.

Do you *have* to do this? In some cases, no. But if you want to be a winner at the game of life, it's a good idea. But also understand what I mean by "winning." It is not simply about having a competition where there is a winner and a loser. Wearing the right attire on Casual Friday makes you a winner, in a sense, but there are no losers. In this example, winning means fitting in and showing respect for and allegiance to a tradition. In doing so, you feel confident and become part of something larger than yourself.

A friend of mine in college was pre-med. Every day during his senior year, he would wear a shirt and tie to class. Not only did he look good to all the girls on campus, but he also made a statement to his teachers, the other pre-med students, and the people who would be interviewing him about who he was—not just a BMOC (Big Man on Campus) but a soon-to-be doctor.

Earlier I mentioned the phrase "going along to get along," and I know that this saying has been turned on its ear over the years to be derogatory rather than positive. I want to recapture it here and put it in a different light. Following codes and traditions that are, at their heart, good is a show of respect. Demonstrating respect for a game or an occupation also shows respect for the other people who are part of that culture. If I bring you to my home and all you do is complain about the rules, codes, and traditions that my family lives by, you are, whether you know it or not, insulting *me*, and that's not nice.

OLD DOGS, NEW TRICKS: Abiding by codes and traditions is what makes you a pleasant person to be with and not a general pain in the behind. And yes, even if you have done something in your own free-spirited, unconventional way all of your life, if you have been noticing some blowback from people who do not always appreciate your irreverence, it may be time to learn the proper rules and protocols and put them into practice. After all, a little polish never hurts. On the contrary, it may get you some perks.

When someone invites you to his or her house for dinner, there may not be an official rule stating that you should bring along a small gift, such as a bottle of wine or dessert. But it is a nice thing to do, and most books on etiquette would suggest it. No one will look down on you if you *do* bring a gift, but if, on the other hand, you *fail* to adhere to this tradition, you could earn yourself a poor reputation. At the very least, you'd be dubbed a leeching cheapskate. Keep it up, and you may even manage to get yourself off some guest lists in due time.

Everyone is given a mulligan for being a scatterbrain now and then, but to carry the reputation of "the ungracious houseguest" or "the woman who would forget her head if it wasn't attached to her neck" is not a good thing. People will avoid making plans with you, and their attitudes toward you will carry over into other areas of interpersonal relationships. "Why should we invite her to lunch? She'll probably forget her wallet and lock her keys in the car!"

Again, learning codes and traditions will make you more confident and comfortable in a more formal and competitive setting. The same goes for most aspects of life. If you and your best buddy run a mom-and-pop business, both of you may be free-spirited nonconformists. But if you sell your company to a big corporation, you may feel like the "flaky guys" if you don't bother to learn proper decorum and other aspects of your new employer's corporate culture. If you want to test this, try going to the pre-sale business meeting sporting a funny hat, a chest-long scraggly beard, a massive mustache, and dark sunglasses. Unless you happen to be one of the original ZZ Top musicians in all your uniqueness, I'd say the deal will be off in no time.

BEING A GUEST: There are some classic questions about who should pick up the check when people go out to dinner together. The answers often are simpler than we make them out to be.

If you are friends and one party has called the other and suggested going out on the town, there is no concrete rule as to who should pay. More often than not, the bill is split or, if the relationship is ongoing, the responsibility is traded off. But questions often arise when one couple orders an expensive bottle of wine and the other couple does not drink any of it. It could be argued that the other couple ordered lobster or chateaubriand, which normally cost much more than other entrées. As a general rule, however, when you order an expensive entrée or one of the more expensive wines on the menu, make sure you give more money to cover the extra cost if you are splitting the tab. If someone else is paying for the dinner, I would refrain from ordering the most expensive items on the menu. You don't necessarily have to opt for the cheapest meal or go overboard by splitting an entrée with someone just to save a few dollars. The simplest thing to remember is to have some discretion and common sense, as well as respect for your dinner buddies.

In business situations, there generally should be no need to wrestle over the check. If you have invited a client to lunch, it is presumed that you are paying. The classy thing is still for the client to make a gesture toward paying, but that gesture should be declined. Now, you might wonder why, if the client knows his offer is going to be declined, he should make it in the first place. The offer is important because it establishes that the client has no obligation to do business with the host simply because he received a free meal. The offer and declination establish this independence. The same idea applies to all the would-be Casanovas out there on the dating scene, particularly first dates. In this case, the woman may be *more* inclined to insist on paying for her half of the meal so that it is *really* clear there will be no automatic quid pro quo later in the evening.

When you accept an invitation to be someone's guest at an event or a private club, always take along money and always offer to pay for anything and everything that you personally receive. However, you should expect that your offer to pay will be kindly refused. At that point, show your sincere appreciation and put your wallet back where you found it.

In this situation, all the players in the drama should know their roles and their lines. There should be no wrestling over the check. If you don't offer to pay, perhaps your wish is to rival Scrooge for stinginess and presumptuousness. If you are the host and you accept a guest's offers to pay, you are being cheap. He or she is your guest. If you invited someone to your home for dinner, you wouldn't charge him or her, would you? Of course not.

GUEST PRIVILEGES: If you are invited to a private club or function, you should anticipate being extended most of the privileges granted to regular members, unless it is not the club's policy to do so. The note here, really, is to the host more than the guest. Magnanimity is a long and thorough chore. I've seen people who think they've done others a great favor by inviting them to their club. Once there, they make no effort to pay the guest fees or give their guests direction as to where things are and what to do when they arrive. They are oblivious and so into themselves that they forget they are responsible for their friends. Meanwhile, the friends feel only discomfort, and any benefits they may have anticipated disappear. The friends have a lousy time.

Being a good host does not mean treating your guests like babies, but neither can you ignore their needs. Remember, you are also your guests' advocate if they run into any problems. If there are "upgraded services" that you yourself indulge in (a snack, some refreshments, a caddy, etc.) understand that, as host, you should offer the same amenities to your guests and pay for them. Guests, again, should offer to pay, but a gallant host will refuse the offer.

I've seen some private clubs where members have different locker facilities than guests. If so, you, as the host, should be the one to explain this to your guests, not some locker room attendant. Also, remember that in addition to the rules, codes, and traditions of the game (or *any* "game") there are the ones unique to the facility itself. Your guests shouldn't be expected to know these in advance—it's your club, not theirs. *You* should know them and guide your guests so that they can fit in.

DON'T INSULT THE HOST: Okay, so this one probably sounds like a no-brainer, right? But if that's the case, why do I still see and hear it so often that it flabbergasts me? Some people's common sense, it seems, is neither common nor sensible.

Someone invites you to a party. You find something amiss—maybe the food spread is a little meager or the creamy guacamole is starting to turn brown. Do you really think that the host's or hostess's intention was to serve you unappetizing food and show you a bad time? Of course not!

Remember that all hosts care, even if it sometimes seems they do not. If you have a negative comment to make, save it for the conversation on the way home and out of earshot. Even a person's best efforts may not always meet with your personal standards, but that is no reason to hurt their feelings when they have extended themselves on your behalf.

QUID PRO QUO: Accept an invitation; return an invitation, particularly if you had a nice time. The key here is the part about having a nice time. If someone tries to show you a good time and it is a disaster, you'll have to think through all the specifics of the case. The dating scene immediately comes to mind again. If you go on a date and feel as much romantic attraction as you would for a plank of dry, rotting wood, then, no, you are not expected to go out again simply because you "owe" the person. Nor do you have to ask him or her out in return. The same goes for being a business guest or host.

Friendship, on the other hand, is different. If you are friends and you wish to remain as such, then you should feel obligated to reciprocate favors. The three foundations of good relationships are respect, civility, and reciprocity. This triad is a staple; it never changes.

But what if there is a large gap between the incomes of two friends? That's where the respect part must come into play. Money is not the only thing to be respected in this world, and it should not be a thing that tears friendships apart. Maybe your friend has invited you out to the most expensive restaurant in Manhattan. Perhaps there is no way you can match that generosity on your salary. Don't feel bad—although I know it is human to do so. Instead, simply think of what you can afford to do to reciprocate. Pasta, perhaps. Invite your friend over for a night of home-cooked noodles at your place. Or a Mexican fiesta with chips, dips, and margaritas. Remember, the quality of an evening out is not gauged purely by the cost of it. I've had miserable nights in the most posh spots in the world and made wonderful memories on a shoestring. But yes, when friendship is involved, always reciprocate in some way. If you want to keep a friend, think of reciprocity as a series of letters of correspondence that must remain unbroken—always answered.

ENFORCING THE RULES: Respect, civility, Right View, Right Intention, Right Speech, Right Action, Right Mindfulness—literally all the teachings of this book come into play when we consider the enforcement of rules.

The very idea of having to enforce rules seems stressful, doesn't it? If you read it like I do, you're getting a sense-memory of the uncomfortable time you had to tell some stranger at your health club, "Um, that's my towel you're wiping all over your sweaty face." Yikes! How do you do that while adhering to all the edicts mentioned above?

My take is to look at conflicts as opportunities, positive opportunities. A situation is only as dreadful as we make it. A lot of what I've learned about success has to do with having the right attitude. If I go into a big tennis match with a positive attitude, I may not win, but I put myself in the best possible position *to* win. The same goes for conflict.

If someone is breaking a rule, a code, or a tradition and it infringes upon you, don't think of it as a dreaded confrontation. Think of it as an excuse for an icebreaker.

RULES CZARS: It's true. Some miserable people use their knowledge of rules and codes as a cudgel to bash down the people around them and make themselves feel superior. This speaks to the issue of Right Intention.

We choose to be happy; we choose to be sad. Most rules czars go about correcting people with a perpetual scowl on their face and a condescending tone. Rules are not about embarrassing other people or making them feel bad about themselves. That approach will only spread misery, not joy.

Don't always be on the lookout for rules violations or a chance to point out someone else's blunder. For the offender, the embarrassment of realizing you've made a faux pas is punishment enough. It is not necessary to have someone highlight it and demean you for it. My rule of thought is that if things seem fine and everyone, including you, is happy, then things must be (basically) right. The purpose of any set of rules or code of conduct is to prevent conflicts and instill fairness. If there is no conflict and everyone is happy because things appear to be fair, then smile, relax, overlook the fact that someone made a blunder or violated a rule, and just have a good time.

OVER-"RULING": With all of this emphasis on obeying and enforcing rules, one might wonder whether it is possible to go overboard with it. It does feel a little like being back in elementary school, where we sit straight in our seats and mind our p's and q's, waiting for words of praise for good behavior. If we ruffle the teacher's feathers, we know what will happen—detention.

I believe part of the answer to enforcing rules is to do so without being judgmental. Being judgmental is *not* Right View or Right Action. It's just not noble. If I diplomatically suggest that you should tip a baggage handler at a hotel, I am not "judging" you. This is not to say that some people who are of "wrong intention" will not take glee in this exchange and use it as a way to make you, the forgetful tipper, feel as embarrassed at your faux pas as possible. I would never do something like that to you.

That being said, if I gently, with careful words and a soft tone, bring this error to your attention, it is not meant to be the start of some great battle between us. How I feel about you as a whole person has not changed, I assure you. If I deliver my suggestion to you nicely, I only wish for you to receive it in the same spirit in which it was given. If so, we can both go along our merry way together. I am *not* judging you. Let me repeat that how you say something is of paramount importance. Always be conscious of your tone so that you do not sound condescending. Sometimes the way you say something is even more important than what you actually say.

If you see someone breaking a rule or disrespecting another person, raise the issue with the one committing the violation delicately and with compassion so that it can be properly resolved. Then make the person equally aware that you are happy he or she took your kind suggestion. Too often, we like to brush things off and not get involved when it would be okay to give our two cents' worth to make things better. If your intention is good and you are conscious of being respectful of the other person with your words and tone (not putting them down), your comment will be well received more often than not.

If you hear someone spouting hatred, do not let this person get away with such venomous comments. Saying nothing helps to perpetuate this unacceptable behavior. Be courageous, take a stand, and call people on their rude behavior. One day, someone might do the same favor for you.

JUDGMENT AND CRITICISM: Abiding by rules, codes, and traditions is not to be confused with being judgmental or being the perpetual critic.

Among the worst offenders in this area are the people who think they are being asked for their unvarnished opinion when they're not. When your little child comes up to you and shows you her macaroni art, is she really asking you for serious art criticism? Of course not. The same goes for a lot of situations in life. Yes, we should be honest with people, but not to the extent that we offer exploratory surgery of all their endeavors. If I give a speech and it went well, my insecurity—which I am trying to overcome—might cause me to ask a person who is part of my inner circle, "So, how did I do?"

If I totally tanked, I most likely already know it and I won't be phrasing it that way. I'd probably say, "How bad *was* it?" But short of that, the best answer to "How'd I do?" is usually the short, generic, "Fine." That will make me feel good about myself for the moment. Later on, if *I* (not you) bring it up again, and if you have some specific critique that you feel may help me in the future, I might be more open to hearing it.

I've spoken to writers who have joined writers' groups to get feedback on their work and have heard mixed reviews of that process. Some groups are great—full of constructive criticism from well-meaning people who have kindness in their hearts. Others include windbags who feel that if they do not have something heinous to say, people will think they don't know anything. Look, sometimes good is good and no criticism is *needed*. People actually do get things right in this world sometimes. If a peer group thinks its only role is to provide negative criticism, the entire exercise is one of sadomasochism. *There's nothing wrong with saying, "That's really great! I liked that."* Of course, this holds true only if it is sincere, which goes back to the issue of honesty, something we should always embrace.

If I break a major rule, you may be placed in a position of having to tell me. If I ask you whether I am doing something right, I may be asking for advice. Life coach practitioners learn to *give advice only when it is asked for or when you ask for permission to give it.* Trust me on this one. I've learned it the hard way. When people complain like a broken record about the same situation over and over again, yet they don't do anything to change that situation, I have learned that either consciously or unconsciously they do not want to do anything about it. I know…it goes against all common sense. They say they are miserable but they do the same thing repeatedly. They are obviously getting some payoff for their misery, which, in turn, keeps them stuck in the situation.

My best advice to you when dealing with such people is to offer only sympathetic comments such as, "Yes, yes, I understand; that's terrible; oh my, you poor thing." There will be times, however, when you feel you are not able to offer the sympathy the person is seeking. Rather than snapping at him or her to "wake up and smell the coffee," it is probably best to end the conversation or leave the room. What's the old saying? The definition of insanity is doing the same thing the same way but expecting different results!

Now, in regard to people who think they know more than others do or can live their lives better, every piece of conversation is not a request for a long-winded, detailed explanation of how the other person is wrong and should do something *this* way. The best rule of thumb is, you live yours and I'll live mine. But if we can help each other from time to time, we should seek the other out when the need arises.

THE UNNEUTRAL JUDGE: Once, when playing the finals at the Ladies Open Championship at my tennis club in Maryland, I was told that the referee was unable to make it that day, but that as a last-minute backup, they had chosen an honorable member of the club who also happened to be the best friend of my opponent. My first thought was, "Gee, why not have my father officiate? He would be just as fair as the best friend of my opponent—ha-ha!" As it turned out, I did win the tournament. To my initial surprise, there were no problems with the referee's calls whatsoever. When I thought about it later, I felt a little embarrassed for questioning the integrity of this club member who I knew to be a person of good character.

Often in junior tennis, players forget the score after a long point. When this happens, they will look up to the stands to see if someone can help them. Parents are always advised by tournament officials not to help the players, but usually they can't help themselves. Every time I have seen this situation or been a part of it, the parents always respond to the player in a mature manner. Without appearing to take sides, they yell back the answer—the correct score. Although the officials do not like for parents to get involved, I've never seen this type of temporary officiating (making one or two calls or calling out the score) evolve into a problem.

(Not all parents are this mature, of course. We've all read the disturbing stories about parents who have fistfights with other parents while watching their kids play sports. It makes you cringe when you hear about parents who defame their kids for performing poorly and swear at the coaches and game officials for making a call against their child. Some people would say these parents should read my books, while others would say we should call the police. Personally, when people are this out of control, I think it's best to call a doctor. A psychiatrist sounds like the right kind. We'll talk more about this subject later in the book.)

So how do we behave with integrity when we are placed in these "un-neutral judging" dilemmas? It happens to everyone from time to time. I believe it is a test of our character, and we must rise to the occasion. A lesser person would rub his or her hands together deviously and think, "Aha! Now victory is ours!" This is not the Zen Game way.

My advice? Enforce the rules properly, but if anything, err on the side of the person with whom you are *not* affiliated. Tell them you will do so before you even begin. Yes, you read that right. It is the noble way.

There will always be close calls that could go either way. Try diligently to call it as you see it, but if you cannot be absolutely sure, call it the other way. The other party is already wary of trusting you. Hence, you need to earn their trust and fortify your own trust in yourself.

RULES STRESS: Don't let all of this talk about rules make you so stressed out that you would rather not learn a new skill or activity. At its core, this issue is all about etiquette. If you are new to a situation, I suggest that you do some preparation, but I also know that it can be almost impossible to know everything in advance. Learning all the rules of any activity often takes years.

If you embrace etiquette, you will understand that common sense is usually at the center of all rules and codes of conduct. Be fair, amicable, and considerate—these things are universal. If you don't know all the details in between, a more experienced person who holds true to these basic tenets should *help* you, not *judge* you.

What can be more adversarial than a court of law? Yet lawyers all take a bar exam that tests their knowledge of the prevailing codes of conduct in the legal profession. These rules were created to establish a level playing field in which lawyers exchange witness lists, have "discovery" whereby they share all physical evidence, and so forth. The key here is the *sharing*. Unlike the drama on television shows, the lawyers never spring any "surprise" witnesses at the last minute. Both sides advocate for their clients, but both are supposed to be primarily in search of the truth. They take an oath of loyalty to the rule of law, not merely to their clients and the concept of winning versus losing.

Even if you do not have mastery over all the rules of a situation, you do have mastery over your own proper etiquette and deportment. If you spread warmth and civility, it can be contagious. Kindness is contagious. If you let yourself get grumpy and strained, you can only spread pain and stress.

KEEPING SCORE: Sometimes I wish we didn't have ratings, rankings, and scoreboards in life. While these forms of keeping score are traditional in sports and other areas of life, I don't believe they support the participants in an activity. In fact, they can create more of a struggle for us mentally and emotionally because we are at the mercy of the scoreboards.

To use an example I'm familiar with, the United States Tennis Association (USTA) has formulated a standardized rating system called the National Tennis Rating Program. This system rates players from a level 1.0 (beginner) to a level 7.0 (world-class player), with 0.5 increment levels between those numbers. Sanctioned personnel rate players at many clubs at prearranged times and places.

The whole idea behind this system is to make it easier for players to find others of similar skill to play against. It's a great system, but only if people regard it as nothing more than what it is—a way for players to have some idea going into a game of whether they match up fairly evenly or not. It goes awry when people think it is an overall judgment of their total worth as a human being, as some do when comparing cars, houses, or occupations. It's just a number!

The point here is, no matter what the discipline, there are ways in which we "keep score." Some cynically say that money is the ultimate scorekeeper. Within a company, it may be position. Some salespeople are so good at what they do that their commissions give them a higher annual salary than the sales managers—their bosses!—earn. Still, a boss is a boss, and position on an organizational chart is still position. The lower-paid boss still has the power to fire the higher-earning salesperson below him on the organizational chart.

With regard to your social life, a lot of insecure people feel that once they've reached a certain status in life, they have to change to an entirely new set of friends. This is the definition of shallowness. People who go into teaching, law enforcement, or social work have knowingly chosen to make less money than they could in some other occupations, but without these people, our society would collapse. I choose to socialize with people I like, no matter what they earn, where they live, or what they do for a living.

I hate it when income, title, or "who's your daddy?" begin to dictate social status. Some adults act like they're back in grammar school, with the "cool kids' table" and all that nonsense. Something to bear in mind is that the people who have a low rating, income, or title today may, in fact, be new to the game (again, I use the word *game* euphemistically). But if they are serious about improving, they might surpass you in a year or two. Why treat them like second-class citizens today? It will not be funny in the future when you get your comeuppance. Trust me. I've seen this happen several times.

From the perspective of the lower-ranked player, why should you trail after people ranked or rated above you as if you were their little puppy dog? Do their ratings mean that they are automatically swell people, and that they deserve to have your tongue and tail wagging whenever you set eyes on them?

Don't keep score in life. That's not your job. Do the best you can to surround yourself with nice people—ones who have similar values to your own. Open yourself up to meeting all sorts of new people, not only those who impress you.

TRADITION VERSUS ETHICS: In any discipline, there are tricks of the trade that come with experience. Sometimes these tricks are simply part of the unstated, traditional means by which people do business together. Other times, they might cross the line and become unethical business practices. The key is to know where the line is when you are following your profession's "traditions."

For example, when salespeople are dealing with a potential buyer who is interested but hesitant, they might say, "I would recommend you moving fast on this; there's been a lot of other interest in it." This statement may be true or it may be a bluff. More often than not, it is a little of both. Perhaps there has been some other interest, but those other parties also are vacillating.

Some good salesmen take their clients out for a good time, spend a lot of money on them, and perhaps buy them some drinks, all in the pursuit of the sale. This happened to my husband and me when we were looking at time-shares (they should call them "crime shares") in Cancun, Mexico. The realtor kept insisting that we have some Spanish lemonade (also known as margaritas) with him. This type of wining and dining happens every day. "Why is it necessary?" you may ask. Basically because it's a distraction, that's why. Instead of sitting in a quiet conference room, boring a hole into the buyers with facts and figures, and building the case as to why they should do business with him, the salesperson distracts them with the other amenities—including getting them tipsy.

Does this behavior violate a code of conduct? If the potential buyers happily go along with it, I imagine not. This approach to selling has gone on forever. People do business with one another for a multitude of reasons, and the best price and service, logical as they are, are not always the only criteria. Some people simply like to do business with people they like. On the other hand, getting people plastered and then forcing their hand on a contract is just plain illegal. Distraction is a matter of degree and of Right Intention.

In tennis, an action such as shouting the moment your opponent is about to serve is definitely against the rules. But giving your opponent a head fake so that he thinks you're anticipating a shot going one way, but then going the other, is simply good strategy. When I try to outwit my tennis opponent on the court *within the confines of the rules of the game*, my intention is merely to win via good, legitimate strategy. If I hit a ball on the second bounce and keep playing the point as if I had hit it on a single bounce—this is cheating. The same goes for all other aspects of life.

On the other sneaker, one of the classiest gestures I have seen in professional tennis occurs when a player feels that his or her opponent was cheated out of a point by a linesman or judge and then misses the next point to even the score of the match. Such noble gestures provide lessons we should carry with us in that other game—the main game—of life.

HOW TO SAY HELLO: When I go places, particularly shopping, I sometimes see two strange extremes in hospitality or lack thereof—both of which trespass on the unwritten code of appropriate conduct for a business's employees.

The first extreme is the feeling of being mugged. "Hello! May I help you? We have some new jackets on sale. Here, let me slip this one on you. Oh my, that looks splendid! Now, if you match it with this scarf…"

"Excuse me, but I just came in here to ask directions."

It can be like that. It's overkill and it's creepy.

Then there's the other extreme. You walk into a store and are completely ignored, even though a number of employees are lolling around. That's bad too. I've even seen this poor conduct taken a step further, where the employees treat you like some sort of criminal. A friend of mine told me that she once wandered around a store, unable to get anyone to help her. She called, waved, did what any normal person would do to get someone's attention, all to no avail. Finally, she approached a salesclerk who was folding garments and gently tapped her on the shoulder since she was ignoring her verbal pleas. "Don't touch me!" was the icy response. Totally freaked out, my friend slinked away, vowing never to return.

Folks, most people simply want a plain and pleasant "hello" when they enter a room of any sort, an acknowledgment that they exist and that the place they have entered is a happy one. If we all did that, the world would be a nicer place.

GET TWO: When you are alone, you only have to worry about yourself. When you are in a group, even if it only has two members, you now have shared responsibilities (I love that phrase!). This means that if you get up to get yourself a drink, the code of good conduct says that you must ask if anyone else in your party wants one too.

Anything you want to do, you need to make the others in your party a part of your plans. A waiter comes by with a tray full of snacks? Don't just help yourself; make sure the others know the snacks have arrived so they can get some too. Or else grab some extras for them. Think of others. Look outside your own private bubble.

According to Forrest Gump, "Life is like a box of chocolates." In my mind, this saying not only refers to the "mystery" of living but also to the fact that we are social animals made to share this earth space with others. Hence, we are destined to be considerate. So during our sojourn here, why not make the best of it!

3
MORE TRADITIONS, HABITS, AND ISMS

Human beings thrive on patterns. In fact, almost everything in life is based on a pattern of some sort. We do something because it is a tradition in our family, profession, or personal life; it is a habit we've fostered for many years (be it good or bad); or it is a well-honed mannerism of ours. Sometimes we do something—or go *against* it—because it symbolizes a particular belief (an "ism") that is in some way entrenched in our thought processes or culture. We often do these things without thinking—they are quite simply in our DNA. It may be something we've done since childhood or something we've picked up along the way.

Whatever tradition, habit, or ism we adopt, we must always consider it in light of our Zen perspective. We may find that our Zen Game renders a particular behavior pattern incompatible with the life we now desire to live—a life of Right Intention and Right Action, in which we can truly become, in all respects, good citizens of the world.

Living a life of Right Intention and Right Action may mean changing one (or more) of our traditions, habits, or isms. There's no denying this is a real challenge. But that is the goal we must set if our existing behaviors and beliefs are not serving ourselves and others well. If we are serious about this, we must be open to adapting to the cycle of change within and around us—change for the positive, with an attitude of Right Mindfulness at our core. Change has to come from within, from a point of observation. We must jump into the melee and put into action that which we know is best for ourselves and others within a communal context. When we have this kind of mindset, we choose the Middle Path within the Zen Game. This choice will fill our lives with respect, wisdom, and compassion.

Let's consider some of the more common habits and behaviors that are within our power to change.

FORGETFULNESS: This section also would be relevant in the previous chapter because it concerns unwritten rules of behavior. But the way

I see it, the real focus here is on a bad habit, one that for some is hard to break. While all of us can be forgetful, does that mean we should receive special privileges *because* of it? I learned during my life coach training that we are all Pavlovian to some degree. If we do something and get a reaction we like, we're apt to do it again and again. Even if the thing we do is wrong, bad, or simply against the rules of common sense and personal responsibility, if we are "rewarded" in some way for it, we are likely to keep doing it. We are drawn to things that will bring us pleasure and go out of our way to avoid pain in any capacity.

Forgetting to bring along the things we need for a specific task is a common example of this bad habit. I see it in tennis all the time. "I forgot my sunglasses. I forgot the new can of tennis balls. I forgot my wallet. I forgot my sunblock. I forgot my serve." (The last one is usually offered as an excuse for poor play, and luckily I have never been asked to lend mine to anyone.)

Yes, at first glance it may seem that the loving, caring, giving approach would be to say, "Oh sure, no problem," and lend the person yours or make some sort of compensation for their forgetfulness. But in this type of situation, we should maintain our structure as a society by adhering more to rules than to emotions.

If Person A has lots of water and Person B is about to die of dehydration, for Person A not to share would be, well, manslaughter. But most times, we're not talking about life and death, are we?

There will always be people who want to be carried by others due to their own *repeated* lack of preparation or sheer incompetence. Is incompetence a disability? Not in the legal sense. There are special public accommodations for the blind, deaf, and mobility-impaired. There are no laws protecting the incompetent, unless we are using incompetence as a euphemism for legal insanity. And no, forgetting your sunglasses is not enough to get you committed.

Things like this tug at our better nature. Yes, we want everyone to like us and we want to get along. But what should the fair trade-off be? If you and I are in a court of law, facing off in a dispute, and I show up with a lawyer and you forgot to hire one, should I send mine home so that we have a more level playing field? Where would it all end?

Life is bigger than we are as individuals. Life and civilized society are about tradition. Rules are created to maintain order and provide a fair and balanced stage on which we all can perform. Whether we are talking about playing a sport, taking the SAT, or getting the Purple Heart, the rules are all about right and wrong, fair and not fair, as determined well in advance of the individual event, so that every situation will not have to be ruled on as a new circumstance.

Yes, in some circumstances there may not, in fact, be a written rule saying we should remember to bring this or that. Indeed, is there a written rule book about going to the beach? Yet if we forget our SPF 30, we're going to bake, maybe even play footsie with skin cancer. We should turn around and go home for some or else swing by a nearby store to buy some. We should not start bugging total strangers, asking them to squirt some of theirs on our backs.

As opposed as I am to hunting animals, a famous scene in the movie *The Deer Hunter* illustrates this point. It involves Robert De Niro's character losing patience with one of his hunting buddies who always fails to bring his boots, his rifle, his ammo—basically, everything a person should bring when they go deer hunting. De Niro's other pals egg him on to let the forgetful guy borrow his stuff. The irony here is that, while the other hunters want De Niro to share, they themselves cannot share because, while they are better prepared than Mr. Forgetful, they only remembered to bring along one of everything. De Niro, the mature, well-prepared man, always knows to bring along enough to cover every contingency. And what does he get for his competence? He's supposed to "carry" everyone else!

Unfortunately, most kids expect parents, neighbors, and teachers to back them up when they are not prepared with the equipment they need for their activities, their studies, or anything else for that matter. What are the long-term effects of overprotecting our young and innocent? Does condoning children's lack of responsibility adversely affect them as they mature into adults? Definitely yes! If you teach kids how to prepare themselves properly and play by the rules in any endeavor, they will not have to learn this important skill later in life. Also, kids always take their cues from adults. If they see adults being unprepared, making excuses, and not playing by the rules, kids will learn from and copy this mediocre behavior. The old saying "Don't do what I say; do what I do" does not work today. Nor did it ever.

When we make mistakes, when we forget things we need, we must bear the consequences. If we do, and if those consequences are equal to the infraction, we will learn from the experience and gain character. If there are no consequences when we make mistakes, what motivation would we have to do things by the rules? Why have rules at all? ANARCHY!

VISIBLE LATENESS: Showing respect for other people is the essence of the Buddha's Noble Eightfold Path. When you are late, it invariably sends a message to other people that "everyone can wait for me."

Here's a good example:

You go into a darkened movie theater. The movie has already started. It takes your eyes a minute to adjust to the darkness. Easy does it. Stand there in the back of the theater, where no one can see you, and get your wits about you.

Would you believe I've seen people in this situation start talking loudly with one another?

"Hey, it started already."

"Oh damn! I told you to hurry."

"Shut up! I can't see a thing. Do you see any seats?"

"No, it's too dark!"

I've heard exchanges like this that were even louder than the movie up on the screen.

If you arrive somewhere late, show consideration for others. It is self-centered to start disrupting the atmosphere for everyone else. Other people arrived on time and you did not. While you may not actually be verbalizing it, you are asking the on-time people to forgive you and allow you to join them. You don't do this by acting like you are still in that big bubble you've cast around yourself, the one where you can be as loud as you want and no one else will mind. We do mind!

If you are late, show your remorse by tiptoeing in and getting to your seat as quietly and unobtrusively as possible. This is true for plays, movies, business meetings, classes—*all appointments.*

EVERYBODY UP: Sometimes the behaviors and habits we fall into are simply the result of not thinking. For example, you're in the same theater. This time you actually arrived on time. Good for you! There are seats in the middle of a long row. Center seats, with the best view. There are two people on one end of the aisle and twelve people on the other. Who do you ask to stand up and let you through, the two or the twelve?

Think! Again, we go through life in this bubble sometimes, not taking time to notice, look, and think. Inconvenience the fewest number of people. If that means you have to go back and around the rear of the theater to go down the aisle on the other side, so be it. Walking is good exercise. Remember to think outside the box and outside your bubble.

DOWN IN FRONT: You arrive *really* early in this same theater (boy, you sure go to the theater a lot, don't you?). No one else is there. Finally, another person or couple walks in…and sits right beside you or in front of you!

Okay, this one is just plain weird. I mean, if this were a lightly attended party in someone's house, I can understand trying to mingle with the few other people in attendance, but a theater is where we sit quietly in the dark to be entertained. Give me my personal space! And furthermore, give me my unobstructed view!

If it is crowded and you have to sit in front of someone, there's not much anyone can do about it. But if you can avoid it, don't think only of yourself by picking *any* seat that gives you a clear view of the screen or stage. Think also of the person behind you. Try to cater to that person's needs as well. As with so many of our behavior patterns, it's often a case of just breaking out of our bubble and taking a moment to *think*.

DOWN IN FRONT, PART 2: All right, so you finally get tired of going to the theater and decide to take in a sporting event. Good choice! Variety is the spice of life.

Remember, however, that not every play is the Play of the Century. When the home team hits a walk-off home run, that's a big deal. When someone hits a three-pointer from half court, that's a big deal. But don't stand up and cheer for every single bit of action. That's weird too. It borders on making you look like you have never seen an athletic event before or have been incarcerated for the past dozen years.

There's a reason they build seats in stadiums. They are to be sat upon. If you were supposed to stand the entire time, there would be railings and nothing more. Employ Right Mindfulness and remember that there are other paying ticket holders right behind you, and they would like to see the game or match as well. You should be jumping to your feet only for those incredible sporting moments when you simply can't help it. The beauty and excitement of the events simply propel you out of your seat— and everyone else out of theirs.

PUBLIC LOUDNESS: Here's another "bubble" issue where people often are so inside their own private space that they don't realize there's a big old world around them.

In Westerns, there's always that saloon scene where two gunslingers start a-fightin' and the barkeep says, "Listen, you two, take it outside!" I wish more people did that in real life. Not the loud gunslinger part, but the barkeep part. We already have too many loud gunslingers.

Modulate your tone when in public. Sure, the acoustics in some places are so bad that you do literally have to scream to be heard. (Have you ever tried to have a conversation in a loud nightclub?) But have you ever sat down for a romantic dinner and discovered that the "Look at Us" family is at the next table?

The biggest thing to avoid, more than simply keeping your voice down, is having a fight with your girlfriend, spouse, friend, or even a stranger in public. If you find yourself involved in some brouhaha, like the barkeep says, "Take it outside." Or better yet, go home and do it. When an argument is unavoidable at home, be considerate of your kids, your pets, or even your neighbors if you are one of those people who like to leave your windows open all the time. Having an altercation is never fun, but you do not have the right to make everyone else's evening miserable too.

So what do you do if someone is bothering you with inappropriate loudness? I've seen folks get so angry when people were talking loudly during a movie that they went up to the culprits and yelled at them even louder. This is not Right Action. The offensive party will get *de*fensive, and now you've got a shouting match on your hands.

Instead, the louder the other party is, the softer you should be. Really. Talking softly subtly guides the other party to match your softer tone. The louder someone gets, the softer I get. Keep your confrontation to the simple issue at hand. Don't judge the other party, no matter how hard that is. Don't say, "You are really ignorant" or even the slightly more appropriate, "You are *acting* really ignorantly." Instead, say softly, "I'm sorry, but we can't hear the movie. Would you be so kind as to keep your voices down? Thank you."

Observe unwritten codes of conduct regarding loud outbursts. If not, as the wise barkeep says, take it outside.

IRRITANTS: Some people do little, irritating things that rattle others around them, whether consciously or unconsciously. In these situations, the best thing you can really do is to concentrate even harder. Do even more to focus on what you are doing, and do not let this person rent space inside your head.

Most of us were guilty of this behavior when we were kids. Do you remember saying some teasing remark over and over again to a "friend" at school and then acting all innocent when he got upset and you were reprimanded by your teacher? Even worse is the enjoyment we felt when we saw the other person was out-of-his-mind annoyed and we continued doing it just to see what would happen next! Hmmm, this is definitely not an experience to look back on with pride. Why did that friend ever talk to us again? Probably because he was the one doing it to us the next day!

Also, try to look for the humor in the situation when you are bothered by another person's mannerisms. That's right. Use your imagination! If you are at a dinner party and the person across from you is eating with her mouth open, try to visualize a squirrel that is busily chomping down on a big nut. It is important to note that you are not laughing at the person. You see, we all have quirky habits, but when we can look for some humor in these gestures, we are better able to tolerate them and maximize the good in the situation. Best of all, we may eventually find that these gestures no longer bother us.

CHANGE: Change is good. Whether we are successful or are struggling, it is still good to change things up every once in a while.

We all get into ruts. We all do certain things the same way every day simply because it has become a tradition for us. Well, some traditions are good and should be followed, while others need to be stirred and shaken from time to time.

Do you know that if you always do things the exact same way, you're not even doing your *body* a favor? Ever hear of repetitive motion injuries? Even the brain and nervous system enjoy the workout they get when we change things up a bit. Always brush your teeth with your right hand? Try the left. Feel like your gray cells have started to go on vacation more often? Try chess or Sudoku. Why? You'll be stimulating other parts of your brain. You'll start having fewer of those "clueless" moments. And you'll be staving off the aging process by using as much of your brain as possible in as many ways as possible.

Sometimes we chain ourselves so tightly to our traditions that they become like bindings tied too snugly. Maybe you have a family tradition of making pasta every Wednesday night. There's nothing wrong with that. But if your significant other decides to mix it up and make meatloaf instead one Wednesday, don't go into a tailspin about it. Change is good!

Personal trainers preach this. Don't do the same workout in exactly the same way week after week. Change it up. Trick your body and it will respond happily. Even when you are dieting, if you do the exact same thing week after week, meal after meal, you may find yourself plateauing because your body has gotten used to the routine. Remember, the body's natural inclination is to survive. *You* may want to lose weight, but your body does not. Your body is still operating as it did in primitive days, when not eating enough meant you might shrivel up and die. To lose weight on purpose (something primitive man never had to do), you sometimes have to trick the body.

Changing things up in your relationship will keep it romantic and exciting. How many times do you know what your spouse, girlfriend, or boyfriend is going to say before he or she even says it? One reason why new relationships are interesting is that you don't know what the other person is going to say. Of course, it is nice to be familiar with another's likes and dislikes, but how nice would it be if, instead of hearing the words "No, I don't want to do that," you heard "Yes, let's try it" for a change?

Always strive to make positive changes, but do not discount the therapeutic benefits of simply making change for change's sake.

"ISMS" IN SPEECH: They say that actions speak louder than words, and I agree with that assessment. But it is still important that we use Right Speech when referring to particular groups of people and not let any "isms" cause us to denigrate others. We need to make our words as fair, kind, and liberated as our actions.

Consider, for example, the common use of sexism in speech. The same person who is evolved enough to hire a woman in a historically male field and ensure that her pay is equal will still go to the company picnic and catcall another male employee by saying he "throws like a girl." Sorry, but that rather defeats all good intent, doesn't it? Or what exactly is the intent, to intentionally demean the other person?

Want some more? How about when a man is feeling emotional and his "buddy" (for no buddy of *mine* would dare be this knuckleheaded) says, "Stop acting like a girl." Ugh! I also take umbrage with some rappers who use misogynistic lyrics. It's disappointing to think that an entire generation of boys and girls is growing up to think that words like "bitch" and "ho" are okay to use.

On a related topic, why is it that gay people are still open targets for this sort of derision? If something is corny, some people say, "Oh, that's so gay!" *Gay*, in this context, is being used as a slur. Unfortunately, some people also misuse the word *queer* in a derogatory way to mean weird, strange, or odd.

Language evolves over time. I do not think political correctness is a bad thing. Sure, some people feel as if they can't say anything without inadvertently offending someone, but the key is to always use common sense. What is common sense? A good way to determine whether a word or statement is offensive is to consider how you would feel if something similar was said about you. Always put yourself in the other person's shoes. All it means is that we try not to hurt other people's feelings. Since when is that a bad thing?

On the other hand, there are people who go overboard with their complaints about sexism, anti-Semitism, or racism. They have every right to speak out, of course, but if it keeps them from trusting a particular group of people, *they are now the victim of their own beliefs*. In all areas, there has been improvement over the years, but I would hope to see a lot more in the near future. What we must not do is let other people's limiting beliefs stop us from trusting each other and treating each other with civility and respect. I've noticed that the best way to get people to change is not to force them to do something or constantly complain about them or their actions, but rather to set a good example yourself.

NO MORE MR. NICE GUY?: When people think of pacifists, someone such as Gandhi probably comes to mind. They envision the frail little man who always turned the other cheek. What we fail to recall is that Gandhi freed a nation—the second most populous one in the world. Pacifism is not all about liking to lose. Gandhi was a winner.

Some people, by habit, always maintain a sweet, smiling, pleasant, courteous demeanor. That's admirable, and it clearly fits with the Zen Game perspective on how to treat other people. However, nothing about the Zen Game says that you have to become a "doormat" and allow others to take advantage of you. The clever way to go is the Middle Path. When you follow this path, you embrace good qualities, but when the situation calls for it, you also let people know that politeness is not to be confused with weakness. Gandhi was *not* weak.

Being a competitor does not make you a bad person. You've heard all the homilies about "striving for your personal best." Yes, some people have perverted them into an excuse for cheating and poor sportsmanship, but taken at their purest, they remind us that we should always do our best. And if our best is better than someone else's best on a given day, then so be it. Do not apologize for giving your all, believing in yourself, and doing well. Excellence is our "Right Livelihood." At its best, it is pure and it defines personal focus. And that is to be embraced.

THE JUDGE'S PANEL: One final habit (of the bad kind) deserves mention here. It's about gossip. It's about staring. It's about judging others. It's about prejudice.

You and your best friend are out having lunch and someone walks by. The conversation immediately stops, and the person is given the once-over and…judged. Judged based on her clothing and her looks in general. It's so blatant that you almost feel like holding up a numerical opinion like an Olympic judge: "The Venezuelan judge gives her a 6.3."

What's this all about? Is it Right?

I don't believe so. I'm an avid reader, and avid readers learn a lot about old sayings through books. Here is one of those old sayings: "Brilliant people talk about ideas, average people talk about things, and dullards talk about other people." If all you're worried about is what the new person in the room looks like or is wearing, you need to drum up some serious conversation skills. And if you'd go so far as to interrupt a conversation to judge what another person has on—well, a thinking makeover seems to be in order. Golden Rule time once more: If you don't like it done to you, then hold off on the judgments! Raise the level of discourse at your table. Be like the brilliant among us and discuss ideas or even things, not people.

4
ALL I WANT IS A LITTLE RESPECT...
AND TO PAY IT FORWARD

This chapter flows naturally from the previous two because it deals with the unspoken codes of good living. When we give to others and respect the world around us, we are traveling a path that nurtures the human spirit on so many levels. The earth has been leased to us to share with all the living creatures that inhabit it. We are not owed anything for living; rather, we owe the environment around us for allowing us to survive within it. As we inhabit this space, we are charged not only with pursuing our interests but also with showing our ability and willingness to live with others.

A kind gesture, no matter how small or insignificant it may seem to be, is our way of paying it forward for the gift of life. In addition, what means little to us may represent a golden opportunity for someone else. We cannot discount the power of living well and right, and not merely in the material sense. By exercising genuine compassion, care, respect, and thoughtfulness, we are employing five of the eight tenets of Zen living introduced in this book: Right Action, Right View, Right Mindfulness, Right Effort, and Right Intention.

RESPECT: We live in a country and an era that appear to be fixated on wealth and fame. We are more interested in what's on the cover of tabloid magazines than in the layoffs many people are experiencing or the starvation occurring worldwide. An engagement ring the size of Jamaica will certainly garner head-spinning news coverage, and a mansion sporting a solid gold commode in the powder room will elicit widespread gasping and hypertension. The catch here is, some people have grown to feel that wealth means empowerment and lack of wealth makes a person a non-person. But here's a news flash: Being rich does not make one "right." Nor does it mean that you are "somebody."

A friend of mine once witnessed a traffic accident involving a bus and a Mercedes. Both drivers exited their vehicles and began arguing. The worst of it happened when the Mercedes driver shouted, "Look what *I'm* driving and look what *you're* driving!" Just as might does not make right, neither does money. Frankly, bus drivers are *professional* drivers, no matter who takes home more money at the end of the day.

One great story I heard was about a longtime U.S. congressman who always entered banquet halls through the kitchen. Why? So he could shake hands with and say hello to every kitchen worker before all the big donors mobbed him in the main hall. That's not only good politics, it's class. And a few extra working-class votes, of course!

PRIVACY: As much as I've learned to open up conversations and spread smiles wherever I go, I also know that sometimes it's "me time." Allowing people to have such time when they need it is a matter of basic respect.

We all get upset from time to time and wish to be left alone. This can be so for a variety of legitimate reasons. Maybe your loved one is ill or another type of tragedy has just befallen you. It isn't important that you justify your plight to others. You have the right to be blue if that's sincerely how you are feeling.

I often talk about focus, but focus does not mean only focusing on ourselves. It also means focusing on others so that we can pick up signals. If you smile and say hello to someone and he or she looks upset, you may try to ask gently, "Is there anything I can do for you?" Maybe you can, and if so, great. But often, people need some healing time. If that's what they ask for, if they appear eager to get away from you so that they can have some privacy, grant it to them. The same goes in reverse. If you are distraught and someone approaches you, let them know that you do not need them right now, thank you very much. But remember not to be rude or take your problems out on an innocent bystander.

And since we're on the topic of privacy, what's with the staring? When a new person walks into a room, people often stop and stare—it's almost impossible not to do so. What you *can* avoid is *holding* the stare. Glance up and then go back to your own business. To keep staring is to invade someone's privacy and make him feel as if he is under a microscope—not good. You'll have him running to a mirror to check for torn seams, mystery spots on his teeth, or even ketchup smears on his chin. Celebrities tell me it's one of the things they dislike most about being famous. No one wants that kind of pressure. The famous discount designer clothing store Loehmann's used to have an open dressing room. Holy smoke, that's what I would call a breeding ground for staring contests. I'm not sure if you've ever tried on clothing in a communal dressing room, but if you can survive it without getting a complex, you deserve a medal!

Nobody deserves to be the center of unwarranted attention. And certainly, people who truly do not deserve such visual scrutiny are individuals with disabilities. Bet you know what I'm talking about here.

I'll never forget a party I attended a few years ago where a woman stared at my friend throughout the event. My friend pointed this person out to me, and sure enough she made no bones about it. My friend was so distracted by this woman that she barely enjoyed herself at the party. When it was time to leave, the woman approached us and told my friend that she'd figured it out. "Figured out what?" my friend asked. She said she'd finally figured out who she resembled. "Who?" my friend said, exasperated. Sarah Jessica Parker. The interesting part of this story is that the woman staring was actually admiring my friend, but because she was so overt about it, she made my friend very uncomfortable. This resulted in a miserable time for her. The idea is this: Try to treat all people the same when it comes to staring—don't do it!

ALL BACKED UP: We've all been through this one. We have an appointment at 1:00 p.m. We arrive at 12:45 so that we can check in, hang up our coat, and collect ourselves. We take a seat and wait. And wait. And wait. Finally, at 2:15 p.m., we are shown in, and the person we had an appointment with apologizes because the client she had scheduled at noon that day either arrived horribly late or wanted to stretch his appointment by another hour or both. *Grrrr...*

Here's the rule: If you are late for your appointment, you may in fact have forfeited it. People have been refused interviews for jobs because they arrived late, and they wouldn't dare say this result was unfair. When you arrive late for a job interview, you are demonstrating exactly what kind of irresponsible employee you would be.

My issue is that more people should use this approach in other areas of life. My time is precious, as is everyone else's. If I have an appointment with my dental hygienist and I am on time, I want to be taken on time, not after I have waited so long that I feel as if I've lost the use of my legs. If the person with the appointment before me arrived late, he or she should have to reschedule so as to accommodate me, the person who is on time. I should not be punished for following the rules. If, on the other hand, I am late and the person is kind enough to take me anyway, I ask whether there is another appointment after me and whether my lateness might adversely affect him or her. If so, I volunteer to use less time than I would normally be allotted or ask to reschedule the appointment on that day or another.

I am someone who *used* to be late. That's right, I admit it. I thought it was no big deal until one day I woke up to the fact that I was not being respectful of other people's time. Perhaps the biggest wake-up call occurred when someone showed up late for me and didn't think it was a big deal. I got some of my own medicine. As I always say, what comes around goes around. I realized that responsibility makes the world a better place. We can all accomplish more because we do not waste so much time. Conversely, rewarding or condoning bad behavior never helps to change thoughtlessness.

Yes, I know, this is all a little pie-in-the-sky. I cannot change the entire world. I can only change myself and the space immediately around me. This means that yes, I literally knock myself out to be on time. If I do not arrive on time, I am willing to accept that "the train may have pulled out without me."

Trying to be on time is my Right Effort. Accepting that there may be consequences if I am tardy is my Right View. Volunteering to receive less time if I have arrived late is my Right Mindfulness. Enforcing these codes of conduct when someone arrives late for an appointment with *me* is my Right Livelihood.

TARDINESS: It's one thing to be late for an appointment here and there because you are backed up by business matters. But some people, it seems, are always late for dates they have made in their personal lives as well. Frustrating, isn't it? After all, any activity is important if you've scheduled it at a specific time. Unlike the utterly incompetent people who have a reason to be late for everything—the baby wasn't feeling well, they received an unexpected phone call, and so on—these people wouldn't dare be late for an important business meeting but are always late for a movie date, a dinner, a barbecue, or what have you. As noted above, this used to be me until I finally realized that such behavior is just plain inconsiderate.

Caring, responsible people are that way with everything they do, not only with select activities. When people you know do appear to be selective about being on time—and it's not you they *select*—I would consider how little they value you and your time.

Look, we all have busy schedules. Here is what I do now: I begin every day thinking I'm going to conquer the world. I put a thousand things on my to-do list and I swear to myself I'm going to get to them all, but then reality sets in. You can't put ten pounds into a five-pound bag. What I do then is prioritize. If I've made an appointment—a specific appointment for a specific time—that commitment is as sacrosanct as a marriage vow. If I had originally thought I might be able to swing by the store to return something but then see that I am running late for the appointment, the store return gets bumped from my to-do list. I can do that some other time. The person I would otherwise keep waiting will not be placated when I explain how much I got done as I stroll in forty-five minutes late for my appointment. On the contrary, I might be faced with a pair of bloodshot eyes and a nasty tongue when I arrive. Not good.

Being late is a combination of poor planning and a bit of selfishness. After a certain age, we all should have a good idea of how long it takes to do things and plan accordingly. If you know it takes twenty minutes to get somewhere, give yourself thirty (or sixty, if you're one of those people who take twenty minutes just to get in the car and get settled) so that you can relax and not arrive frazzled. That also gives you extra time in case something beyond your control occurs, such as traffic, cell phone calls, or the zillion thoughts in your head.

As I've hinted above, however, sometimes allowing an extra ten minutes for traffic and such is not enough. If you do get caught in a situation beyond your control, you can use one of those little gadgets called a cell. It's interesting to note that accidents happen more frequently when we are rushing around in life. If you have such accidents often, it is an obvious sign that you should slow down—don't run, walk! Now if you are in a hurry and you accidentally rip your brand new silk shirt and must make a U-turn to your home or the nearest department store, you shouldn't be embarrassed at all to admit such a thing. That's being of Right Intention.

If you find yourself with a persistently tardy person in your life, confront the situation directly. If it continues to happen after you have explained your dilemma clearly and fairly, then move on. The same goes for most things. Give respect to get respect, and if you don't respect yourself, you can't expect anyone else to do so either.

BEING RUSHED: The subject of rushing deserves more consideration here. When you spend your days feeling rushed, you won't have the time or the mindset to be respectful of others. You won't be on your Zen Game.

In some cases, it is not your own behaviors that cause you to rush, but rather the expectations of others. There are two reasons why other people might rush you. One is that it is a strategic tactic. They think that if they can mess with your timing, they can get you off your game, so to speak. The other reason is that they simply live life at a faster pace than you do, which makes you feel rushed when you try to match it.

In the case of it being a tactic used against you purposely, sometimes the answer is as simple as giving the opposite back. Do everything in your power to slow things down. Talk slower. Take a bathroom break. Raise your hand or take both hands and give the universal time-out sign. All of these things will slow down the pace so it's more to your liking.

Think of the pushy salesperson who keeps saying, "You have to buy now; buy now! Or else it will be gone and you'll be sorry." Maybe that's true, but more often than not, it is just a strategy to get you to do something you may later regret. Stand back, take a deep breath, and take control of the situation by saying, out loud or to yourself, "I will do things at the pace that makes me most comfortable." Move and dance to the beat of your own drum. Or as my father has always taught me, it's best to tell people you will get back to them.

All of these same tactics will work when you are dealing with "rushers." These people don't have an evil agenda for world takeover; they're just in a big hurry. But the problem with being in a big rush is that it is nearly impossible to be thoughtful and nice at the same time that you are rushing. People in a hurry hardly ever say "Please" and "Thank you." They're in too much of a panic to get somewhere. They rush to get past us on sidewalks and in hallways and airports. More alarming are the speeders who cause life-or-death near misses as they dart in and out of traffic. I'm sure you are familiar with these drivers. They cut you off and speed past you, and then you wait behind them at the next traffic light. My beloved father-in-law, who repaired and sold cars, would always say when a reckless driver cut him off, "I will see you in my shop." It's true! Drive like a maniac, and you will eventually pay the price.

Of course, it's not always other people who cause us to rush. We all encounter situations that are beyond our control and can throw us into rushing mode. For example, we live an hour from the airport. We check the traffic report on the day of a trip and everything seems fine. We leave *two* hours early, yet we inevitably run into the world's worst traffic jam and arrive at the gate two minutes before our flight is about to go wheels up. We're under stress now, but what we often don't realize in such situations is that we are stressing out all the innocent bystanders around us.

Okay, so in this case, maybe we don't have any other options but to rush, unless there's another flight an hour later. But I've found that in most situations, there are always ways in which we can avoid these rush-rush scenes.

The first is through good planning. Everything takes longer than it should, so as I have illustrated, if you figure it takes an hour to get somewhere by car and you absolutely have to be there on time, leave yourself far more time than it should take. A good rule of thumb is to double the time you know it takes to get there. If you get to your destination early, you can relax, have a cappuccino, read a book, maybe even get some work done on your laptop or BlackBerry. Good preparation is the best tool for avoiding the stress of rushing.

If you prepare properly but things still don't go your way, think about whether there is a backup plan you can use. You're killing yourself to get to the day-care center to pick up your child before the place closes, and now you're caught with a flat tire? Call another mom or dad who is going there anyway and ask if he or she can help you out in your time of need. Trying to fit too many things into too little time? Mentally reprioritize your schedule and figure out what you can drop and leave for another day. Then relax and do the things left on your to-do list well, rather than sloppily due to all your rushing.

At the end of your days, you will not likely be pondering why you didn't get more things done on any one day of your life. What you will leave behind in this world is the overall impression you have made. Quite simply, when you rush you don't have time for etiquette. If, on the other hand, you were the person who always seemed relaxed and considerate of others, taking the time to remember your Zen Game, you will have left behind a legacy of love and happiness.

NOISEMAKERS: Unruly children, out-of-control barking dogs, boom boxes. While sometimes they are inevitable, they can be a form of disrespect when they are not handled properly. Yes, children need parenting and attention. Dogs need to get fresh air and to run and be walked.

Boom boxes…well, there is no need for them at all with the invention of iPods and other headset devices.

It is disrespectful to play loud music and rupture everyone's ear drums when you are not on your own property. No one should have to suffer blasting boom boxes in public places. Although the supposedly cool dudes playing the music love it, the people within earshot have mixed opinions. Some may like it or think it is okay, while others will find it a terrible distraction. It is not too far off to assume that some of them may be condemned to lifelong hearing problems. I've even heard my friend's mother say the music was so loud and the bass so strong that the vibration rattled her bones. The rule of thumb is this: When in public, I don't need to hear your sounds, and you're not obliged to hear mine.

This message also applies to people who play their car stereo so loudly that people a block away with their windows closed can hear it. Not only are you disturbing the peace, but statistics show that sales of hearing aids are up among young people due to excessively loud music. You may think that hearing aids are only for people who are way old, but think again!

Now, if you go to someone's house and he has unruly children or barking dogs, you must accept that this is his home and the way he lives. You are a guest in his home, and while you may find such things somewhat distracting, it is his home, not yours. If he asks for your opinion and you want to convey it diplomatically, that is fine. Also, don't be afraid to let your host know if you are allergic to dogs or cats.

On the other hand, if you and I have a date together—a dinner or perhaps even a business appointment—you must remember that there are some places and situations where those adorable two-legged and four-legged angels in your life do not belong. If you can't get a babysitter, then go out sometime when you *can* get one. Unless, of course, we are scheduling a play date and everyone has agreed that noisy children are fully welcome.

If someone else violates these codes of conduct, don't let it blow your top off. Just be direct and explain the nature of your objection. Give your fellow man a way out. Be in the moment. Remember to exercise Right Concentration.

YAKKERS: Have you ever been talking to someone face-to-face or on the phone and said, "I've got to go"? Of course you have. There are times when all of us must end a conversation, no matter how wonderful or exciting the other person is.

It's interesting to see how people react to these simple words. Some will practically hang up the phone before you even have a chance to say goodbye. Although the ending of the call is abrupt, this response is respectful of you. Then there are the people who hear these words, sense the time constraint, and start talking faster. Still others just keep talking as if nothing was said at all. Both of these responses are disrespectful. Even when the person wants to say "just one more thing," that one thing can turn into two or three things and last several minutes. These extra minutes can make you late for an appointment or mad that someone is trying to take advantage of your good nature. You may even avoid talking to the person again for fear he or she is going to try to hold on to you when you have other things to do.

Have you ever noticed that it is always the same people who must be told that you have to go? The difference with other people is that they are showing Right Mindfulness throughout a phone call. They sense consciously, through your words, tone of voice, and overall energy, that you have to go for one reason or another—to get back to work, to keep an appointment, or simply because you are tired of talking and your hand is getting numb from holding the phone to your ear. All of these reasons are valid and should be respected.

The bottom line is that when people say they have to go, trust that they don't mean five minutes from now or even one minute, but right now! Most people hate to be the one to end a call, so when you hear these words, either in person or on the phone, give them the gift of respect. Apply Right Action and say goodbye. Let them walk away with smiles on their faces, rather than worried that they are going to be late for their next appointment.

MORE ON YAKKERS: I have a group of friends I play tennis with regularly. If we go to a club or public court and no one else is around, we joke, laugh, and gab between games. But once other players arrive, we tone it down to respect the other people on the court. We know the codes and traditions and we respect them.

Have you ever been to a movie theater where the movie is accompanied by unrelenting audience commentary? Or to a church service where the six-year-old sitting next to you is fully engrossed in his PSP space game and shouts victory over the invading aliens every twenty seconds or so? Oh, and here's one that hits you directly in the pocket: Have you ever had a massage that was *not* relaxing because the masseuse talked your ear off the entire time? Talk about a waste of money! Remember to apply Right Action and self-control in all situations, and you will receive more joy and less resistance from others.

TO GIVE IS NEVER TO GO WRONG: How many times have we driven by someone who is stranded on the side of the road and thought to ourselves, "If only we had more time to stop and help them"?

Have you heard of Thomas Weller? They call him the "Mother Teresa of the freeway" because he has helped thousands of motorists. He is sixty years old and cruises around the freeways of San Diego looking to help people who are stranded or have car trouble. It's interesting to note that Weller was inspired to be a Good Samaritan after someone rescued his car from a snow bank. The "San Diego Highwayman," as he is called, accepts no payment. He only hands people a card that asks them to assist someone they may encounter who needs help.

Naturally, you want to be smart about making such a gesture yourself. It is important to be especially cautious late at night and to be aware of gangs flagging down your car. And if you see someone who is wearing a black suit, black shirt, and black tie and holding a violin case, I would drive on. I'm sure you get the idea!

Countless times we pass by homeless people on the sidewalk and do nothing to help them. We feel sad for these less fortunate souls, but because we are in a hurry, we do not take a few seconds of our precious time to offer them some change from our pockets or even a silent prayer for their well-being.

We make judgments too often about people who have a hand out or are asking for money. Are they *really* homeless? They don't *look* homeless. Are the stories they tell us true? What do they do with the money they are given? Are they using it to buy drugs and liquor, or are they really buying food with it?

The answers to these questions are not important. It is more important to be mindful of what is going on around you and recognize the power you have within you to make a difference in these people's lives. I have found that little acts of kindness—such as giving directions, giving change for a dollar for a meter, or giving people money when they say they need it—can make a big difference for them.

I heard a lovely story about how a nice single girl met the man of her dreams. They had just started dating and didn't really know each other very well yet. A television show came on discussing homelessness. Political commentators and social activists flapped their jaws loudly and long about what should be done about the dilemma. All sides seemed represented in the debate. The young lady turned to the young man and asked what his opinion was. He stared thoughtfully at the television set, but said nothing. Finally, he said, "Let's go." He grabbed her hand and helped her on with her coat.

It was early on a cold evening in the dead of winter. They lived near a major city that had a very large homeless population. He led her to his car and drove to the closest large discount store. She still had no idea what was on his mind, but she didn't mind shopping, so she went along amicably.

Once in the store, he headed for the large "bulk" items. He found big bags filled with cozy, warm, one-size-fits-all tube socks. In bulk, the price was right—a dozen pair of socks for only a few dollars. He gathered up as many as he could carry and encouraged her to do the same. She thought she had gotten involved with a madman, but his smile was infectious and so, as illogical as it all seemed, she went along.

Finally, once they were back in his car, she asked him what his plan was. He answered, "I have no idea what the answer to the homelessness problem is. It's way too big for me to solve all on my own. But I do know this: It's a cold, cold night and there are people only a few miles away who might likely freeze. I'm going to help them out, if only for tonight."

He drove to the city. Once they arrived, they headed for all the places where they knew homeless people might be found: subway stations, park benches, etc. Whenever they came upon someone, they gave the man or woman a pair of brand new tube socks. Some asked for two pairs—one for their feet and another to use as gloves. They went around and around until they had given out every pair they had.

She later said that this was the moment she knew she had met the man she wanted to be with forever. This was a person who lived a life of love. He did not get hung up on the intellectual or philosophical arguments of a social problem. He took the Right Action with the Right Intention.

People were cold. He gave them warmth. Period. Life is as simple as you choose to make it.

Whenever I am in a hurry and don't think I have time to stop, I know that it is necessary for me to stop and pay attention to this person in front of me who is in need. It's in times like these that I reflect on the words of my husband's grandfather, Nathan. He always said, "Better to be ripped off than not to give to someone in need." The message behind these words of wisdom is that there will indeed be times when people lie, deceive, and trick you. But unfortunately, we don't always have the foresight to separate the connivers from the ones who are truly in desperate need of our help. By being more mindful in our busy, everyday lives and having a conscious intention to always see the best in all people, we strengthen ourselves more than when someone gives us a hundred compliments. It's natural in life to be cautious of people. Heck, by the time you are an adult you've been jilted, lied to, and conned on at least 455,997 occasions, give or take few! It is why some people would say it is "normal" to mistrust people. Yet, when you incorporate your Zen Game into your everyday life, you also train yourself to give people the benefit of the doubt.

No, I'm not looking through rose-colored glasses, and I'm not saying that you will avoid all con artists. But the reward is that you will attract like people and will have the personal pride and satisfaction of knowing that you are giving and being your best self. Know that each action you take to help others is an expression of your love for yourself, your appreciation of life, and your respect for your fellow man.

COMPLIMENTING THE VICTOR: Some people get so hung up on winning and losing that they lose any passion they have for the purity of an endeavor. When I see someone doing something amazing, even if that action steals my thunder, I am truly ecstatic for that person. You can show your Right Intention in these situations by acknowledging the other person with a simple yet elegant compliment.

When you can earnestly appreciate an activity and compliment people even when they are beating you or performing better, it shows class and confidence. As we often see in life—sooner rather than later, hopefully—winning isn't everything. If you love an activity, a great performance is like a work of art. Champions can't help but acknowledge a winning performance, even if it's from their competitor. This holds true in any aspect of life. I've seen artists admire the work of a contemporary in an exhibit and openly admit it. I've seen tennis players put their hand to their racquet to applaud an opponent for a well-executed shot. Ego shouldn't come into play here. Let other people have their fifteen minutes of fame, and show that you are mature enough to handle it.

Now, what happens when a patient goes to a doctor for a second opinion, and this second physician catches something the first one missed? Should the first doctor shun the second doctor if they bump into each other in the hospital cafeteria? No way. The heart of the matter is caring for patients, *not protecting one's ego*. In matters such as this, there is no place for pride and pouting.

When complimenting the other guy, don't do it condescendingly, sarcastically, or when it is not merited. When you see something that is admirable, put aside your own petty jealousies and show respect. It's a good thing, and it may halt those nighttime bouts of heartburn you've been complaining about lately.

Ladies, this same advice applies if you have a tendency to look at other women as your competition. When you can show respect and acknowledge another woman for her beauty, intelligence, or athleticism, you increase your own happiness. You show to others your own confidence and empower yourself. In my practice as a life coach, too many women have confided in me that they feel unduly sensitive when they are near a group of women. Usually there is one person in the group who tries to instigate something and get the other women to jump on board with comments such as, "Look at her....Who does she think she is?" These comments are mean-spirited and unwarranted. Ten out of ten times, the people who think in this manner are the most insecure people you will ever meet. The act of belittling another woman oddly makes them feel better about themselves.

Women who behave like this are only setting themselves up for disappointment in life. The universe does not reward such behavior. As a matter of fact, it sends it right back to them like a boomerang. The result is not a pretty picture, only more misery for that person. These jealous types usually walk around being mean and angry with the world, never figuring out why their lives are a struggle. They think they have every right to pick apart someone they don't even know. They would never admit to their ill intention and wrongdoing, even if someone pointed it out to them. Often they think they are fooling people with their arrogance and condescending ways, but in actuality, everyone is aware of their insecurity and how miserable they really are in life. They are also unduly cautious of this person because they could be the next one she talks about behind their backs.

I always say, *all* women can be the queen, just as *all* men can be the king. Sometimes I think we do our gender a great injustice by not being as sisterly as possible, supporting and cheering on our sister-friends as much or more than we do men. I suppose women can learn by example from men. You rarely see a group of men putting down another man or scrutinizing and belittling a complete stranger who enters the room. Being of like gender should not make us more competitive, catty, and petty with one another; it should make us more collegial. We can all be winners. After all, we are all works in progress, we are all connected, and we are all in this life together.

SELF-DEPRECATION: A famed movie critic takes the stage and says, "Far be it from me to be opinionated, but..." and everyone laughs. It is called self-deprecation—poking good-natured fun at ourselves—and in the right hands, it's funny. As with any form of humor, however, it is dangerous when handled clumsily, and it can turn an attempt at respect into one of disrespect.

Some people actually use self-deprecation in a mean-spirited way. They say things like, "Well, I may not know much..." to imply that the person they are talking to has somehow impugned their intellect. My response to this is, if you feel someone has insulted or disrespected you, it is not appropriate behavior or Right Speech to respond in a self-deprecating manner. These situations can be handled in a more appropriate way.

In this case, self-deprecation is like a backhanded compliment. If your intent is to let someone know that he or she has hurt you in some way, approach the person directly and maturely and try to resolve the issue. If you cannot or do not want to do this, then decide once and for all whether you simply want to cut this person out of your life. It is your right to do so, and ending the relationship without incident is more proper than getting in some "last licks" as you go.

Self-deprecation is also of Wrong Intent when the person delivering it wants to *appear* humble. Putting yourself down to convey humbleness creates an odd façade that invariably makes both parties feel uncomfortable. In general, people will think you are *genuinely* humble when you respect other people, don't put others down, and don't put yourself above them. So why project something that is not natural? When we overtly try to sound humble to others, it looks and sounds phony.

Now, if for some reason you feel that you are lacking in a particular area, focus instead on the areas where you excel. No one is a champion at everything. The rocket scientist may not be able to tell a joke well. The star athlete may not be able to do math in his head. We all have our attributes and our deficiencies. Bemoaning our deficits is a way to ask for pity, which is a big no-no.

When something bad happens to us, it is okay to share that news with a close friend. But it is annoying to others when we complain about our lot in life through endless self-deprecation. This tactic will elicit a reaction more akin to travel sickness than respect.

BEING "TOO" NICE: When someone uses the phrase "too nice," I think of "Yes Men." Only egotists need Yes Men. People who are more evolved and self-confident want the truth, and at his core, a Yes Man is a liar. A very nice liar, but a liar all the same.

They say you must give respect to get respect. But before that, you must respect yourself. A person who has no self-respect will never be respected.

Please don't agree with me when I am wrong. Yes, be diplomatic. Yes, be sympathetic to people when they need it. But always remember to use Right Speech by making sure your comments are truthful and appropriate.

A person must never be afraid to be honest and say what he or she really feels, if asked. Some people feel they have to apologize for their honest thoughts. In fact, some seem to feel they have to apologize for everything, even for just being alive. That's what occurs to me when I am around someone whose every word is, "I'm sorry." Sorry for what? If you just stepped hard on my foot, then by all means, say you are sorry. But don't be sorry simply for existing.

If we are playing cards together and you make the wrong move because you're not familiar with the game, you don't have to apologize. It's just a game! If we are playing tennis doubles together, the same applies. As long as I can tell that you care and are doing your best, I can deal with it. Do you think I've never missed a shot? And since I do miss shots, please don't expect me to apologize every time I do. If I did that, I'd be hoarse from talking, rather than tired from playing.

Don't let me win. I want to earn it. I won't respect you for giving a game away to me. Sure, if you're Venus Williams and you want to give me a point or two to make up for the disparity in our abilities, fine, but do so from the outset, not during the match. (Venus, are you listening? Call me.)

TAKING FRIENDSHIP FOR GRANTED: Most of us put on our very best behavior for strangers. As we've all heard, "You only have one chance to make a first impression." There's nothing wrong with that. But what about people whom you already know quite well? Shouldn't we still want to demonstrate good behavior around them?

Sometimes I wonder if this is a lot like the situation I mentioned earlier in which a person who is nice to you at dinner but not to the waiter is not a nice person at all. Perhaps we have made such people a friend or a friendly acquaintance (almost a friend) because their initial pleasant demeanor made us like them. But if they now take us for granted and treat us shabbily, then that is who they really are.

It's like drinking. I never quite believe it when people say, "Sorry I did that to you. I was drunk and didn't know what I was doing." Most experts will tell you that alcohol is like truth serum. When people are drunk, they act like they really want to act, not like someone they're not. Not everyone who gets drunk acts like a jerk. Some fall asleep. Some get very mellow and more amorous. If someone has too much to drink and starts slapping you around, it's because he or she has been bottling up that rage all along. What he or she actually has, along with a drinking problem, is an anger management problem, as well as very negative feelings toward you.

Life is a litmus test. Yes, we all have our bad days and no one is perfect. We must acknowledge this fact before we judge. But if some people are always acting like a jerk toward us, they might be just that—a jerk. Why would they still want to hang around with us? Maybe it's because that's simply who they are. They let their real self loose once they feel comfortable enough to do so—so long as you allow it. But once that is revealed, it is up to you to decide how you want to proceed.

I once had a friend who liked to talk continuously during our get-togethers. His conversations were all about him and his life, and he never let me get a word in edgewise. A lot had to do with the fact that he always thought he was right and everyone else was wrong, so there was never any need to hear what I or anyone else had to say about anything. He never asked my opinion, and it was rare that he inquired about things that were happening in my life.

All relationships are about give-and-take. A good question to ask yourself about any important relationship is, "What am I getting back from it?" When you invest time, energy, and heart, you should always get something valuable in return. Such relationships might not always be fifty-fifty, but they should vacillate around that number. Eventually I concluded I was wasting my time with this person. Time has proven that I was right.

Some people's main character flaw is that they don't realize how hurtful their behavior is. Or perhaps such people like to test the limits of a friendship. When that happens, it is not wrong to confront them privately but directly and tell them how their behavior makes you feel. Sometimes, they will take it to heart and make a more conscious effort to demonstrate better manners. If not, you have just learned that this is not a person most people would choose to have as a friend.

LISTENING: There's a lot of talk these days about ADD—attention deficit disorder. It is very, very real in some people. And yet, more and more people either claim to have this disorder when they do not or are accused of having it when they don't. Why? Because they engage in "selective concentration."

Selective concentration is, "Yeah, I heard the first few words you said but then this really hot blonde in a 'barely there' dress walked by and everything went blank." That's not ADD, it's thinking with something other than your brain. And in the process, you've managed to offend someone.

As this example suggests, all of us receive signals from others that they do not place a high value on us. But we place a high value on ourselves, and rightly so. So one thing you can say, preferably in a humorous way, is something like, "Hey, my eyes are over here." Or else you can keep mum with the blowhard and think to yourself, "Oh well, I guess I don't rate as highly as the blonde does. My best play right now would be to have a discussion with someone who values me more." And off you go to greener pastures.

Some people think they can ignore others or be irresponsible and then offer the excuse, "I'm just a lunkhead" or "I'm just spacey." Most people would be insulted if they were called these names, yet these people relish the offbeat, self-deprecating humor of referring to themselves that way.

Think about it: In these situations, we are both victims and perpetrators. When you are talking to someone who is long-winded, for example, the situation is a shared dilemma. She should be more aware that she is so wrapped up in the sound of her own voice that she can't stop pontificating. You, on the other hand, are mentally drifting away, thinking, perhaps, of how to break through and get your own chance to talk or about the twittering little birdies overhead that sound so much more melodious than this windbag in front of you.

Everyone deserves their say. Everyone deserves to be heard. I hate the idea that children should be "seen and not heard." Children are just little people. Ignoring them only teaches them negative things about the world around them. Hear them out; see what it is they are trying to say. It may be a cry for help, something witty, or something silly, but give them a chance. Instill in them a sense of personal value. Some kids grow up to be troubled adults because they have no sense of self-worth. Why? BECAUSE NO ONE LISTENED TO THEM!

If you are engaged in a conversation, go out of your way to watch the other party. Are you losing him? If you know you've been talking a long time and he seems to be fading, maybe you've been too greedy with your time together. Ask him about himself. People love the chance to talk about that, so you can wake him from his comfortable little nap with this change of strategy. Don't let it all be about you.

But what about people who won't let you get a word in edgewise? Do you jump up and down and wave your hands in front of them? Or do you simply zone out? Then what do you do if you are on the phone? I try to send out subtle "I'm bored" or "I have something to say to that" signals as much as possible, but only after I have given them ample respect and time to make their point. That is, only at the point that I'm about to pluck the hair from my head one by one and make a handbasket out of it.

Another tactic is to throw out a question to them that is completely different from the subject they've been expounding on like a broken record. I find it usually gets them off their tangent. If you can't distract them with a question or a change of subject, then you may have to be more abrupt. But when you do so, don't simply tell them off. This approach will only force them into a defensive posture, and from there, no one can learn. They may also turn stubborn and drive you to complete frustration with more relentless banter. At the very least, it wastes a lot of your own precious energy and can even get you into a foul mood, and we certainly don't want that. Instead, say, "I hate to cut you off, but I think Pepsi actually *does* taste better than Coke." I know, it isn't much fun when a conversation turns into a competition for time to speak. But if a subtle or direct comment does not work, perhaps a zany or offbeat remark will do the trick.

If your windbag still doesn't get it, you may simply have to excuse yourself for better environs. Again, disengage. The longer you sit and get frustrated, the more likely it is that you will lose your temper and say something you'll regret.

The other art to listening, truly listening well, is not to let your mind drift while the other speaks as you try to think of what it is you have to say in response. How many times have you been ready to tell someone something and then forgotten it as you were about to say it? At the moment, it seemed so important. But even though you never shared the thought or story, in the end it really wasn't so important.

Use Right Concentration when you listen, which means, in essence, to listen. Be in the moment. When you are busy thinking of your response, you are living in the next moment, the one that has not yet happened. We often think that everyone is so interested in every nuance of our lives, but the truth is that sometimes the less we say the better. Let the other person do all the talking—why not give other people that gift? It really is a gift to truly listen to people and not interrupt them or try to top them with your own stories. They will usually walk away and say, "Wow, I really like that person. I just had a very stimulating conversation with her (*even though they did all the talking*)." You will even look very wise to boot!

Do you know what makes a person charismatic? Listening. Yes, listening, not talking. John F. Kennedy. Bill Clinton. Ronald Reagan. These men are three of the most dynamic public speakers of all time. And yet, people who have met them say they were most drawn to them because, no matter how small and unimportant they might have felt in the presence of such accomplished men, Kennedy, Clinton, and Reagan made them feel like the most important person in the room when they spoke. Each of these presidents knew the art of active listening, of making the other person feel special. They also knew how to initiate a conversation by asking good questions and appearing to really care about the answers. This is something we should all strive to do.

To be a good listener, lean and arch your body in attention in the direction of the speaker. Make eye contact the entire time he or she is speaking.

Nod, make facial expressions where appropriate, and engage the speaker with simple answers, such as "Yes, I agree, really, that's fascinating….I've never heard that before." If you agree with the speaker, let him know you are on his side and admire his astuteness and eloquence. If you disagree with something he says, engage intelligently and diplomatically.

"YES" VERSUS "NO": There may be no more overused word in the world than "no." When in doubt, "no" is often a great default answer. But "no" can also be a form of disrespect, indicating that the listener really has no intention of giving any real, sincere attention to the matter being presented.

"This tastes bad. Here, taste it."

"No."

I believe that in the world of business, "no" is the "no-brainer" answer to almost every inquiry. On the other hand, the businessperson who says "yes" instead of "no" often is the one who becomes more financially successful. "Yes" requires thought and ingenuity; "no" requires…lips and a voice box.

I have friends with food allergies. They go to restaurants and ask if dishes can be slightly altered so that they can enjoy them. The restaurateur makes a big deal about it and they feel guilty. So what do my allergic friends do? They go somewhere else! Good for them. The chef who is willing to help out those with allergies and do it with compassion gets the business.

Getting to "yes" often benefits everyone. For example, I enjoy traveling with my wonderful dogs. But have you ever tried to find a hotel that is pet-friendly? They are rare. Why? Because somewhere along the line, saying "No pets" became a rule and a tradition. And mindlessly following tradition became the norm. But when I find a pet-friendly hotel, I support it with all my vigor.

What is the harm in setting aside a handful of rooms for us pet owners? I say I have no idea. But I figure it's because "no" comes easier than "yes" in this age of parroting the other guy. Before defaulting to "no" because it's a "rule," consider examining the issue at hand. Perhaps there is a great opportunity awaiting if you think through how to get to "yes."

CATCHING A CHEAT: Everyone in life, including yours truly, makes mistakes. But what should you do when it seems obvious that someone is cheating—cheating you?

My first move is to give them all the opportunity in the world to come clean. We're back to that old adage about always leaving your adversary with a way out, a back door through which to save face.

This strategy may take a while. When people cheat, they are as aware of it as we, the victims, are. Of course, people's first inclination is toward self-preservation, and that means they will defend the cheating. What is incumbent upon the victim is to press the issue without raising the temperature to a thousand degrees Fahrenheit. This means we can continue to repeat or rephrase our allegation. Where we fail is if we lower ourselves to the cheater's level by losing our temper.

The idea is to give cheaters multiple opportunities to reverse themselves, knowing that the world will not collapse around them if they do so. That is the most important part that *we* play. Even if we find it hard to forgive, we must allow the perpetrators to believe that we will help facilitate a soft landing for them. That's our only chance to resolve the conflict peacefully without the use of intermediaries.

So what if it doesn't work? Well, all we can do in life is to try. If it is important enough, we may have to bring in some higher authority to mediate. Then things may get a little complicated, or perhaps hopeless is the right term. But more often than not, the simpler method is to just walk away. Yes, that's right, walk away.

If I go to the auto repair shop and am quoted a price of $250, but then receive a bill for $400, I will go through this process. And if it absolutely does not resolve itself the way I wish, I pay my bill, take my car, and go on my way. Sure, I could call the police, file a small claims case, call consumer protection, and all that rot, but that's very time consuming. Isn't my time worth more than the $150 that he overcharged me? I'd like to think so. If the amount were larger—and this is all relative—I might well find it in my best interest to invest the time and energy it would take to resolve the issue fairly. In this case, all that happened was that the auto repairman lost my patronage for all the years that followed and that of every member of my family. So he was the one who ended up getting the short end of the stick, in my opinion.

Occasionally I will run into acquaintances or strangers who have "short-changed" me, and they ask me why I do not use their services anymore. If I feel these people are open to my comments and will not be defensive, I will tell them diplomatically that yes, I felt I was not treated fairly. Although it would be much easier to make up an excuse that protects both of us, I feel that by taking the time and energy to state my case, I am in a way giving such people a gift. They may not see it that way initially, but if they listen and seriously consider my words, perhaps they will see a pattern in their behavior. Usually they have treated other people the same way and lost a lot of business or a good reputation because of it. When this golden opportunity does not arise, I take my business elsewhere.

HUMAN SUNSETS: Who doesn't want to live a long life? That being said, look around you and see what life is like for many people who reach their eighties, nineties, and above. It's often not pretty—and I don't mean that in a cosmetic way.

Life takes its toll on us. The body starts to go, and eventually the hearing and even the mind can begin to fade. It's sad, especially when you're watching a once-vital loved one begin to break down. Have you ever seen the movie *Cocoon*? It's about a group of seniors who find themselves regaining their youthful energy. For someone who's reached the sunset of life, this would be a fantasy come true.

When the body starts to malfunction, it often tries the person's patience as well. Elderly people with hearing loss often feel they have to shout for others to hear them, and sometimes the things being said are not meant for many ears to hear.

The younger caretakers of elderly people sometimes feel frustration and embarrassment. That's understandable. But what we must always try to do is think about how we ourselves would like to be treated if this were to happen to us. *Unless an elderly person has been put under your care by a doctor, I encourage you to give him or her the free will that he or she deserves as a human being.*

Kindness and respect are ever so important. And remember, almost everyone in the outside world feels empathy, more than any other emotion, for us and our elderly relatives. The pressure we feel is something we are putting upon ourselves. The public at large is very forgiving of these sorts of situations. Always remember this when you are straining to keep your patience and having to repeat things over and over again. The elderly deserve our respect. They are our human sunsets. Look at them with awe when you consider how much they have seen and learned and how many changes they have witnessed and adapted to over their long lives.

5
DRESS NOT TO...BE NAKED
(AMONG OTHER THINGS)

Living from a Zen Game perspective means learning to be comfortable with ourselves in every way, including our manner of dress and the way we project ourselves to others. When we dress well, we do much more than enhance our appearance. We reflect our confidence and self-esteem and demonstrate that we care about and respect ourselves inside and out. We also show that we care about and respect others. There is a lot to be gained from wearing something that fits well and looks attractive. The idea is to strike a balance between what we want to project and what other people expect of us.

It has been my experience that by the time people are thirty years old, they have a good idea of what looks good on them and what does not. This is true for both men and women. As adults, we no longer dress for other people, as we did in school, or to shock the establishment. Rather, we learn to dress for our shape, size, complexion, and so forth.

Most men and women want to project a certain image at work, so they learn to dress in a way that conveys authority and credibility. Once we have learned how to dress for success, we won't need to pay a lot of conscious attention to it. By always dressing with Right Intention, we will feel comfortable and will synchronize who we are and what we are projecting to others. This image will help others to feel comfortable with us.

DRESS TO SEXCESS: I grew up at a time in tennis when skirts with matching tops were the norm. Now just about anything goes. The same is true in other areas of life where there used to be rather stringent dress codes. I now see businessmen in ripped jeans, T-shirts, and a two-week growth of beard. This is not only considered acceptable, but some women find it sexy as all get-out.

Which brings me to the point of this section: sexiness. Dressing to appeal is fine. Men and women have always tried to attract one another and always will. If they did not, civilization would end because there would no longer be procreation. But this doesn't mean we should not have any limits on the way we dress.

There is a place for everything. Even if you are a nudist, the world has places for you. On the other hand, sexuality can be like a hammer, a blunt-force weapon, when it is used in the wrong place at the wrong time.

If I am having a business meeting with a man, I can accept it if the standard attire in his office calls for shirts but no ties. But if he is wearing a button-down shirt, I do not care to see it unbuttoned down to his navel, even if he looks like 007 Daniel Craig. Daniel, if I were single and you came over to my apartment dressed like that, it would be one thing. But at a business meeting, *no*. It's distracting.

I started with a male example on purpose because the remainder of this section is addressed mainly to women, who often have a problem with unduly sexy attire. I am a woman and I love to dress attractively. I want my man to be proud to have me by his side. But I can look sexy (at least I like to think so) in a classy way when I am conducting business for my books or giving lectures, rather than wearing a shirt cut down to here and a skirt hiked up to there. To dress in such a way demeans me as a professional and embarrasses my mate. How could I expect anyone to take me seriously if I went out dressed like Daisy Duke or wearing tight, low-rise jeans that barely cover me?

Yes, guys, I know some of you are reading this and saying, "Oh, I wouldn't mind." Oh yes, you would. Trust me, I know. Over-the-top clothes that reveal too much make everyone a little uncomfortable unless they are worn in the right place (after work hours, in restaurants, on the beach, in nightclubs). Guys, if your lady dressed that way for work, you would feel uncomfortable and you might even begin to wonder what's up. Also, the people who work with her and dress more professionally would feel equally uncomfortable—men and women alike.

There simply is no need for this. Before you go out, take a close look at yourself in the mirror. Do you look good? Is your choice of clothing in line with the dress code of the place where you are going? Is your clothing clean and in good repair? Does it flatter your figure, or does it show off your greatest embarrassments? If your considerably sized front is popping out, it's a good idea to change your outfit. If you can clearly see the "SWEET THING" tattoo in gothic print just above your butt, you need to change into more modest high-rise pants or choose a shirt that adequately covers that expanse of skin. In the workplace, especially, this type of attire sends a negative message. If you wear a skirt to work that reveals your thong, you are not showing that you are willing to work your way to the top of the ladder, but rather that you may be ready and willing to *sleep* your way to the top. (Sexy lingerie is acceptable, however, because it makes you feel good without advertising to the world, "Look at me, I'm sexy!" I've found that the sexiest people are those who don't feel the need to tell you they are such or push it in your face.)

Men, I'm talking to you here too. If you've got a big ole belly, running around in the shorts that you wore in college ten years ago is a definite no-no. You know the ones. They are a struggle to put on because they're several sizes too small. I know you hate change and you think these itsy bitsy shorts look cute on you. But let's face facts.

Some attractive people think that if they dress in a very revealing way it will empower them, make them popular, and do more for their careers. Perhaps this is true in acting or in the music business, but in other professions I beg to disagree.

I once took a class on elocution and my wonderful instructor said, "One of the best looks for a woman who is speaking before a crowd is a turtleneck. In that way, all eyes are drawn to her expressive face and her mouth as she is talking, not to any other part of her body." Having all eyes on your face when you talk is far more empowering than having people staring at your chest. When you are focused on the front or back of a man's pants, or on a woman's chest or legs, it does not lend itself to getting a lot of work done!

I think television has done us all a great disservice in this area. No one in real life dresses like the characters on TV. Every female character on television with a serious career has her shirt cut down to her navel and her skirt resting at the top of her thighs. No schoolteacher would go to work like this. No policewoman, no lawyer, no doctor. And yet those are the occupations of these characters.

Dress appropriately. Show respect for your occupation, your employer and co-workers, your friends and family, and yourself.

BUTT CRACK: Have I gotten your attention? Seeing the words *butt crack* in print has the same effect as seeing the actual thing in public. I personally apologize to you, the reader, for having to read these words just as I, personally, do not like to see people's actual crevices when I'm out and about.

Styles come and go, but I wish some would go away far sooner than others. We now have this thing where men walk around with their pants falling off. In the past, butt crack exposure was a dubious privilege granted exclusively to construction workers and the like. In the fashion context, the effect has been mitigated somewhat by the high-riding boxers worn under the pants. Do I feel like looking at a man's boxers, designer or otherwise, protruding from his falling-down pants? Not really. The look doesn't quite do it for me because I think it's a bit of an old, worn-out fad. However, colorful boxers are a small step above seeing naked rump peeking up at me while I'm trying to down a sandwich for lunch at the corner café. Why, the sight could be enough to ruin your appetite.

This is not just a male phenomenon. With women, it is more often low-riding, hip-hugger jeans (accompanied by candy-colored or polka dot thong panties playing peekaboo when the lady sits on a chair). Hey, I admit, with the right body, this look can be sexy (not the panties but the jeans). But like anything else, there are limits. Tight jeans hanging on hips just so are one thing; looking like you forgot to pull up your pants after a bathroom break is another.

One overriding (as opposed to low-riding) issue, as these fashion trends come and go, is how appropriate (or inappropriate) your attire is in the circumstances. What *is* fashion, anyway? In the animal kingdom, it may be a bird's plumage. But when we find ourselves discussing the appropriateness of clothing, we are often talking about overt sexiness—that is, dressing to attract. Granted, there may be times when we want to attract others in a sexual way. Even if we are already in a committed relationship, we may want to "flaunt what mama gave us." That's fine, so long as it's okay with that aforementioned significant other. I suppose in the Zen Game world, if you dress with Right Intention you will always feel comfortable, convey confidence, and project to others that you respect who you are.

COMFORT: Fashion can be downright uncomfortable at times. Ladies, perhaps you enjoy wearing a short skirt on occasion—I know that I do. Well, there's short and then there's so short that it looks more like a belt than a skirt, causing you to pull and tug constantly at the skirt so that it covers the bare minimum. That pulling and tugging? It's uncomfortable and a real hassle. So what has been accomplished? I've worn something that I thought would have certain positive attributes, but those positives were overridden by the discomfort of the pulling and tugging. Simply put, no matter how nice I may or may not have looked, I was physically uncomfortable.

Is fashion worth discomfort? That's a tough one. I happen to love a man in a tuxedo (James Bond fetish). I've met some men who find them to be very comfortable, although it seems that the majority think the opposite. So what does a man who finds tuxedos uncomfortable do when invited to a black-tie affair? In that case, all you can do is bite your lip and sally forth. Wearing what is expected of us in certain instances, even if we don't enjoy it, is making the Right Effort.

I try not to be physically uncomfortable in my clothing if I can avoid it. Even if an outfit looks great, if it causes actual physical pain, what will my overall experience be while I'm wearing it? For example, some women can wear heels higher than the Eiffel Tower and be comfortable, while others cringe in agony. I believe it is possible to make compromises between comfort and appearances. How much fun can a person be having if she's in pain? You may find yourself not only having a bad time but also being less than your best to others. That's a classic lose-lose situation.

One last word on fashion comfort: Years ago I heard that one of my favorite baseball players, Johnny Damon, took to wearing a thong in order to break a hitting slump. It worked so well that then teammate Jason Giambi tried it too. Now, why would a man, an athlete, wear something that most men find incredibly uncomfortable (not to mention quirky)? Distraction! Athletes who are in a funk sometimes need, among other things, to get their minds off their troubles. What a simple way to do that—wearing uncomfortable underwear!

OVER-DRESS/UNDER-DRESS: Now that we've just spoken about *underwear*, let's talk about another "under": under-dressing.

As I mentioned earlier, we are becoming a much more casually dressed society. Watch some old movies on late-night television and you'll see that there was a time when men wore fedoras everywhere, women never went out without white gloves, and it wasn't unusual to see your next-door neighbor cutting the grass while wearing a shirt and tie.

No more. Young guys now strive to make their hair look like they just rolled out of bed, people go to Broadway shows in Bermuda shorts and sandals, and men wear baseball caps in church. Arguably, it's a new and not entirely better era.

Now, before you paint me as some sort of schoolmarm, understand that I'm not talking about looking attractive per se. I'm addressing the concept of being too casual in the way we dress. My mother always lectured me, "Better to over-dress than to under-dress," and I believe she was right.

Do I mean that you should put that fedora back on, don the white gloves, and wear a shirt and tie to mow your lawn? Of course not! Furthermore, cocktail dresses at a football game or tuxedos at a tractor pull are more than a little over the top. But outside of the ridiculous, you'll rarely go wrong if you "pump it up" a bit. Look, there is a reason why every man in Palm Beach wears a blue blazer with white trousers and black loafers—it looks good and women love it, and if it gets too hot you can always take the blazer off. The rock band ZZ Top got it right when they sang, "Every girl's crazy 'bout a sharp-dressed man!" Likewise, the beautiful models in Monte Carlo are dressed to the nines. Don't expect to see them wearing old jeans and T-shirts.

I'm not saying you need to primp and fuss every time you go out. As a matter of fact, the smartest look to me is when people are well put together but don't look as if they spent the whole day getting ready. You have more important things to do with your life than spend hours on your hair and dress.

However, a little bit of extra attention to the way you dress will create a good impression with others, and it will give you that added bit of confidence as well.

LEADING AND FOLLOWING: Have you ever been to a fashion show? I have, and the clothes the models wear are gorgeous. Of course, they would look gorgeous wearing a burlap bag because they are so beautiful. But here's the thing: Can *everyone* dress like these models and pull it off? In my opinion, no. If you think long and hard about it, you would have to agree.

Whatever your age, take a look around at people the same age as you. Look at what they are wearing. Would every outfit you see look good on you? Even if you are a supermodel, I would venture that the answer is "no."

We all have different bodies, faces and hair. A great look is idiosyncratic. My father has told me that when the Beatles first invaded America, every boy in town tried to grow a "Beatles" haircut. On some, it looked great, while on others it looked like a circus wig. Do you have old pictures of yourself that you never show to people? We all do. Is it because of a hairstyle that you now know was a terrible mistake, or an outfit that was so trendy and looked so bad on you that you hope no one remembers you in it? Once again, join the club. We *all* have experienced these embarrassing moments.

Fashion trends will come and go, and many of us will be tempted to join them. On some of us, a trend will "take." We may even wear it for years after it has ceased to be trendy—and it will still get us compliments. Why? Because it just "fits" us. If Britney Spears showed up in Laura Ashley clothes to give a concert, people might not recognize her. It's just not her thing. But what she does choose to wear looks good on her and fits her image as a top entertainer.

What you see in the top fashion magazines or on the Paris catwalks is not necessarily what you will see people sporting at the office or on the streets where you live. Why, you ask? Because being a "dedicated follower of fashion" often fails us. People want to dress fashionably, but they also want to be practical about what they wear at work, at home, or when going out.

So here's my best tip on the topic: Be a leader, not a follower. Ditch the catwalk looks and fashion trends if that's how you feel about it and follow your own instincts. Otherwise, take a hard look at yourself, be honest with the image in the mirror, and ask yourself *why* you want to follow a new trend. Is it simply because it looks "kicky" and worth a try? Then what the heck—dive into the adventure! But if it's because you feel you have to change your look just to fit in, ask yourself whom you are trying to fit in *with* and what kind of people they are if they don't accept you as you are, looking your best in your own personalized way.

COMFORT REBELLION: Just as I know people who will suffer through stiletto heels and the like just to look hot, I also know folks who consider having to wear a tie an act akin to being waterboarded. They will actually avoid going places where they must dress in a certain way.

In the end, this is your personal choice. I agree, frankly, that if you are totally miserable when you must dress up, then maybe you should avoid having to do it. You'll be happier, and you won't poison the air around you as you grouse about what you had to wear.

On the other hand, I believe there are fashion compromises available if you are willing to take notice. Let's take footwear. Ladies, if you loathe heels, there are flats and near-flats available that look marvelous, if only you take the time to look for them. Guys, some of you wish you could live in sneakers. Well, the sneaker is an ever-evolving thing; it has come a long way from the canvas high-top Chuck Taylor All-Stars that all the girls and guys wore in grade school and that are now back in fashion for both kids and adults. Today we have sneakers that don't even look like sneakers. While I might not suggest you try them with a tuxedo, you may find some that are quite dressy while still retaining their light weight and flexibility.

There are people who belligerently flaunt improper attire and show up purposely underdressed for a place or an event just to make some sort of point. This is a bad idea—Wrong Intention. If I invite you to a black-tie affair and you show up in a T-shirt and shorts just to make a statement, I will in turn make *my* statement: "Out!"

Fashion involves other kinds of compromises as well. For example, when girls get married they often ask their bridesmaids to buy a dress that vacillates between an iridescent peach and pink. Not only is the color unbecoming, but the design is something you would never wear except when asked to do so by your dear, sweet friend or, perhaps, under torture. Naturally, all the bridesmaids swear they will have the dress altered afterward so that they can get their money's worth, but of course they never do. Instead, they wear the dress once on their friend's special day. They smile for the pictures and never let the bride know how much they dislike looking like the icing on a cake. This is a beautiful example of being a good friend as you put someone else's happiness before your own.

It's one thing if you are being asked to compromise your values, morals, and ethics. It's quite another if you are simply being asked to wear a dress. If certain types of apparel bother you, be creative and use your investigative skills to see whether there are new or alternate styles that will suit both you and the event. Short of that, ponder the invitation and decide what is more important—staying home and being totally comfortable, or attending the event and being a little less than comfortable for a limited amount of time. Occasionally, it is Right Effort to "take one for the team."

TO DRESS YOUR BEST, CALL AHEAD: So, how do we avoid improper dress? One of the best methods I know is to call ahead. If it's a get-together at a friend's house, it's not out of line to ask, "What will people be wearing?" You're probably not asking for anything more specific than whether it is a dressy or casual event, but the answer will give you a clue.

This is also an area where people who open up their house to others can really demonstrate good hosting techniques. If you are a host, *do* tell people what to expect apparel-wise. If you are inviting guests to swim in your pool or play tennis on your court, don't expect them to read your mind and know that you own these things and plan to open them up for guests. If you are a guest, on the other hand, don't show up in a swimsuit simply because you know the host owns a pool. Maybe that was not the plan and not the nature of this particular party. I can just envision having people over after a funeral and some dingbat showing up in swimming trunks!

The Call Ahead is also perfect for restaurants, clubs, and other public accommodations. I'll tell you a funny story: My husband and I were going to a supper club to see the fabulous Bebe Neuwirth. We didn't quite know where the place was, so I called and asked, "What is your address?" The owner replied, "Smart casual." I suppose he'd received so many calls from people asking about the dress code that he simply parroted the answer he had given most, without stopping to think about what I had asked.

But seriously, men run into this issue far more often than women do. Some very fancy restaurants require men to wear jackets. If you arrive without one, you get stuck wearing some funky thing they have hanging in the closet. This is no fun at all. So unless you know exactly what the dress code is at your place of destination, call ahead and find out what is appropriate. In fact, whether you are going out *on* the town or going out *of* town, it's best to find out the weather conditions, the activities planned, and the dress for the evening. This tactic will allow you to be the best you that you can be.

TRAVEL CLOTHING: Travel produces a fashion quandary for most of us. First off, I know there is still a good chance I will be seen by others. This is obviously the case if I am taking a plane or train. But even if I am driving somewhere, I'll probably be using a rest stop and stopping for a meal. On short hops, I may run into folks at the supermarket or pet store. When people see me, I don't want to look like I've been mucking stalls all day.

But travel has its own quirks. If you wear a suit or dress on an airplane and then have to sit in cramped quarters for a few hours, you are bound to deplane looking like one big wrinkle. Then there is the issue of being comfortable in that cramped space. Even if I am not in a dress or a suit, I don't want to be wearing something too tight because the sardine-like conditions will only make me feel tighter than a pig in a blanket.

Can you still look good while traveling? Of course. All it takes is the ability to think through the situation. Pick out something that looks nice on you, but avoid things that wrinkle easily or are too tight. Another trick I've picked up concerns footwear. I love to free my feet whenever appropriate. When I'm on a plane, I bring along an extra pair of socks in my purse. That way, I can slip off my shoes and slip on the socks and have that barefoot feeling that is *oh so good*. Hey, travel is uncomfortable, and discomfort makes us miserable. Me, I don't like to be miserable, so I take personal responsibility for my own disposition by making myself look good and feel good. You should too.

KNOW THYSELF: Know what kind of clothing you will require when it comes to hot and cold extremes. If you are always cold, bring a sweater wherever you go. This is even pertinent in the hottest of heat waves if you may be going somewhere indoors. For example, most movie theaters crank up the air conditioning, so even though it is a hundred degrees outside, it may be sixty degrees in the theater. If that bothers you, bring along a sweater or a light jacket just in case.

There's nothing worse than people who are always hot or always cold who then make everyone else miserable by playing "Thermostat Terrorist." These people get into armed battles with the rest of the world because they want to turn a room into a freezer or a steam bath to suit their own quirky body temp. Dressing comfortably also means knowing if you're one of these "hot" or "cold" people.

Don't be afraid to ask questions when it comes to outdoor activities. If you've never been to a live football game, you might not know that there's a big difference between being outside for a few minutes as you go from your front door to your car and sitting in the stands at a game for several hours while cold winds blow through you and the seats feel like blocks of ice. I went to Ohio State—I know! When that happens, even if the thermometer says forty-five degrees, you will probably be more comfortable dressing as if it were fifteen degrees. Be sure to wear layers so that you can "ride the (cold) wave" as winds and temperatures rise and fall.

The simple rules apply here: Always be prepared, and do what the cowboys do—remember that you can take off something you don't need, but you can't put on what you don't have.

OOPS!: Remember the scene in the movie *Legally Blonde* where Reese Witherspoon is invited to what her romantic rival says is a costume party? She shows up in a Playboy bunny outfit and finds that it is not a costume party after all. I enjoyed a similar scene with Renee Zellweger in *Bridget Jones's Diary*, but let's go back to Reese Witherspoon. Your first inclination is to feel sorry for her, but you also can't help thinking, "My God, I would die if I was in her situation!"

You can take away this piece of advice from *Legally Blonde*: In real life, things like this happen (except, hopefully, the part about someone pulling a purposeful prank on you). And if you live long enough, they may even happen to you.

My loving husband got it wrong once when he was certain that a party he had been invited to was black tie. He and a friend of his showed up in tuxes, only to find that they were incorrect. Everyone else was dressed casually, and here were these two good-looking guys in their tuxedos. Because they were the only ones dressed so formally, I'm surprised that people didn't start giving them their drink orders!

In both of these examples, the heroes (for my husband shall *always* be a hero in my eyes) did what heroes ought to do: They shrugged it off and moved on. In *Legally Blonde*, Reese showed her spunk by effectively saying "to heck with it" and holding her head up high and "working it." My hubby had a few beers with his pal, and before long they were laughing like schoolboys at their dilemma. The point is, if you get caught in a total fashion faux pas, what the heck can you do but take it in stride?

Another awkward situation occurs when you go out and something utterly terrible happens to your clothing. The waiter spills an entire entrée on you. You look like chicken vindaloo on an oversized platter. What can you do? You try to clean yourself up, you accept that everyone there probably saw the accident happen, and if you put it in context, you realize that every person there has probably had a similar thing happen to him or her over the span of a lifetime. Accidents happen. If you can laugh about it, you will ease everyone's tension. The more you freak out, the worse everyone else feels. No one is laughing at you; trust me on this. People are sympathetic, even if you spilled that bowl of chowder on *yourself* and cannot blame it on a waiter or another person. *Allow* people to sympathize with your plight by keeping your cool.

If you are terribly, terribly uncomfortable—and yes, there are certain meals I would not want to wear for an entire evening—consider the pros and cons of going home and changing or simply calling it a night. Just don't go away angry. Remember that into each life a little marinara sauce must fall.

What about liability? This is one of life's two-way streets. If you are the cause of someone getting plastered with béarnaise sauce, be a good citizen and treat it as you would a traffic accident. Introduce yourself to the victim and volunteer to properly clean or perhaps even replace the ruined clothing. If you are the victim, expect the same. If you do not receive such a noble response from your food dumper, try not to make a big scene. But understand that accepting responsibility for ruining someone's clothes is the Right Action to take. Attempt to convey this as firmly as possible without allowing other extraneous issues to cloud the one issue of controversy.

NAPOLEON: I was recently surprised to hear the number of male world leaders today who are of less than average height. Vladimir Putin of Russia is only around five feet five. His hand-chosen successor is, I believe, about an inch shorter than that. These are only two examples, but there are scores of others.

So what of it, and why are we talking about it here? Well, we are told that the average height of an adult American male is about five feet ten. This means there are just as many men who are less than five feet ten as there are taller.

I rarely hear women grousing about their own height, but for men, this seems to be an issue that they erroneously link with virility.

I find that men of almost every height tend to be most attracted to women who are shorter than they are. Maybe it's engrained in them from caveman days. I certainly can't tell men to whom they should or should not be attracted. But if you are a guy who dismisses a woman who is appealing to you because she's an inch or two or three taller, think again.

Yes, some women are the same way. They won't give a shorter guy the time of day. It's sad, but again, it's hard to tell other people whom they should or should not find attractive. But when two people find that certain spark between them, consciously dismissing it because of some perceived issue of height seems just loony to me.

And what does this have to do with fashion? Heels! Yes, in some relationships where the woman is taller, the woman is either forced by her man to wear flats or chooses to do so herself because the two think that the world at large will laugh at a couple where the man is shorter than the woman.

People, let me ask you all a question: Have you ever laughed at a couple because the woman was taller than the man? I'll bet any amount of money that the answer is "no." People don't care! Oh sure, they might notice it in the same way they notice anything about you—your hair color, your weight, what you are wearing—but it doesn't *define* you, either as an individual or as a couple.

A completely confident, evolved man has no trouble being in the company of a taller woman to whom he is attracted on some level. And if she wants to wear high heels because they make her look or feel good, the confident man says, "Go ahead" and means it. I'm sure that Napoleon's short stature wasn't one of his concerns when he wooed his Josephine or set out to plunder half the civilized world.

If you are in a relationship where your mate makes you dress a certain way because he or she would feel like less of a person if you were to dress the way you like, then you've got troubles. Fact is, there is nothing sexier than self-confidence, and if you don't have it, make it a priority to get yourself some, no matter what your height, weight, age, or whatever. Always try to look your best, but accept that some things can't be changed—such as height—and that these things should not rule your entire existence. Live, love, laugh, and dress in a manner that allows you to look your best.

MAKEUP: Some women have such a hard time with makeup. Most of it is not designed to endure the sort of sweaty conditions women face when running around like headless chickens—taking care of family, doing the shopping, rushing to work, etc. As a result, many women choose to not wear any makeup at all. For this reason, a lot of people are surprised to see how attractive these women look when they ditch the stresses of routine life and go out into the world of leisure. Yes, many of us clean up quite nicely.

Once off the daily grid, how much makeup is the right amount? The best look is a natural one. Some men may think they prefer a woman with no makeup, but as my friends in the modeling business will tell you, a little makeup that is properly applied is more flattering than none at all. Well-applied makeup will accentuate and highlight the beautiful parts of your face, conceal dark circles under the eyes, even out skin tone, and make a blemish just about disappear—things *any* woman, no matter her age, will appreciate. Ironically, a good makeup job will accentuate your beauty while making you look like a natural beauty who doesn't wear any makeup at all. Indeed, if you look like someone slathered it on you with a cement trowel, you're going in the wrong direction.

So how do you get it right? Perhaps when you were a teenager, you didn't have a mom or an older sister who was a whiz at such things and able to teach you how to use makeup. If you are having trouble, see a professional. Heck, even those ladies at the finer cosmetic counters in good stores can teach you a thing or two. My only advice here is to take a good look at the person behind the counter. If *she* looks like she's in the opera, then try another place, unless that's the look you want.

TANS: The healthiest tans are the ones that come in a bottle. True, they used to make everyone look like an orange, but they're getting better every day, so give them a try. Lying outside without sunblock and slowly baking like a lobster is a quick road to skin cancer, and that doesn't look good on anybody.

And lastly, remember that the peaches and cream look suits some people just fine. Look at Nicole Kidman. She loves to swim outdoors and always wears a long-sleeve shirt when she does so. It's obvious that she protects her skin, and the result is that she's gorgeous—a beautiful lady with pure alabaster skin. A dear friend of mine from Belize named Shelly has beautiful dark skin. She never leaves the house (even in the winter) without putting on her sunblock. She knows that this daily effort is worth it from all the compliments she gets on her radiant skin. The more we apply Right Action toward our well-being, the healthier we will be and the better we will feel.

6
WE ARE FAMILY

It so happens that I am not a parent. On the other hand, I do have beloved children; it's just that they run on four legs and their hair takes longer to brush! All kidding aside, when I was a tennis pro, I taught many children and spent many years watching them grow up. I am grateful to all the children who have touched my life for reminding me of such important things as expressing your feelings, enjoying the simple things in life, and living every day in the moment with imagination, curiosity, and enthusiasm. Allow me to share what I've learned over the years from tending to the youth of America.

People who take a Zen Game approach to life affect more than just themselves. When we strive to always be mindful of the eight pillars, we cannot help but influence those around us in a very positive way. Perhaps no one is more susceptible to outside influences—both good and bad, unfortunately—than children because they are so impressionable. So let's talk about some parent/child issues and family matters in general, and about how we can imbue a Zen Game attitude within the next generation and those closest to us.

BE THE SHINING EXAMPLE: Perhaps the most important lesson for all of us is to always be our best self. Whether you realize it or not, people are watching you. So give your kids or anyone else who is watching something to emulate. Ditch the "do as I say, not as I do" approach.

We all know that kids ask a lot of questions—why, why, why? We also know that saying "do as I say" is sometimes easier for the parent than having to explain things to the nth degree. But you will find that this archaic expression only works temporarily. When questions are not sufficiently answered in a child's mind, they will indeed come up again and again and again.

MINI ME'S: Teaching by example is especially important because children emulate everything they see, whether you like it or not. As a parent, you are your child's greatest influence, no matter how many Miley Cyrus posters she has tacked on her bedroom wall.

So what happens when you face the conflicts that arise in everyone's life? Your children see how you handle those conflicts. If they witness you having a tantrum during participatory sports or at a political rally, they will do so too, no matter how much you tell them otherwise. Why? Because they are "Mini Me's." They saw you do it, and now they subconsciously want to be like mom or dad. Parents are their heroes, even when they don't act like it.

Yell at a store clerk? They will too. Gossip viciously about the neighbor? So will they. Tell a blatant lie to someone? Your child will think that lying is proper etiquette as well.

They say that parenting is a major life event because it forces maturity on us. This new role must be done properly and accepted introspectively. The moment we see that shining newborn face, we must look within ourselves and realize that nothing will ever be quite the same again. Our worst behavior will be seen by this little witness with an elephant's memory, and so we must make a pact with ourselves to grow up and clean up our act. Maybe we were prone to bad behavior before, but now we *really* have a reason to turn over a new leaf.

SAFETY: Until now, we've discussed the idea of the Zen Game in mostly existential terms—the importance of being a nice person and, in doing so, making the world a slightly better place. But with kids, and with ourselves as well, living life with a Zen Game attitude also keeps us *safer*.

Take the example of learning to be prepared, an aspect of the Zen Game that we discussed earlier. Being prepared for any event or activity means we will not be as rushed when we need to be somewhere. It is when we rush that we tend to have accidents—car crashes or smacking into other pedestrians as we race down the sidewalk. Those things are far more critical than simply being late.

Here's another safety issue to consider whether you have kids or not: cell phones. I see people walking down the street texting into cell phones and BlackBerries with their heads down, oblivious to the world. Step off a curb incorrectly while doing that and you'll break an ankle or step in front of a car. Do it while you are pushing a stroller or in charge of watching a toddler and the ramifications can be ever worse. Keeping your eye on the ball is a good metaphor—multitasking with cell phones can be dangerous!

ALCOHOL: We talked about drinking earlier, but when kids are in the picture, the rules change. Some parents allow their children to drink even though they are underage. Granted, this is sometimes a cultural thing—in many European countries, for example, parents may serve wine to their teenage children at dinner. But the issue here in America is legality. Should you really teach your children to "wink" at laws? I don't believe that is the Right View to take.

If your children see they can sidestep laws while in your presence, they will rarely make the distinction to alter that behavior when you are not around. But no one will be winking if they get pulled over by the cops when they are seventeen and drunk. Getting into trouble with the law at a young age can ruin college plans and some career plans because these things tend to follow us around for a while. What is the upside? Is it really so important to have alcohol that it is worth getting thrown off the football team or having your college admission rescinded?

Parents, your children's respect for the law—indeed, for rules in general—stems from *you*. You set the tone on rules and behaviors. The same goes for drinking to excess. I don't believe it's a good thing, period, but going back to what I just said about parenthood being the catalyst for "growing up," if your children see you smashed, they will think it is fine for them to behave that way as well. This isn't good, even if they do wait until they are of legal age to drink.

STRESS: Your child is about to step onto the stage at his high school in the title role of "The Importance of Being Earnest." Or she is about to walk into the testing room to begin her SAT for college. What mood and attitude do you want your child to be in? Stressed out of his or her mind? Probably not.

You, as the most important adult in your children's lives, have within you the ability either to calm them down or to put them on edge. Why do damage to their performance by inducing stress?

Ten minutes before an important event or test, there is nothing new you can impart to them, no new knowledge. At that moment, they are what they are. The best you can do is to offer one simple piece of advice that may act like a hypnotist's "magic word" and remind them of something they already know. The key word here is "simple." You might say something like, "Remember to keep your head up; be proud of yourself." (This was good advice my father always gave to me—to be proud that you did your best!) Beyond that, leave kids alone in these situations and realize that what they need to do in the last few moments is to get themselves into the zone.

Bolster them up. Relax them. Let them know you love them no matter what the outcome. Show them love. Make sure they are filled with self-love and positive thoughts. Don't stress them out. Smile.

IRRITABILITY: Our families see everything. They see us at our best and they see us at our worst—when we step proudly onto the stage to accept our degree or when we spend a week with the toilet bowl, afflicted by the world's worst bout of gastric flu.

We allow our families to see sides of us that we would never allow anyone else to see. However, if we let loose enough with these "inner demons," it becomes much easier for us to slip up and let them escape at the most inopportune times.

All of this, of course, is a two-way street. Let's say you are about to step into a room for the most important interview of your life. It's the job of your dreams, the one you'd do almost anything for—including chewing your fingernails to the quick in anticipation of the interview. You're stressed. You forget your wallet and lock the keys in the car. Your nervous tic is having a field day and your right eye is winking repetitively, of its own volition. Nothing your spouse or parent has said was the cause of your current condition. It is simply that you are too tightly strung at the moment. So who do you take it out on? Your loved one, that's who!

It's wrong, but it's also somewhat understandable. You've gotten into a "fight or flight" mode, and that reaction is as old as ancient man. So what are the roles to be played, and what is the Zen Game way of playing them?

First off, work on the irritability issue. Learn de-stressors such as relaxation and deep-breathing techniques. Practice constructive, meditative thought. In the world of sports, prodigies learn and practice constructive and meditative thoughts as children, and this practice undoubtedly benefits them throughout their lives.

In addition, realize that there are second chances at almost anything in life. Little is truly do or die. We often lose sight of this truth and find ourselves stressed unnecessarily. For information on how to get better control of your emotions and perform at your best in every situation, please check out my books *The Victory Dance: Placing Yourself in the Winner's Circle in*

Sports and in Life (for adults) and *Victory Dancing for Teens: Smooth Moves for Getting to the Winner's Circle*.

On the other hand, what if you are the *victim* of this irritability? Well, fighting fire with fire is rarely the answer. If your child is stepping out onto a football field and snaps at you, this is not the time to grab him by the arm and chastise him. A confrontation at that moment will only accentuate the problem.

Wait until later, after the event is over, and have a calm discussion about the issue. Look at it as a problem to be fixed, rather than focusing only on your desire for an apology. Irritability is a problem that needs to be attacked because, along with everything else, it will come between your family member and his ability to succeed in his endeavors and develop interpersonal relationships. Work together to mitigate the problem, so that in the future, going to work or competing in an activity will not always be a trigger for bad behavior caused by anxiety and stress. Always know that for every problem there is a solution. Learn to put more focus on the solution than on the bad behavior.

INDIVIDUALITY: One thing parents sometimes have a hard time dealing with—much like spouses and bosses—is that everyone is unique. As parents, we tend to think that we are a certain way and thus our children will be that way too. Sometimes they are like us due to genetics, but not always and not in every way. The same goes for managing people in the workplace.

As individuals, we have our own way of working through issues. Some of us like to be left alone. Others like to talk it out endlessly. Still others like to be distracted from the matter at hand so that they can calm down and realize that everything in the world is not focused on this one task. There is a larger context in which every activity fits, and "the big game" is not really the most important thing in the entire world.

Our Right View should be to recognize this individuality and respect it. We should not always try to "fix" people to make them more like us if their individuality is not truly hindering them.

Are you in doubt about the unique, and possibly confusing, behaviors of your children? ASK! When the time is right, quietly ask them, "When you get upset (or nervous, or confused, or whatever) like that, what can I do to help?" Once they have given it due consideration and answered you thoughtfully, LISTEN TO THEM! Unless they are in complete denial or are truly doing harm to themselves, avail yourself to your children (and others) in the manner *they* feel they need, not in the manner *you* feel they need.

I've always liked this poem about children by Lebanese poet and philosopher Kahlil Gibran. It comes from *The Prophet* (published by Alfred A. Knopf, 1969):

> …Your children are not your children.
> They are the sons and daughters of Life's longing for itself.
> They come through you but not from you.
> And though they are with you yet they belong not to you.
> You may give them your love but not your thoughts.
> For they have their own thoughts.
> You may house their bodies but not their souls,
> For their souls dwell in the house of
> Tomorrow, which you cannot visit, not even in your dreams.
> You may strive to be like them, but seek
> Not to make them like you.
> For life goes not backward nor tarries with yesterday…

This approach with your children is an example of Right Mindfulness, and it will help to facilitate your children's Right Concentration.

MEA CULPA: We all mess up from time to time. Within families, though, the issue is complex. For one thing, we see or find out about each other's mistakes—albeit minor ones—far more often than we do other people's: putting "dry clean only" clothing in the washing machine, burning the fish sticks, backing out of the garage incorrectly and scraping something, and so forth. Yes, I've done every one of these things and a few more.

The thing is, as a family, we must then be that much more forgiving. This is one part of the formula. The other part is to admit to a mistake we've made instead of trying to hide it. This acknowledgment is important. It mitigates the possibility that you will later be seen as someone who cannot be trusted or who argues that "it wasn't my fault."

Getting along within a family is one of the greatest challenges any person will face in life. Fifty percent of all marriages end in divorce. The key to being in the 50 percent who stay together is kindness, forgiveness, understanding, and honesty. These traits are also paramount in helping our children become good world citizens.

We've talked a lot about kindness, understanding, and forgiveness. These are the hallmark traits of living your life with Zen Game. Part of what makes all these elements work is the *mea culpa*—"I am culpable"—admission of guilt. When you mess up, admit it. And go lightly on the excuses. They only tend to lessen the positive effect of the apology. Mea culpas save marriages, they save families, they help make strong and forthright children, and they make us better people once we step out of our house and into a sometimes challenging world. Kids are always apologizing to their parents, but if you have never apologized to your kids, you have not fully opened your heart to them.

NOT MY KID: Life is conflict. If you have a spouse but no children, you have only one other person coming home each day and telling you about his or her adventures and misadventures. Have kids, and there are that many more dramas in your life.

As parents, we must learn to respond to those dramas in a constructive way. Many parents have a kind of hair-trigger reaction when little Jimmy comes home with a problem: the Mama Bear Syndrome. Someone did something to our little bear cub?! Well, we'll see about that! This maternal or paternal feeling is a good thing. It's an expression of love and responsibility. But it also can lead to errors in judgment.

The first and most important thing we must do is gather information. Little Jimmy may be upset and crying, but we still need to get all the data. If little Jimmy says, "Yeah, so I told Bobby that he was fat and ugly and then he punched me in the nose," we have to stand back and realize that *our little angel* was the one in the wrong. If we had flown into a rage and stomped over to Bobby's house without first getting all the facts, we would have had egg all over our faces. Why not even ask little Jimmy what discipline he thinks he deserves for his actions? Getting kids involved in the problem-solving process helps them to own up to their mistakes and teaches them how to ameliorate a sticky situation with a Zen Game attitude.

Secondly, even in cases where our little angel *was* a victim, there are still nuances to consider. Do we, as parents, *have* to jump in? If we never make a distinction, how will our children ever be able to fend for themselves? Depending upon the scenario, we might want to consider advising our child on how to deal with a conflict, rather than dealing with it *for* him.

Lastly, there are the times when children do need an advocate. Heck, there are times when *all* of us need advocates. That's why we have lawyers, the police, and *60 Minutes.*

In all three cases, we do, though, have to show love, love, and more love. Even when we find out that our child is the one who did something wrong, rather than the one who was wronged, our admonishments must be filled with love and teaching. A mistake is an opportunity for learning. People who never screw up never learn anything.

SACRIFICE: Parents who pay for lessons and tutoring for their children are making a financial and logistical sacrifice. Is it always worth it?

This is the question parents must ask themselves from time to time, and the answer is often gathered, again, through observation. Are you paying out tons and tons of money on piano lessons, but your daughter never practices? Have a talk with her and discuss what you are observing. Perhaps there is a better way to spend your money and further your child's individual development.

Does your child understand that you are *making* a sacrifice? If things come too easily to children, they may enjoy the activity but not respect and properly appreciate the gift they have been given by their parents. Some kids from poor families struggle to excel at activities despite not having the resources for private lessons and the like. This is to be commended. When Little Superstars begin to get a "star attitude," bring them back down to earth by helping them realize how good they've got it. If they don't understand the big picture of that sacrifice, maybe they should have to get a summer or after-school job to pay for those lessons themselves. That can be quite the eye-opener.

GIVE A MAN A FISH...: We all know the old saying, "Give a man a fish and he will eat for one day. Teach a man to fish and he will never go hungry again."

This philosophy has been applied to national political discussions for decades, but it also comes up in our day in/day out lives with our children and family members as well. Tell me if you haven't experienced this one:

"I can't open this e-mail attachment."

A huff and a roll of the eyes. "Move aside; let me do it for you."

We rationalize it by saying, "I can either take one minute and do it *for* you, or I can sit here for an hour and explain it to you. And I just don't *have* an hour."

Uh-huh. And what about when it happens again? And again?

We ought to look at the big picture sometimes when people around us ask for our assistance. Yes, maybe it will take a little longer to teach them or point them in the right direction so that they can find the answer themselves. But if we choose this approach, haven't we accomplished the long-range goal of making them better, more self-sufficient people?

And what about the process? If we always do things for young people, they will never learn to be a problem solver in life. They will have learned that the way to solve problems is to ask someone else to do it for them. What kind of lesson is that? There is a wise Buddhist saying that, as adults, we are challenged to help people raise their competencies, not simply to fix their problems for them.

By teaching our family members how to help themselves, we can not only teach them one skill—the solution to their immediate problem—but also the *process* by which self-sufficient people address *all* of their problems.

Take the computer example. Understanding how to use online troubleshooting guides and such can solve a whole slew of potential problems. What about knowing how to call free tech support? And then there's the tried-and-true "owner's manual" that so many folks just put in a drawer and forget to use. By teaching a person how to use these tools, you will make him or her a far more equipped and competent individual.

THE GIFT OF STRENGTH: What is the most important thing a parent is supposed to give a child? Love, of course. But can we love too much?

Love is and always should be a constant. But love takes on many forms, and when it becomes a possessive type, it can be damaging.

In the end, parents are charged with making children strong enough to make it on their own. This comes from building up their self-confidence to a point of strength, without going so far overboard as to make them delusional fools. Our job is to let them know that they can accomplish more than they thought possible, but that they also must know when to ask for help. We must imbue them with strong character, the knowledge of right and wrong, and the strength to take Right Action. We must make them independent, overcoming our own desire to do everything for them because we love them so much and they are so very precious to us. In the end, it is love that drives us to do this, but our mission is to create strength within them and also to "cut the apron strings."

KIDS WILL BE KIDS: I met a man once who was always complaining about the noise and traffic near his house. He lived in a high-rise on a busy street.

Now, had he bought the place and suddenly saw the city plow this big road in front of it and direct tons of traffic there, I could sympathize. But that street had always been there and had always been busy. Furthermore, he was in a high-rise, not on an isolated farm.

The same goes for children. They have a lot of energy (or at least they should), and they make a lot of noise. Good for them! As long as they act reasonably and don't trash the joint, we should let them be.

The problem is that some people do not understand this idea. For example, most swimming pools post schedules, and it is usually easy to see when kids will be there and when they will not. If you like to swim laps in peace and solitude, check the schedule and see when lanes are set up for lap swimming. Go then and swim in quiet. But if it's "open swim," don't get irate because you're trying to do those laps when a bunch of splashing, squealing, and playing children are in the pool. That's what kids do.

Kids are not invited everywhere, of course, and if someone brought a ton of kids to a fancy restaurant for a wild birthday party when I was having a romantic night out with my hubby, I would be upset. You'd think it would be unnecessary to say, but since it happens more than it should, let's say again that kids' parties belong in kids' party places, not in adult venues during adult hours. At the same time, if my man took me out to eat at Chuck E. Cheese, it would be insane of me to complain about the racket. As long as all of these rules and codes of conduct are being met, try to be a little understanding and realize that you were once a child too.

WHO'S THE BOSS?: Whenever you hire teachers and coaches to assist your child with some activity, there has to be a point at which you decide who the coach is—you, the parent, or the person you are paying.

If, as a parent, you disagree with the approach a tutor or coach is taking, it may be appropriate to ask questions when the time is right. But if you're going to attend every practice and boorishly undermine the coach, why are you bothering to pay this person in the first place?

At some point, you must reach a decision about whether or not to turn your child over to this other authority figure. Once you do it, make it a clean break, except in cases where your child comes to you with personal issues that need to be addressed. There can only be so many cooks in the kitchen making the stew.

Another seldom-mentioned issue is credit. It makes me boil when I hear a "superstar parent" brag about how they were their child's "personal coach" when I know for a fact that they were not. Sure, as a parent, your role is invaluable. You may have also helped your child a lot in a particular field of interest. But if you gave your child her first two years of beginner piano lessons, then turned her over to Maestro Fingerfast for the next twelve years, don't go around bragging that it was all about you. Be truthful, be humble, and give credit where it belongs. That's the Right View to take and the Right Effort to make.

RESULTS: We are all driven by results. When the boss asks if you have finished a particular task, he doesn't want a list of the things you *chose* to do that day; he wants to know if you did precisely what you were asked to do. He wants results.

With kids, it's a little bit different if the "result" is winning or losing. When we send children out to compete in the science fair, they shouldn't have to worry that if they don't bring home first place they shouldn't come home at all.

The result we should be seeking from our children is that they have done their best, period. The problem is, children sometimes put so much pressure on themselves that even the most innocent question or comment can send them away sulking.

"Did you win?" Sure, it sounds innocent enough, but with some kids, it means that anything other than first place is a loss. And who wants to say, "I'm a loser"? Try, "How did you do?" or one of my favorites: "Hey, champ…how did it go?"

Children can be like sensitive, raw nerves—if they are rubbed the wrong way, or merely nudged, they can hurt like the blazes of hell. A parent's response to them when they've been in a tough test of skill, strength, or brainpower requires timing, good sense, and diplomacy. You might say it takes more skill than attempting to negotiate a nuclear weapon test ban treaty among hostile parties. Always let them know that their value to us, to themselves, and to the world is not based upon the results of any one competition or test. They are valuable, period.

APPROPRIATE AGE BRACKETS: Child prodigies are great, but they are rarer than most parents think. A Mozart comes along once a century, not once a week.

Once parents see talent in a child, they sometimes feel they have to push them along at a pace faster than the speed of light. I have seen eight-year-olds being pushed into classes with twelve-year-olds. What's that all about? Why is it necessary?

As a life coach, I've learned the importance of the psyche and the role it plays in every aspect of our lives. A child's thoughts, emotions, and behavior are the most important thing to take into consideration in these situations, not the "feeling" that talent has some sort of expiration date and must be moved along on a certain timetable.

If a child is sincerely bored by a lack of competition or mental challenge, I would suggest looking first for a more challenging class for eight-year-olds before throwing him or her in with kids so much older. For one thing, he or she will get nothing out of the experience socially. And yes, in the end, the social aspect of an activity is one of the most important things a child can get out of it. Children learn to grow emotionally by being with their peers and interacting. A kid much younger than all the others is likely to be isolated socially.

This happened to a very dear friend of mine who skipped a grade in junior high. Before he skipped the grade, he was popular among his friends and excelled at sports. When he was moved ahead, the students in his class changed, he had less association with his old friends, and he did not perform as well in sports because he was now playing with kids who were bigger, stronger, and older than he was. He said that for a few years, he felt alone, unhappy, and out of place.

Always make sure the child is happy. If it appears that you must move him or her into a higher age bracket to achieve this happiness because he or she is losing interest in the activity due to boredom, do so with caution. Then watch carefully to see if it takes. You don't want to cure a problem by introducing a worse solution.

But most importantly, don't push too hard, even if you see incredible talent in your children. Talk to them about what you see. Praise them, ask for their opinions and give them options as to what they can do with their talent *if they choose to do so*. Don't create an unhappy Superkid.

SLOW STARTS AND ROUGH PATCHES: So your princess has always wanted to be a ballet dancer. She begs mommy to sign her up for a class. Excitedly, she puts on her little outfit. She lines up and…feels as if she is on an alien planet where everyone else knows what is going on and does it well except her.

She is crushed and crestfallen. She only assumed the best and instead feels embarrassed and cloddish.

Good parents, this is your cue!

It is rare that we begin any new activity with immediate success. So should we only keep working at things in which we succeed right away? Wow, imagine how scientifically backward we would all be if that were the case. Scores and scores of failures preceded almost every single medical and scientific discovery in history. How many poor animals died before the first organ transplant was successful? How many poor humans died before it was successful on people? Should scientists have quit after the first failure? There are tens of thousands of people alive today who would give you a resounding "no!"

Parents, remind your kids of this when they are crying after that first ballet lesson. Try to make them focus on the "fun" part of the activity, not the embarrassment of failure. But listen, also. There are people with weak ankles who literally scream in pain when they put on a pair of ice skates. Unfortunately, we aren't all physically or psychologically cut out for every activity. But realize that this is more the exception than the rule. Show children love during these trials and tribulations and give them strength to face all of the world's challenges.

There is another variation on this theme: slumping or plateauing. Here, your child has become good at a certain activity but then hits a wall. Others are progressing, but your child is not.

In some cases, this may, in fact, be the end of the line for the child's ability. We all have our talents, and merely loving an activity is not enough for us to excel at it. This love will only take us so far, even if we work at it. This experience can be nature's way of telling us we have some other talent we should be pursuing, while leaving this other activity in the "purely fun" category.

But there may be another answer here as well. These slumps and plateaus may be artificial walls that we need to attack and get over, under, or through. Think about changing coaches or teachers. Internalize and regroup. So many people go through an activity by rote. They don't stop to think about their choices.

I'd like you to read one of my favorite quotes, which I used to run across in golf magazines several years ago. The quote was part of an advertisement showing one of golf's great competitors, Greg Norman. The copy read like this: *"There are no natural-born golfers. No man's ever entered the world with the innate ability to drive the green on a par-four. Or hit a one-iron 280 yards. What golfers are born with is desire. Desire to work. Desire to sweat. Desire to learn. Desire to have someone watch him someday and say, 'Look, now there's a natural-born golfer.'"*

It's always been my belief that to be one of the best, you have to at least start with average ability. Then you must have the best teachers and the desire to devote your life to it. Whether your child wants to be the best at something or simply the best he or she can be at it, it may be helpful for you and your child to read my book *Victory Dancing for Teens*. There is a chapter called "How to Create a Workable Action Plan," where I suggest tracking the progress you are making in a particular activity. You and your child can use this journal to collect your thoughts as your child works toward achieving his or her goal. What worked and what didn't? What needs work and what doesn't? Many people never progress beyond mid-level because they don't become introspective enough about the task. It might be necessary to acquire Right Concentration to move ahead.

PLAYING THROUGH PAIN: I always talk about how the world does not rest upon your performance in any one competition or situation. I stand by that statement. It really irks me when I see coaches and parents pushing a kid to risk injury (even serious injury) over some game that will be forgotten days later.

Sometimes televised sports do us an injustice when they show Olympic gymnasts making jumps on damaged tendons or racehorses running on cracked hooves. We are encouraged to cheer these feats of superhuman (or super equine) resilience.

But is it healthy? No.

Don't look at these feats and think that they justify sending your child out to play football with a bruised spleen, baseball with a torn rotator cuff, or a basketball game with a high fever. This is insanity. As a parent, you are not teaching your child anything other than reckless behavior. How would this differ from suggesting they drive a car without brakes to get somewhere on time? You are teaching that the end justifies the means and that even the most logical and prudently placed obstacle should never stand in their way.

Your child's safety, health, and long-term well-being are more important than anything else. It often takes more character to walk off the field when you are injured than to stay on it and blow it for your team. What is better, for your child to perform at 25 percent or for his or her backup to perform at 100 percent? Probably the backup. Also, understand that it is often prudent to live to fight another day.

CLASSY WAYS TO QUIT: We are raised to hate quitters. To us, they personify losing. But let's examine quitting for a moment.

When a competitor retires, he or she is, ostensibly, quitting. Isn't it sad when boxers keep fighting even though they can't do it anymore? And dangerous too. Some keep doing it for the money, while others simply don't know when to leave the stage. In the end, we all quit something sometime.

What about when your child wants to quit an activity? Children have mercurial personalities that swing wildly from extreme to extreme. One day they love horseback riding; the next day they hate it. Parents are tested regarding how to help them negotiate through all of this drama.

It all begins with listening. Listening is an *active* sport. It may require us to ask questions and follow-up questions.

When children say they no longer enjoy an activity, be sure to give them enough time to consider this decision thoroughly. Time is the key. Suggest they go to the next practice and see if they feel the same way. If they do, you might suggest they miss a practice and then gauge how they feel after that. Do they feel guilty or as if something is now missing in their lives? Or do they feel as if the world has been lifted off their shoulders?

The whole idea behind this tactic is to prevent them from quitting *on the field*. Unless they are injured, they must realize that they have made a commitment to perform *that day*. No, they do not have to perform again tomorrow if they sincerely do not want to, but they must carry through with the responsibilities they have committed to *today*.

If a child is taught that it is okay to quit things right in the moment, he will walk out on tests in school if they are too hard, he will walk out of jobs if something seems too stressful, and he will walk out on relationships the moment there are stormy waters. This is not good. Quitting should always be a well thought out decision, and you, the parent, must help facilitate this mindset in children when they are young and need your guidance.

GO FOR IT!: Want to know one of the very best things you can say to your children as they enter the world? *Go for it!*

This applies to acting, mathematics, signing up with the ROTC (Reserve Officer Training Core), anything. Go for it! Carpe diem! Seize the day! You only go around once, so when you've decided to try something, give it 100 percent and go after it with a smile.

Ah yes, the smile. A smile sets the tone for everything. The difference between gritted teeth and a smile often is the real difference between a happy life and an unhappy one. I've known some miserable winners and some happy losers. But in those cases, the winning and losing I am talking about concerned an isolated game or event. Happiness versus anger is the true meaning of winning as opposed to losing. Teach this to your children. When you send them into the unknown of competition or new experiences, smile and tell them to "Go for it!" You will set the tone for a true Zen-like victory.

7
PARTNERSHIPS

It is a popular parlor game to ask, "What would you take with you on a deserted island? *Who* would you take with you on a deserted island?" In certain ways, we are all on a deserted island with someone else. Marriages consist of two people on a deserted island. You and your boss are two people on another island. You have made a commitment to another person or have been placed in a situation where you have to try to make a relationship work. Yes, compared with a real deserted island, we can leave these marriage and work situations if they become unbearable. But doing so would involve some bruises to the soul and psyche, so we figure out how to make them work.

In my life, I have met all sorts of people, and some of them you might not want to be on that island with: know-it-alls, divas, prima donnas, Mr. and Ms. Snob. So let's now talk about the rewards that flow when we execute the Zen Game in our relationships.

THE POWER: This may sound strange, but in a way, adults who are treated badly by their bosses have to accept some of the blame for allowing it to get to that place. Very, very few of us are in inescapable dilemmas. But this chapter is not about leaving a bad situation; it's about how to avoid getting into one in the first place.

It has been said that many unhappy people are in imaginary prisons of their own making, and I tend to agree with that. One of the reasons we allow such a situation to exist is that we have relinquished our power in exchange for something we need or want.

Let me speak in metaphor. If I were to ask you if you would allow yourself to be verbally abused by your boss for minimum wage, you would likely say, "No way!" But suppose I said, "What if you were paid a million dollars a year?" Suddenly, it's a tougher question. *Why?*

The "why" is about the Power. In a perfect partnership, all parties have relatively equal power. Sure, someone may be the manager or boss, but that does not mean he or she is all-powerful. If the boss is desperate for employees, the power shifts to the employee. See what I mean?

When we are directed by our needs rather than our wants, we rarely relinquish all of our power. But we often have trouble separating our wants from our needs. We *need* a bed to sleep in and a roof over our heads. We *want* a luxury cabana in the tropics. We *need* food to survive. We *want* surf and turf at the finest restaurant in town.

Imagine that you are seventeen years old. You are still living with your parents and you *want* some spending money. You get a job at Burger King and the manager there is abusive. You have the power to hand in your apron and go down the street to McDonald's. You do not *need* this abuse. But now you are a little older and you *need* a job. How much are you willing to put up with? How much power will you surrender?

I firmly believe that the Zen Game approach to life is to find that wonderful Middle Path we spoke of at the beginning of the book. So many of us surrender all of our power to get ahead, but what is "getting ahead" if we are miserable?

Getting ahead may mean getting that job with a fantastic law firm. But what if the boss takes the power we give him or her and treats us terribly, ruining our quality of life? Well, let's look at "wants" and "needs" again. You *need* a job and you *want* to be a lawyer. There's nothing wrong with having wants. It's just an issue of analyzing and strategizing how and where to get those wants satisfied.

So this is a great, prestigious law firm, but if you're miserable, what's the damage in taking your J.D. off the wall and marching down the street to another, perhaps lesser firm? Will you make less money? Probably. But consider your quality of life. If you work about sixty hours a week like most Americans today, that doesn't leave an awful lot of waking hours in which to spend that money. Yes, $250,000 a year will buy you more than $100,000, but at what price on the psyche?

The same goes for relationships. Lots of men and women inspect their potential partner's earning capacity and pedigree as much as their looks or anything else. Fine then. But how much power are you willing to surrender for that rich wife or husband? How unequal a marital partnership are you willing to endure? And for what?

Does this mean we shouldn't try for that job with the most prestigious company and the big salary? We shouldn't try to get to know the new rich woman or man? Of course not! It means that we must place a value upon ourselves and respect ourselves. That is *our* power. Again, remember that the boss is not automatically the one with all the power. Power is not inherent. It is given and it is situational. It begins with self-esteem, and that transcends any outward societal measure of power and value. If we enter into any relationship feeling that inner power, we will be on an even keel with whomever we are matched, no matter what the roles. It all begins inside our own head.

Remember, no matter who we are and where we come from, we all possess an inherent power. We can hold on to it or we can surrender it. In partnerships of any kind, the best situation we should be looking for is one of equal or near equal power. That is the path to real happiness.

SETTING BOUNDARIES: Step two in making sure you are getting into and staying in a good relationship: Get off to a good start.

I consider myself to be a nice person. But let's say, hypothetically, that I hire you to work for me and the first day we're together, I happen to be in a horrible mood for one reason or another. I snap at you without good reason. Maybe I'm so lost in my own personal dramas that I don't even realize I did it. You, for your part, take it. You want this job. Because you want it, you've convinced yourself you need it. Maybe you do need a job, but you do not need *this* job if I am a total tyrant.

Because I snapped at you and you took it, what happens next? Even though it may be completely subconscious on my part, I may have just discovered that you are a person I can mistreat. Now, I did say that I'm a nice person, but maybe because you let me get away with it from the start, I begin to view you as someone who brings me back to that "bad place" I was in when I first met you. You become my personal punching bag. I see you, and all the anger and frustration I've ever felt or am dealing with bubbles to the surface. You become like a safety valve to me, where I spew out all the steam that's been building up.

This is an unhealthy relationship for *both* of us. How can we prevent it?

First off, even though our roles are boss and employee, if I am unacceptably rude to you, you have every right to employ all the Zen Game tactics we've been talking about and let me know how you feel about my actions. Don't try to be rude to me or beat me at my game; go about it in all the right ways. If I am, indeed, a nice person, you will establish with me that you have "personal power" (self-esteem) and do not wish to be treated shabbily. If I am a nice person, I will realize the error of my ways and will apologize and amend my manner around you. If I am not a nice person, I will blast away at you even harder and even think I have a right to talk to you this way because you are working for me. The situation will be untenable. Advice to you: abandon ship.

It is important to set boundaries in every relationship we enter. The more transgressions we let pass by unanswered, the harder it will be to salvage the relationship. Once roles have become ingrained, they are hard to change.

TEAM SHORTHAND: Playing doubles in tennis is a tenuous exercise sometimes. You and another person are a team. You win or lose based as much on your ability to work as a team as on your individual abilities.

So how does a team engender that sort of winning teamwork? The easy answer is, "through practice." But even so, the game moves quickly. There is little or no opportunity to discuss the game once you step onto the court. Maybe a couple of words between points, but that's about it.

So again, how does the doubles team work together successfully? Shorthand. That's a nice way of saying they shout to each other a lot.

"Mine!"

"Yours!"

"Deep!"

"Short!"

See, no long soliloquies. There are millions of other team-like activities that work under similar conditions. Commodities brokers in the pits. Speaking of pits, how about race car pit crews? The list goes on and on of people who have to shout shorthand instructions to one another to get a job done right. *But*, there's still a wrong way and a Zen Game way to communicate with others in teamwork shorthand.

When things are moving at a rapid pace, the heartbeat races. Stress and tension abound….Or must they?

Right Concentration. This is where it belongs. Sure, if we are in totally unfamiliar territory, it's normal to panic. If I had to deliver a baby in the back of a taxicab, I doubt I would be at the top of my Zen Game. But what if I were an obstetrician? Then it would be unprofessional to stress, bark orders, and get angry and annoyed when others do not immediately comprehend my shorthand—not to mention a terrible way to bring a new little angel into the world. This type of behavior only shows others that we are out of control. It lowers their opinion of our abilities. I certainly would not want to be in the stirrups when some obstetrician was freaking out. I'd probably grab a nurse by the collar and beg her, "Do you have anybody else in this hospital who can help me?" And I wouldn't even be the one he was addressing harshly.

Proper team building requires that each team member learn and agree upon certain forms of shorthand—verbal, written, and nonverbal. Additionally, there is no need for a terse or agitated tone, and definitely no reason for an abusive one. No one—and I repeat loud and clear, **no one is above or better than anyone else**—regardless of your family lineage, your title or job status, or how much you are worth. I'm sorry I had to shout that, but it really is one of my pet peeves.

As I said, treating people humanely and with civility is not just good manners. It is a demonstration of professionalism and inner calm that lets your team members know you have the situation well in hand and are competent.

MIND READERS: Along with using shorthand, sometimes the members of a team that has existed for a long time can almost sense what the other person is thinking. This is great—when it works.

The truth is that it often does not work. Many times, this failure is not a big problem. If I am out with my husband and I start snapping my fingers to the music, hinting that I want to dance, I hope my husband will pick up on this nonverbal cue and ask me to dance. But if he doesn't get the hint for one reason or another, no great harm has been done. If, on the other hand, I lambaste him later as if some enormous problem occurred, then I am acting like a jerk.

Mind reading is based on assumption, and we all know the old joke about what happens when we "assume." The saying goes that it makes an "ass" out of you and me. When mind reading doesn't work, don't get frustrated. Try something more direct instead, such as asking him to dance. What's that other old saying…? "Ask and you shall receive."

OVER-DELAYED GRATIFICATION: I preach patience all the time. One of my favorite expressions is: God, give me patience…and give it to me NOW!

But shouldn't some forms of patience come with an expiration date?

I talk to friends who say, "I hate my job, but I only have to put in five more years before I can get free health insurance for life." Well, that's a pragmatic approach. But how miserable is miserable, and are some investments not worth the payoff in the end?

Our lives are only so long. Yes, we may tend to feel immortal, but we're not. We sometimes say things such as "Five years from now…" and "Ten years from now…" without really thinking about the ramifications.

First off, will we actually live that long? You know the old saying, "Man plans, God laughs." It's true. Beyond that, though, imagine resigning yourself to, say, a job you loathe for "only" five or ten more years. How old will you be then? What ages will pass you by as you wake up every single morning, dreading your daily existence? And for what?

Going back to my life coach training, there are two questions one must always ask oneself: "Does this work for me?" and "Does this benefit me?" In the case of having to put in a certain number of years at a job to obtain benefits of some sort, the "benefits" part is right there in the situation being described. *But is it working for you?*

Quality of life is an important issue. Again, going back to the idea that we create imaginary prisons of our own design, did you ever stop to think that maybe some other job at some other place might also provide you with those much-needed health benefits for life after five pleasant years? It's your life! Do you want it to be happy or do you want it to be miserable? You can make these decisions.

When you decide to delay gratification, stop and really look at how much time it will involve, in what situation, under what circumstances, and at what payoff. If it still looks like a good deal, fine then. But if you dread getting out of bed tomorrow and a whole slew of additional tomorrows into the future, begin to think outside the box. Consider coloring outside the lines. Break out of your imaginary prison—you might find a paradise waiting for you somewhere.

ACCEPTING THE THINGS YOU CANNOT CHANGE: This line is, as most of you know, part of the wonderful "Serenity Prayer" used in 12-step programs. But it stands alone quite well when assessing what makes for good partnerships and teams.

Some of the best sports coaches over time have been the ones who learned to work with what they were given, not what that wished they had. When basketball coach Pat Riley was with Magic Johnson and the LA Lakers of the 1980s, he had an up-tempo game known as "Showtime," with lots of running and gunning. Years later, when he came to the New York Knicks, he had no Magic Johnson, no Michael Cooper, no James Worthy. He had players with entirely different skill sets—big, slow bruisers.

What did he do? Well, he had only two potentially successful answers: Either toss out the entire squad and trade them for "Showtime" clones, or adapt his own coaching skills to *the players that he had*.

Your husband, God forbid, is in a car accident and loses the use of his legs. What can you do? He can't get them back. I pray that you appreciated what he could do with his legs when he did have them, but those days are now over. Today is a new reality.

Again, you have two choices, and one is, of course, the most moral and Zen-like one: You accept him as he is today and work with him to make both your lives as special and wonderful as possible. Why? Because this you cannot change.

Embrace life. Love the little things that make up each day. You'll be miserable and cantankerous if you are always wishing for what you don't have or for the way it was in the "good old days." Appreciate and be creative in using what you've got now to make yourself as happy as possible. What you don't appreciate today could be another thing you will be wishing you had tomorrow!

WHAT ARE YOU WILLING TO TOLERATE?: I once heard a good piece of relationship advice: "Pay careful attention to the things that irk you about someone you are dating, because if you marry that person, those things will only annoy you more."

No one is perfect (except my husband, and he's taken). No matter how much "smoke gets in our eyes" at the onset of a relationship, if we stick around long enough, we will find something about our paramour that gets under our skin. He belches songs. He won't eat his vegetables. He claims he's not colorblind, but you'd never know it from the way he selects his clothing. He always grabs the newspaper first, then puts it back together with the middle page on the first page and the second page as the last page. Before you read the paper, you have to spend fifteen minutes putting it back together. Admit it—you do it or your spouse does. There's one in every family.

Well, guess what? He's got just as long a list on you. "Who, me?" you ask, aghast. Yes, you!

Can some of these transgressions be changed? Can you get another person to change?

I like to substitute the word *modify* for *change*. No, I do not believe you can really "change" someone. I believe, at best, you may be able to *help* someone change himself or herself, but the only time "change" really occurs is when people choose to change. I'm sure you've also heard the pearl of wisdom that when you work on bettering yourself, everyone around you magically changes for the better.

Modification is another story. It may take all of your Zen Game to do it, but if you've got that "Stripes go with checks, don't they, honey?" husband, the best you may be able to do is to group the pants, shirts, and ties that go together in his closet. I wouldn't go so far as to pick his clothes out for him. I think even parents are doing their children a disservice when they do this for them past grade school. But by categorizing your husband's clothes for him a few times, through repetition he will better learn what goes well with what. Everyone will benefit in the long run. You haven't actually *changed* him, but you've modified the situation and even taught him something in the process.

The real question behind these examples is, "What are we willing to tolerate? What are we willing to accept?" All of these irks and irritants are relative. I could live with a man who has bad taste in clothing if everything else is pretty darn good. I could not, on the other hand, marry a bigot. Matching outfits is an artistic talent that some people have and some people don't. Bigotry is hate, and I do not mess with haters.

Your situation with a life mate, a boss, or a buddy will always involve some amount of tolerance on your part. Before committing long-term to such a relationship or breaking it off, analyze the good and the bad. Ask yourself, "What am I willing to tolerate?" Then set out with realistic expectations for the future. If you've made a decision to stick it out with this person, focus on their positive attributes, rather than the ones that make you huff, puff and roll your eyes.

Also, consider where you choose to input certain information. It annoys you that he doesn't eat his vegetables? Maybe you shouldn't look at his plate so much when he's eating. Instead, why not look at his face? The face you fell in love with...those expressive brown eyes and beautiful mouth, not to mention the adorable dimple on his chin! The point is, there are lots of tricks to getting along once you've made the commitment to do so. But whatever you do, understand the lack of perfection we all have and appreciate the things that drew you to this person in the first place.

KEEP 'EM GUESSING: Some of the best relationship advice I've ever received was this: Don't be afraid to mix it up sometimes. I talked about this earlier in the book, but it's a very important point. If you are proactive about mixing it up, you will reap great rewards.

Ever watch a couple who have been married for centuries? They finish each other's sentences. It's cute, right? Well, sometimes yes and sometimes no. Sometimes it's an indication that they *think* they know each other so well that each has become a cliché to the other, and that's not good.

Switch things around once in a while. If you're the one who never wants to see action movies, suggest a "shoot 'em up" instead of your typical chick flick. Always like going out to nice restaurants with fine tablecloths and tall candlesticks? Be the one to suggest a pizza once in a while. Whatever. Just try to become less predictable when it comes to these innocuous issues. In all romantic relationships, we enjoy mixing it up, so to speak!

Now, here's another tip: The next time you want to say "no" to something, pause and think about it. That's right! Too often we blurt out "no" when it's really just a knee-jerk reaction. Suppose your spouse calls you up from work and says, "Darling, I'm taking you to a hockey game this weekend." Instead of chiding him with, "No way, you know I don't like hockey," why not say to him, "Well, that sounds interesting. Let's talk about it when you get home tonight." Then really consider attending the game with him. By pausing after a question, we are less likely to give an automatic reaction. And by saying "Let me think about that," "Let me get back to you on that," or "Let's talk about that later," you are showing great respect to your mate.

You want communication like this to flourish between you and your partner. When you open up a communication line with this type of dialogue, you will constantly be rewarded with the same behavior in return. Everyone will be satisfied because everyone feels honored. Let me tell you, in a marriage or any long-term relationship, for that matter, it's the little things that will kill you, not the big ones.

NEVER BE EMBARRASSED BY THE ONES YOU LOVE: I've known people who stopped going out in public with their spouse because he or she gained a lot of weight, had a bad accident, was undergoing chemotherapy, or became senile.

Come on now, we must be supportive of the ones we love.

This support may be as major as pushing someone in a wheelchair or as comparatively minor as being with someone who now walks with a limp. Either way, how dare we feel that another person's physical appearance can reflect badly on us? And how dare we claim to love someone if we feel they embarrass us when all they are doing is being themselves? It would be one thing if the person we were with poured a punch bowl on himself, tore off his clothes, and shouted, "Party!" That's about actions, not appearances. Right Mindfulness and Right View mean knowing love and how to show love, and we do that by standing by our loved ones no matter what their appearance. This includes people in our lives who were born with physical disabilities. They give their love to us; we must give them our love in return and show pride as we accompany them out into the world. Love looks not with the eyes but with the heart.

I AM MORE THAN YOUR GARBAGE PAIL: We all need to vent sometimes. Some of us do it alone, waiting until no one is around so that we can throw a pillow against the wall and scream. Go ahead, do it. It can be therapeutic sometimes. Better to throw a pillow than to take out your frustrations behind the wheel of a car. I once heard of a glass company that set up a room full of defective pieces of glass—factory seconds—and encouraged frustrated workers to go in, put on some safety goggles, grab a sledgehammer, and smash the place up. Then they would go back to work, having gotten it all out of their system.

Other folks prefer the "buddy system." The moment they have a problem, they pick up the phone and vent to a friend or relative. That's okay too, but there is a greater need to set limits when a second party is involved in your renewable personal catharsis.

Do not come to me only when you want to vent. Do not vent to me every time we speak. If you do either of these two things, you are using me as your personal garbage pail, and I don't like that. Once in a while, fine, especially if it is something new. The real problem, as I've found it, is "the never-ending saga."

"Bobby works too hard; he's never around. I feel like a widow."

Okay, when this is a new wrinkle in your life, I want to be there for you as your friend and I'm glad you shared. We can talk it out, and maybe you will even want some advice from me. Fine again. We can even do some follow-up together. In fact, it would be a Right Effort on my part to ask about how you and Bobby are working things out the next time we speak.

Where does this car careen off the road? When you call me every day and just drone on and on and on about Bobby the Workaholic, Bobby the Workaholic, Bobby the Workaholic. Enough! Why, I'd rather talk about plate tectonics than all of this garbage you are continuously dumping on me. Once people get into a rut like this, they become so self-absorbed, having found a nice guy or gal who will patiently listen to their tale of woe ad nauseam, that they begin to forget that you, too, have a life. Suppose a friend of yours starts neglecting to ask, "And what's new with you?" You know you've gone past the signposts that read, "Danger Ahead! Unbalanced Relationship!"

When people use others as a human garbage pail, great damage is done. For one thing, another person's problems begin to ruin *your* day. Imagine that you pick up the phone one day with a smile on your face. It's been a swell day, but now "Mona the Moaner" is starting in about her Bobby again. How can you get off that call in the same good mood? You can't, unless your ears decide to protest against this outrage and simply shut Mona out.

It's not fair, and unless you set limits, it will continue and continue. When a friend goes over the line, diplomatically stop her and explain that you love and care for her and empathize with her plight, but that you want your relationship to be varied and rich in texture. For that to be so, you need to talk about more than one subject. Furthermore, you are telling her this *for her own good* (that line always works and rightly so) because she is obviously obsessing on this problem. And when a person does that, they ruin their overall quality of life.

When you have had it up to your back molars with this type of situation, the best advice to give someone is, "I know it's bad, but every once in a while, think about something else. We've talked out all of your options and there's nothing we haven't covered. So now all we're doing is repeating ourselves, running over the same old ground. Do yourself a favor and look for some pleasure somewhere in your life. I know it's out there for you; you just have to look for it and find it." This is how you help your friend and this is also how you help yourself.

BREAKUPS AND MAKE UPS: Here is a very touchy variation on the "human garbage pail" problem.

Your friend calls you to complain and complain about her significant other. You might hear something that propels you to say, "Well, I wouldn't put up with that. I would leave him."

Don't do it.

No matter how tempting, say *anything* except that. Why? Murphy's Law. Inevitably, the two will get back together, and as irrational as it sounds, they will *both* hate *you*. That's what you get for having an opinion.

What makes this situation tougher is that it is often very subversive. Suppose, for example, that you have restrained yourself from blurting out your negative opinion and a call to action. But then your complaining friend leans upon you and asks you directly, "Should I leave him? Should I?"

Don't take the bait. I'm telling you; don't do it. It always comes back to haunt you.

People have to come to these decisions on their own. This is what I have learned as a life coach.

You can be a good friend by facilitating their decision making. Toss rhetorical questions their way and make them ponder and come face-to-face with their own life and their future with this other person. But what you must avoid doing is *making the decision for them*. When you talk it out and act as a mirror for them, you may get them to say, "You know, I think I'm going to leave him." If so, fine. If not, fine again. The point is, let *them* say those words, not you. And if they want to give you credit for their decision, emphasize your role by saying, "It wasn't my decision; it was yours. You reached it all on your own." In that way, you have been a helpful friend, but you also have given yourself immunity if your friend changes her mind and goes in a different direction. Don't let your friendship be the collateral damage of two other people's relationship with each other.

HOW MUCH GOOD NEWS IS TOO MUCH?: Can you imagine being Derek Jeter's mother? "Derek won the American League Rookie of the Year award!" "Derek was the All-Star game MVP!" "Derek was the World Series MVP!" "Derek was named *Sports Illustrated*'s Sportsman of the Year!" Let's face it; this is one deservedly proud mother.

If we're lucky, life can be an embarrassment of riches, at least for a time. It may not be as grandiose as Mrs. Jeter's, but perhaps on a smaller scale.

The question is, with whom does she get to brag about Derek and share her joy? *How* can she share her joy?

Look, I hope it's not true, but perhaps Derek's mom had to learn the hard way what I'm about to tell you: There is a pecking order regarding *whom* you can share *what* joy with and *how much* of it you can share. It goes like this:

Immediate family. I'm sure Derek himself can call his mom after every joyous moment of his life and give her every detail, and she will revel in it. I'm sure Derek's mom can call *her* mom, if she's still around, and do the same thing. This is the nexus of our lives. This we all can do without shame or restriction.

Best friends and extended family. Yeah, they'll want to know what's up in your life. But with these people, you have to watch, listen, and learn. Uncle

Eddie may be just as excited to hear about your triumphs as your mom was. He'll want you to call him up the second you hang up with her and give him all the good, good news that's happening in your life. So you can renew the joy that has come your way in life by sharing it with Uncle Eddie. You'll make him and yourself happy.

But then there's Cousin Mark. Mark, while not wanting to be completely in the dark about what's going on in the family, has a cynical, jealous side to him. When you run into him on Thanksgiving and he asks what's new, you can give him a few of the biggest headlines, but watch and see how much more, if any, he wants to know. A couple of highlights, delivered once or twice a year, may be all he can handle. That's fine. Well, no it's not, because Mark should develop Right View about others' successes, but we're not here to change Cousin Mark. We're here to make him and ourselves as happy as possible. If we tell Mark too much, he may say something snarky and we'll all feel bad, so let's avoid that.

The same goes for work colleagues. The challenge here is that colleagues may be even more difficult to read than Cousin Mark, whom you have known all your life. Work colleagues may look you in the eye, smile, and nod their head in approval as you rattle off all the good news, yet inside they are fuming and hating you for every detail you give them. Well, you don't have to be a psychologist to know that when people either overtly or secretly respond negatively to your success and happiness, they are suffering from a lack of self-esteem. Your success highlights their lack of success. Instead of realizing that everyone can be happy and successful, they see it as only one way or the other.

Okay, so what do you do when you sense someone is not genuinely happy for your success? Consciously choose that you will not take this behavior personally. Why? Because it is all about them, not you! When you consciously choose to use your Zen Game, you will have compassion for people like this and your life will reflect the best of you.

The rest of the world. When I meet new people, they are apt to ask what I do for a living. It's a common query. I'll say, "I am an author and a motivational speaker." Indeed, I am more than that two-word description, but cocktail talk does not require that I carry my entire curriculum vitae with me. If the person asks for more details, I'll add a little more and then a little more. Conversation may come around to the fact that I am a life coach and neuro-linguistic practitioner and a former tennis pro. Fine then. Or maybe it won't. Fine as well.

My listener may ask for a few details or for many. If she asks a lot, we may get into areas where I am being asked to list my accomplishments. The point is, though, that I should be of Right Mindfulness and give out only as much positive information about myself as the person directly asks of me. If I say, "I am a radio show host," let it be someone else who says, "Nancy interviews luminaries, celebrities, and experts in their fields on her show every week." For me to say it is just plain gross.

Indeed, others may find it obnoxious if we go on and on when things are going well for us. We must always remember that while joy comes from within, external factors do play a role in our lives. Sharing our good news with others is a part of life, but it must be handled as deftly as telling someone that a great tragedy has occurred. We must be of Right Concentration. We should not become so caught up in our own excitement that we fail to notice the signs that we are being boorish with what has become, for our audience of the moment, bragging.

BAD INFLUENCES: Ever meet a person who was one way when the two of you were alone, then took on an entirely different personality in a different setting? It's creepy, isn't it?

Multiple Personality Disorder aside, some people are chameleon-like. This is odd (I think), but it happens nonetheless. The thing to watch out for, if you are someone who is easily swayed by the crowd, is to be careful of your choice of crowds.

I know I'm making it sound as if this entire thing is something to be corrected within one's personality, but let me give you an acceptable example: Let's think about the person who is basically shy and introverted. Perhaps she doesn't want to be that way all the time, but there it is.

Shy Sally has this friend Rita, who's a party girl. Sally would like to be a little more like Rita. When Sally is around Rita, she lets her hair down a bit and becomes more animated. Rita brings out a different side of Sally. She makes Sally feel uninhibited and allows Sally to break out of her shell, something she is loath to do on her own.

This is a healthy example. An unhealthy example is the partnership between Shy Sally and Gossipy Gloria. As her nickname suggests Gloria never met a person she didn't have dirt on, and she's proud to spew it. When Shy Sally, who's half woman and half chameleon, hangs around Gloria, pretty soon she's gossiping up a storm. Maybe she's even scooping dirt on Party Girl Rita. How's that for gratitude?

In a perfect world, a perfect person would find perfect personal centering and be able to dream it and be it when it comes to who they are and how they act. But we are not all perfect. And, yes, some of us need another person around to complete us. If that's the way it is with you, choose your friends carefully. Think about the kind of people they are and how they act, then think about how you act when you are around them. Does your manner change for the worse? Do you go home and feel guilty for having acted in a way that does not make you proud? If so, consider ending a partnership that does not bring out the best in your behavior and finding a healthier one.

DOMINATION: This goes back a bit to the issue of power. You see a wife who is utterly dominated by her husband or vice versa. You see a domineering parent or a spoiled child. All of these are unequal relationships. Not only are they unhealthy in and of themselves, particularly for the one being dominated, but they make even casual bystanders uncomfortable.

The need to dominate and/or control others is not healthy. If you constantly feel this need, you should seek counseling. So, too, should people who always seem to find themselves in situations where they are being taken advantage of and disrespected as a human being.

There is nothing wrong with having the ambition of being a boss—the top person in some cluster setting. But not all bosses domineer. The best ones rarely do.

Rely upon the Golden Rule when you are in a position of power: Think of how you would want to be treated as a lower-ranked associate and then act that way. Speak to people the way you want them to speak to you. If you are in a high enough position to have "gofers," what's wrong with using a little "please" and "thank you" when you have them make copies or get files for you? That's the Zen Game way. Furthermore, you are likely to get a more inspired effort from those around you. An effort driven by fear is rarely inspired and often rife with stress-related mistakes.

There is that old mafioso question: Would you rather be loved or feared? The correct answer is neither. The best answer is "respected." There is no doubt our first president, George Washington, embodied this winning attitude.

NEW PARTNERS/NEW ADVERSARIES: We all take a bit of time to find our comfort zone around new people. The best thing I've learned, as I've mentioned, is to *make sure that I have control of the space immediately around me.*

I do not need to depend on this new person to feel comfortable. My personal comfort and confidence is my problem, not theirs.

I would never suggest that you immediately treat total strangers like your best friend, but at least treat them like someone you'd be pleased to meet. I have heard friends and even some family members say they like to have lower expectations of people so that they don't feel let down so much. Or, by expecting the worst in an upcoming situation or with people in general, they will be delightfully surprised if the experience is good. I see the intent behind this approach. They want to protect themselves. But I also see it as expecting mediocrity in people. The prism through which I view the world is that I expect the best in people. This practice is the opposite of putting up your guard.

You might be wondering, "Isn't that what they say about a sucker being born every minute?" Not the way I do it. As with our legal system, I say people are innocent until proven guilty. Surprisingly, I like to think that by doing this we somehow exert a bit of control and can nudge others toward their best possible behavior.

When I am really nice to hotel clerks, I am assuming that they are competent and will provide good service. And, as a result of this approach, I believe I stand the best possible chance of *getting* good, pleasant, competent service from them.

I think there are a few people who are unfailingly nice and honorable. I also think there are a few who are simply bad and incorrigible. But the vast majority lie somewhere between these two extremes, I believe. They can go either way, depending upon the stimulus they receive. I make conscious decisions to try to bring out the best in the people I meet.

GENDER ROLES: I was a child when women were burning bras, and I thank God for women such as Billie Jean King who believed in equality and equal pay for male and female tennis players. Here are my thoughts on the subject: I simply feel that I want to be paid in a gender-neutral manner and be respected in every way without regard for whether I am a man or a woman.

That being said, it sometimes surprises me when I encounter women who are "throwbacks" on the feminism trail. In some cases, it's a generational thing, and there's not a lot I can say to a sixty-something woman who thinks a certain way about herself and her relationships with men. On the other hand, what I loathe is when otherwise intelligent, talented, and accomplished women act one way around other women and a completely different way in the presence of men.

Ladies, you are not truly empowering anyone by subjugating yourself before men. That only demeans you. A man who is threatened by the presence of a strong, intelligent, and talented woman has issues to work out—such as, thinking offhand, his own frail or dubious masculinity. *He* has the problem, not you, and you cannot fix those problems by feigning incompetence.

Does this mean you should "castrate" your man—or any man—in public? No, not at all, especially if his actions point toward previous castration (so in essence he has already castrated himself). In fact, my best advice is for you to throw such sexist phrases out of your lexicon. To "castrate," in this case, means to demean and demoralize. This is something you should never do to *anybody*, male or female.

Here is my point: If you are smart, be smart. If you are athletic, be athletic. Be the best "you" that you have worked hard to become. Be all good things, all positive things. Your assertiveness does not make the person you are with weak.

Yes, when matched with any other individual, talents will be relative. If I am with a rocket scientist, she is likely to be the smarter one. If I am with a couch potato, I am likely to be the more athletic one. On the other hand, if I am with tennis professional Serena Williams, *she* will be the more athletic one. The same goes for your run-of-the-mill rocket scientist if he or she is hanging out with a Nobel laureate. This is all fine and good. Be your best at all times. But do not allow gender to dictate whether you are allowed to be who you really are. Those who cannot accept you for your talents do not deserve to be around you.

HIDDEN TREASURES: Did you ever go up to a person who appears to be shy, reclusive, and out of place in a public setting? Occasionally, they turn out to be fascinatingly wonderful people. I call people like this "hidden treasures."

Give people a try; give them a chance. Sometimes the people who are easy to get to know—gregarious, loud people—don't have a lot to offer other than their lack of inhibition. They can occasionally be rather shallow and self-centered. Sure, once in a while it may be great to meet a really accomplished person who regales you with tales of their successes and adventures. But that's not communication—that's putting on a show. And hey, I pay good money to see a show once in a while. But is this type of person likely to become a *friend*?

A friend shares the stage. A friend cares about you and what is going on in your life as well. Showboats may make acceptable acquaintances, but they are the shallow swimmers in the sea. "Hidden treasures" are the deeper swimmers, and they are more likely to make better friends and lovers.

"I TOLD YOU SO": If two people get lost while driving somewhere and one says "Go right" and the other says "Go left," someone is going to be wrong. So be it.

Once they have arrived safely at their destination, does anyone sincerely believe that the person who was wrong doesn't realize it? Of course he or she does. Perhaps the graceful thing for this person to do would be to say, "Wow, I should have listened to you."

Maybe she will say that. Or maybe she won't. Maybe she won't because her ego is bruised. Maybe she won't because the entire situation was so stressful that making apologies has a rather low priority at that moment.

When you are right, is it really necessary to receive accolades for it, particularly from some other person who was wrong? Grow up! You know you were right. Be glad in that. I'm sure it's a bit of an ego boost, but be gracious and keep it to yourself. Don't go spiking life's metaphorical ball in another player's face. "I told you so" personifies Wrong Speech.

"LIAR! THIEF!" Sometimes you have to break up a partnership, and when you do, there's a right and a wrong way to do it.

An entire book could be written about this, so I'll try to be brief. For the moment, let me focus on situations in which you believe the other person in the relationship has been dishonest in some manner. Maybe it's a boss who promised you a raise and later claimed he didn't. Or it's an employee who you know stole from you, although you can't quite prove it.

Notice I stopped short of describing a truly litigious situation where you really have the goods on someone in a definite criminal or civil act. We'll leave those for the lawyers. Getting ironclad proof that someone has wronged you in a criminal or civil manner is often difficult. It can also be costly and eventually fruitless. If someone lied to you and then denied it, you could walk around with a tape recorder for years thereafter trying to get him to admit it or tell the lie again. But all you'll have done is ruin your own quality of life over this obsession with thinking and saying, *"J'accuse!"*

Let's deal instead with the more commonplace: You sincerely know in your heart that every time your housekeeper comes over, another piece of your jewelry goes missing. Or you've gathered enough evidence to make the case that your boyfriend has been cheating on you. Can your evidence hold up sufficiently in a court of law to get a conviction? Probably not, so don't go there.

What should you do? Obviously, as your "case" is piling up, it would behoove you to confront the person delicately, directly, and professionally about your findings (therefore, don't show up at his or her door with a pitchfork and flaming torch). But what happens when a thief or liar gets caught? They usually lie some more.

So where are you now and what do you do? Frankly, in the Court of Real Life, you don't have to have an ironclad case, so long as you don't let things get out of hand. If you think someone you hired to work for you has stolen from you or lied to you, but you couldn't conclusively prove it in a court of law, you can still sit him or her down quietly and say, "This isn't working out. I'm not happy, and I've developed some trust issues that I can't overcome. I won't pursue this any further, and I won't impede your ability to earn a living elsewhere, but for now, things are over between you and me." With the cheating…well, there are a lot of illegal things that you might think of doing to him *in your mind (only)*, but this would not be Right Mindfulness. Remember, this isn't a soap opera on television; this is reality. In real life, what you give out will always come back at you, so look out!

To summarize: If you have truly grown to distrust someone you are in a relationship with and you can't overcome those feelings, end it. But do it legally, respectfully, and professionally, and do it in a way that, should there be any further repercussions, you are legally on safe ground. You can usually fire or dismiss someone without having to raise or defend cause. As for lousy boyfriends, they're a dime a dozen.

JERKS VERSUS JERKY ACTIONS: No matter how perfect I am—I mean *you are*—you will still probably do something regrettably jerky at some point in your life. It's inevitable. A great challenge in life is to separate the jerks from the jerky acts.

Since we all say and do jerky things sometimes, we've already discussed how to approach such situations. First off, we discuss the situation, *not* the person: "I am *not* saying you are a jerk; I am saying that I feel you did or said something jerky."

What happens next is the point of this section.

A truly good, kind, noble person will cop to it and apologize. Bear in mind, some people apologize in an indirect fashion. They walk away mumbling to themselves then send you a dozen roses the next day, unsigned. That's an apology, and you should be grateful for it. Different personalities work in different ways.

But here is where we separate jerks from merely jerky actions. People who commit a jerky action will apologize or offer a mea culpa in some way. Jerks will defend themselves to the death. A jerk is never, ever wrong. They have never done anything wrong in their lives. Jerks are defined by their singular inability to ever realize that they are acting like a jerk.

If you meet a person like this, run for cover. They will cause you nothing but misery. They are God's little tests to let us know how we are able to withstand obstacles in life.

VENDORS AND BUYERS: If I hire you to landscape my lawn, or if you hire me to give a speech at your next convention, this too is a type of partnership. We have entered into an agreement—and in most cases, a verbal one. And you know what they say about verbal contracts: They're not worth the paper they're not written on.

I like these partnerships to be casual. Why? Because a casual approach to things implies that the relationship is friendly and cordial. I want to like my tailor or seamstress. I want her professional opinion on how my clothing should fit me, even if I may not agree with her all the time. But as part of this relationship, I'd like a little leeway regarding errors and problems. If I come to pick up a suit and I say, "I think you made the pants too long," I'd like you to agree with me, the customer, and say, "Oh, here, let me fix that. Sorry." Why? Because I hope this will be a long-term relationship. I don't want you to get defensive when this happens; nor do I want you to go to some little price sheet you have in order to argue with me over how much such an alteration will cost. In return, I will come back to you time and time again, for I respect you and you are (sort of) my friend. This is a balanced relationship.

These casual relationships between buyer and vendor only work when both sides are fair and honorable. In some cases, unfortunately, one party wants that casual, friendly relationship while the other is rubbing his or her hands together, figuring out how to take advantage of the other.

A man hires a landscape designer. They agree on the scope of the work and the price. As the job goes on, the landowner is so happy that he decides to add dozens of additional touches, involving significant time and product. The contractor starts to draw up an estimate for this new work, but the customer says, "Nah, that's all right. Money's no object. Just do it." The contractor, happy to get the work and pleased that he seems to have cultivated a loyal new customer, sets about his business.

The job is completed and the contractor turns in his final bill. The customer says, "Holy cow (or maybe what comes out of the back end of cows)! I can't afford that! Here, I'll give you half."

What is the contractor to do? He didn't have a written contract for the additional work. He trusted the customer to honor his word ("Money is no object"). Meanwhile, this scenario was all a ploy by the customer to put himself in a position of power. How can the contractor "take back" work that's already been done?

It's not fair.

If you are the victim in circumstances such as this, I feel for you; I really do. Yet I still believe in honor and giving trust. It may mean that we have to seek legal redress when we are burned in this way, and it may also mean that we will have to be more discerning about doling out trust in the future. But I refuse to withhold trust entirely from the world.

I want to live in a Zen Game world. That means I must do whatever I can to follow that Noble Eightfold Path. Along the way, I hope to influence others to do so as well. Be trustworthy, and never take advantage of someone else's trust in you.

SPECIALISTS: You go to your doctor, a general practitioner. He discovers something that he feels requires treatment from a specialist and so refers you to one. That's nice. It's so nice that I wonder sometimes why everything in the world doesn't work this way.

You are taking piano lessons. You chose this teacher because she is well known for her expertise in ragtime and that's what you wanted to learn. Your progress with her has been fantastic.

Now you would like to delve into "free jazz." If you've already developed a good and cordial relationship with this particular teacher, you should raise the issue of your new artistic direction. Maybe she's also great with free jazz. Or maybe she's not. If she isn't, her Right Mindfulness would be to say, "I'm not very well versed in that area, but I do know Blues McCoy, who is fabulous with jazz." She should then make sure that Blues knows how you got to him so that he can, perhaps, return the favor sometime by giving her a referral.

Now for the pitfalls in this scenario. Your ragtime teacher says, "Well, I'm not that good at free jazz, but I'll do what I can for you." This means you won't be getting world-class instruction in this new area. Be direct yet diplomatic and ask if she knows someone else who specializes in free jazz. If she's insulted, that is her problem, not yours. If you've done it the Zen Game way, you will have expressed yourself respectfully, letting her know how much you appreciate what she's done for your ragtime playing and how you will be happy to send more clients her way for that particular style.

Do not feel guilty. People often try to make others feel guilty unfairly and selfishly. Now, I'm not going to name names, but you guilt throwers know who you are. For your own good and the good of others, cut it out! For those of you who are naïve about asking for referrals or feel that you don't want to upset people, I say, do not fall into that trap. Do not stay in this sort of partnership out of guilt.

HANGING OUT: When I was a tennis coach, I loved it when one of my students would linger after her lesson and help me pick up the balls and do other assorted housekeeping duties. Yes, of course, I enjoyed the free labor, but in exchange for that, I would try to give something back to the student, perhaps some additional suggestions about her game.

This is such an important life lesson. In college, do you know who attends optional tutorials and study sessions and uses the professor's office hours the most? Not the students in jeopardy, but the *best* students, the "A" students.

What does this tell us? It tells us that practice makes perfect, but also that another form of practice is the less-structured process of "hanging out" with a mentor. The student/teacher partnership need not end when the class period is over. It can continue for as long as both parties are interested and available.

Great athletes have forever hung out with other great athletes that they admire. Why? Not just out of wide-eyed fandom, but because they sought to forge a casual partnership in which they could learn more and improve their performance. Established experts in nearly every field enjoy passing along knowledge to a new generation.

Take advantage of these win-win partnerships, but whatever you do, make sure that you do not just blatantly "use" people. Be willing to give back to your mentor so that you establish yourself as a forthright and appreciative person. If Martina Navratilova had given me her time when I was coming up as a young player, I would have gladly moved her furniture if she needed a hand!

PERFORMERS AND AUDIENCES: A partnership rarely recognized as one is the relationship that occurs between a performer and an audience. It presents some unique challenges, all of which should be met in some way by both of the participants or groups of participants.

First off is for the audience to show respect for the performer. This is an acute situation because the person on stage often can see and hear us. It is surprising how many people are oblivious to this reality.

It's one thing if you walk into a darkened movie theater, find the movie boring, nudge your partner, and suggest the two of you leave. For the time being, we'll set aside the potential rudeness of this action to other members of the audience. Instead, let's take the situation of a live performance and consider the implications. If you are attending, say, a Rolling Stones concert at Madison Square Garden, Mick and the boys likely won't know you were even there, let alone that you got bored and left. But I relate to this more as a public speaker. If you nudge your neighbor, I can see you; I can hear you. If you get up because I am boring you (impossible!), it is not nice. I tend to believe that once you have decided to spend your evening at a lecture, a poetry reading, a piano recital, or a religious service, you have made a commitment to be in partnership with the speaker/performer. You should honor your end of the bargain by sitting respectfully until the event ends or a proper intermission or break occurs. (We will discuss situations relating to the audiences of sporting events later in this book.)

But I am calling this a partnership, so you have every right to ask, "What about the responsibilities of the performer?" Yes, they too exist.

For one thing, the performer does have a professional responsibility to be on time and to be well organized or rehearsed. This doesn't necessarily mean you can expect perfection, but rather that care and consideration have been taken. If I am a violinist, I may practice my instrument all day long, but you, as a connoisseur, may find my performance lacking simply because I am not very good. This is in stark contrast to me showing up forty-five minutes late, drunk and out of tune. That would be an example of me showing you, the audience member, no respect at all.

Another way this partnership can go awry is in the direct interaction between performer and audience. Remember that schoolteacher who only called on you when you were drifting off into la-la land? She was making a point and exercising discipline in the classroom by embarrassing you. It's not a method I thoroughly embrace, but we all recognize that it happens on occasion. Outside of that scenario, though, it is definitely not Right for either party to embarrass the other. If I pay to hear you give a speech, you do not have the right to single me out just to embarrass me any more than I have the right to disrespect you on stage by heckling you or drowning you out with noise. There are, of course, some comedians who are known for heckling the audience, and in these specific cases the audience expects it. This interaction is a part of the partnership. In fact, those brave souls who wish to be insulted actually try to grab seats as close to the stage as possible. Vive la difference!

When I am speaking publicly, I look for eye contact. I do not want to embarrass the people who have given me their time. If someone is looking at me, riding the wave with me as I speak, that's the person I tend to call on if I decide to get interactive. Also, remember the teacher who *never* called on you when your hand was raised, *only* when you were, in fact, drifting off? Again, that's fine and good in a fourth-grade classroom, but it's totally uncool once you've grown up. Call on the person who is excited and waving his or her hand at you. It'll make for a better exchange, and that's why you are there. Speakers are entertainers.

GROUP PARTNERSHIPS: Being in a group is an opportunity for us to be at our best or our worst. You've heard of "mob mentality," right? That's what I'm talking about here. Some guy with a funny mustache hits the stage and riles up a crowd, and pretty soon everyone is goose-stepping off to Poland. Not good, not good at all.

But groupthink can bring out the best in us as well. It's all about how someone in a group begins an action and others either go along with it or argue against it.

Good example (versus the marching into Poland example): A friend of mine told me a story of taking his son to visit a college. In the cafeteria, there was a group of upperclassmen at a table. A "newbie" student came by—either a freshman or another visiting high schooler—who was all alone. She lost her footing and spilled her lunch tray and all of its contents on the floor. She looked upset, embarrassed, and confused.

The group of kids at the nearby table could have done any number of things. They could have ignored her, laughed about it, let out a sarcastic cheer or…what they actually *did*, which was to jump out of their seats immediately, boys and girls both, and help her. Two kids started cleaning up, one consoled her, another volunteered to refill her tray with one of everything she had spilled, and, finally, one invited her to come join them at their table. What did they not cover?! Every single thing a person in this situation could have possibly asked for was given without asking. My friend told me that at that very moment, his entire family looked at each other and said, "Now *this* is a great college!" And their son promptly made the choice to attend.

This situation is a spin on that phrase "corporate culture." At places large and small, a tone is set. We often do not know how it happens, but most logically it begins at the top and travels downward. My friend tells me that ever since his son has been attending this school, he has seen similar scenes almost daily—good, loving behavior exhibited by everyone from the college president on down. If a tone is set in a group partnership where neighborliness and good manners are the norm, then so it shall be.

If we are the leader of a group, whether it is simply a handful of people at a table or a multinational corporation, we have the ability to exert our influence on that group through the way we act when we are in it. If we are at our best, this mindset spreads.

Do we have to be the "leader" to do this? No. I doubt there was a true "leader" at that college cafeteria table. Their response was engrained "groupthink." It was the accepted cultural reaction in that environment. Obviously, it was initiated by someone, somewhere, at some time, and then passed down over the years. But again, don't think you have to be a leader or even an official part of such a culture to have a positive influence on it. Be your best at all times—of Right Mindfulness and Right Action—no matter who or how many people are around you. And don't think twice about whether others will follow you. If you are in the Right, then go for it and *be* Right. Those who do the same are the Right people for you.

CASTING FOR TEAMS: Very few sports seem to require the melding of varied and various talents as much as basketball does. It is common to see a team trade for or draft a number of high scorers, only to have the pundits say, "They'll have to bring five balls out onto the court." The implication is that these five guys will not be able to play nicely and share with only one ball to shoot.

This idea translates to the business world as well. Some folks are leaders, while others are followers. Others are wired to be the "perfect vice president," someone who is a leader but is most adept at supporting a slightly stronger personality.

We are all different, yet we can all add to the success of an organization or a team. Team building involves everyone realizing their strengths and weaknesses and embracing their differences. Interestingly enough, few teams succeed when everyone has the identical skill set.

If you are ever in a situation where you can simply hire or select the cream of the crop to work with you, consider yourself blessed. But always remember, this situation can be a curse as often as it is a blessing. A team full of strong leaders may find itself getting pulled in a thousand different directions rather than moving forward together. Sometimes, clever casting of disparate parts—people with specialized strengths that complement those of others—is the most successful formula. Think about that when you need to put together a team of any sort, business or sport.

8
SPORTS AND
THE SPORT OF LIFE

"AND THE WINNER IS..."

If life is a game like any other, I can think of no better way to break down everyday situations than with analogies from the world of sports. In addition, there are many issues involved in the playing and watching of sports today that could use a little (or, in some cases, a lot) of the Zen Game mindset.

It is my intention in this chapter to help you be your very best self in the sports arena by employing the eight noble principles of Zen. People who master the art of playing sports for the joy of it will automatically enjoy the experience more and play better. Okay, now you're asking yourself, "How can I play better at my sport by applying Right View, Right Intention, Right Speech, Right Action, Right Livelihood, Right Effort, Right Mindfulness, and Right Concentration?" Simple! The sooner we can be at peace with winning or losing, the sooner we will project the kind of energy that magnetizes more self-confidence. Confidence creates happiness and positive energy. Remember that the idea with Zen Game is to "Win at the Game of Life Without Selling Your Soul."

People who are not at peace with winning or losing typically are not playing a sport for the joy of it. They're focused on the results of the game instead—often because they are seeking a way to assert superiority over others. Unfortunately, the bravado of "I am better than you" can get the best of these people. Feelings of superiority are as poisonous as feelings of inferiority when it comes to performing well and playing well in sports. The fear of losing puts an added weight on our shoulders. Instead of playing with confidence and enjoying this wonderful adventure and great opportunity, we play with catastrophic thinking (it's all or nothing). This additional stress will inhibit the way we think, the way we move, and the way we perform.

When people are desperate to win, they only push away the thing they want the most. We must appreciate everything we have and enjoy it exactly as it is in the moment. Our greatest gift is always in the moment and in believing that we are a winner regardless of the outcome.

By surrendering any attachment to the outcome, we are in flow with the universe and will see that the universe is in flow with us, helping us to enjoy the experience to the fullest and play our best game. When we are in balance with the universe—be it on the soccer field or the playing field of life—we create a balance for ourselves that shows in our energy, attitude, and performance. It is when we stop expecting to win at everything that we begin to manifest and harvest positive opportunities. This is the energy that naturally attracts the outcomes we seek.

THE PSYCH OUT: I'm not a proponent of the competitive tactic of "psyching out" an opponent, either in sports or in life. I respect that some people engage in this practice, but I question whether or not it really helps them. It involves an awful lot of misspent energy—energy that could be put to more constructive use.

Now, here is where it gets interesting, because the problem does not fully lie with the perpetrator. Other people add to the problem by condoning this behavior, often because the person is famous, notorious, or considered a "star." I see it with superstar athletes all the time. People let them get away with a heck of a lot more than the guy who is lower down in the ranks. It's the same story with corporate giants. Some people are in such awe of these men and women that they turn a blind eye to their tantrums, disturbing behavior, vulgar rants, and psych outs. The harm in lionizing this kind of behavior occurs when it begins to spread to others. For example, it is one thing for a major league baseball manager to yell at an umpire throughout the game to intimidate him into giving his team some better calls. But imagine if someone did the same thing at a company picnic softball game. He or she would be acting like some sort of lunatic.

As far as I'm concerned, icy stares, yelling, loud complaining, and all the rest have no place in a competition or negotiation, particularly if there are not millions of dollars at stake. It takes all the joy out of the endeavor, like letting air out of a balloon. Besides, it's hard to turn it off when you're finished. Pretty soon, the brat in the boardroom becomes the brat everywhere, and what will that get him or her in life, other than disliked?

In life and in sports, we can either choose the aggressive approach, where every action we take is meant to dominate and intimidate others around us, or we can simply win people over with a smile and positive, intelligent words. If you have figured me out by now, you know which stance I would rather take. A gentle boss can avoid a stomach ulcer and migraine headaches and achieve much better results than does a tyrant who talks down to employees. The same goes for a spouse who manipulates his or her other half with prickly words and cruel remarks to get what he or she wants. Generally, this treatment only engenders more bitterness and, in some cases, a desire for retribution.

So the main thought here is, do we want to make allies or enemies in life? When we're dealing with others, we must always give careful thought to what kind of person we want to be—an inspiration to others or a thorn in their side? Even Scrooge realized that his attitude would not do if he wanted respect from others. It took three otherworldly creatures to drum that into his head, but ultimately he came to his senses.

Nobody wants to be around such people *unless* they feel they are getting something from it. I've seen women put up with their husband's verbal abuse because he buys them expensive jewels and a country club lifestyle. Well, it's a heavy price to pay for the women, I say. The real question is, who is using whom? It's obvious that they're using each other. Hey, if both parties feel satisfied and are getting what they want from the relationship, so be it.

Now, it's a different story if one party is duping another. When you feel someone is trying to usurp your power, it's time to apply Right Concentration and Right Action. The first thing you can do is to use the "mirroring process." For example, when people are conning you, you can respond back to them by saying, "I feel as if I am being conned." To be effective, let them know how you feel with as little emotion as possible. By mirroring back to these people what they are doing through words, you are letting them know that you are on to their game. It's impossible to avoid these "tricksters" in life, but by setting up your own personal boundaries you are choosing the best way to respond to a controlling person and a difficult situation.

INTENSITY: "Intensity" is becoming a misused word in the world of sports and beyond. More and more these days, behavior that is labeled "intense" is really just behavior that is out of control.

Why do we admire this theatrical "intensity"? I believe it is because of the entertainment value. No doubt the media plays it up as well. We see images of this behavior in magazines, newspapers, and advertisements. When someone acts out in front of millions of fans, it gets replayed over and over on televisions across the world. People who do not know a thing about the game understand tantrums. However, when we call this behavior "intensity" instead of recognizing it for what it really is—merely unfocused and out-of-control emotions—we send the wrong message to young people.

All athletes who play to the top of their ability and sometimes push their own limits are showing Right Concentration and giving Right Effort. That, to me, is true intensity. Hey, I could phone in my performance and gesticulate a lot, and you might be conned into believing I was giving my all. But those antics are not a true demonstration of maximum effort. When you are playing with "Zen," you are in the moment. Your mind and body are working together as one. That's why everything flows so smoothly and effortlessly that you are "in the zone."

A person must be balanced mentally, physically, and emotionally for optimum performance. When you are mad and playing with anger, you are overloaded. Mentally your judgment is clouded, physically your muscles and body feel tight and contracted, and emotionally you feel like a ticking bomb. With Right Effort, you never want to give up. You use all of your true "intensity" to try your best—this time, the next time, and every time. You don't make everything mean so much. You just learn from it. You don't waste precious energy getting mad or putting on a show for someone's entertainment.

I've heard some professional athletes say that they play well when they get themselves mad. But in a sense, they are playing with fire. If you think of your emotions on a meter, with feeling cool and numb on the far left of the meter and feeling hot and out of control on the far right, it is best to stay in the middle or a little toward the cold side. This is the place where you are aware but feel neutral—not too hot, not too cold. Once you start to get heated up, you can use this extra energy in your favor, but you must be aware that it is hard to control the fine line between mad and energized and angry and out of control.

When I was playing tennis competitively, I would *hope* that you would become overintense and get out of control. I would hope that you'd get so wrapped up in your own little personal drama and trauma that one mistake would lead to another. Now that I play for enjoyment, I would prefer not to play with someone who has this mindset. It takes all the fun out of the game for me. I don't even like to watch this type of poor sportsmanship as a spectator. If I want drama, I'll go to a movie or play.

This lesson carries forth in all aspects of life. Have you ever seen a child throw herself on the floor in a tantrum to get what she wants? The parents' job is to ignore that tantrum so it doesn't happen again. Paying any kind of attention to such behavior and giving in to a mere toddler's demands will only help create a weak personality in him or her. If you nip this attitude in the bud, on the other hand, as a parent you are telling the child that one cannot achieve much in life with emotional outbursts and hysterics. In fact, the result of all that effort will probably be a massive headache, a feeling of exhaustion, serious embarrassment, and a hoarse voice for a week.

It's useful to consider what the implications are of handling such situations correctly. When you stay positive, clearheaded, and with Right View, Right Intention, and Right Mindfulness, you are better able to control almost any situation. I learned this lesson when I was training my two puppies. The more I got mad at their aggressive, destructive behavior, the more they did it to get attention from me. When I let them know they did wrong with a stern voice and ignored them for a short period of time, they were less likely to repeat the behavior. The change didn't happen immediately, but after a few times they learned that this behavior did not pay off for them.

For those of you who think that winning by whining has its payoffs, why not ask yourself this question: Do you want to gain a reputation as someone who whines and throws a tantrum every time a little bit of adversity comes your way? If you want to be the King (or Queen) of Uncool, that's the way to go. But again, as much as you'd like it to be so, the reality is that the world does not revolve around you, me, or anyone else, for that matter. If you want to be respected and to be someone that others want to be around, I suggest you change that tune of yours as quickly as you can say, "Cut it out, man!"

People who have to stir themselves up to perform are beaten before they even begin. Focused people can see right through this façade. Sometimes it comes in the form of cockiness—an attitude that is meant to intimidate but is actually easy to detect as being false and no more than mere bluster. People who curse themselves out loud demonstrate a weakness that is rarely pitied. We often accept this behavior from good players of all ages and in any sport. Yet it does not set a good example for anyone, especially our youth.

LOSING: We put too much pressure on the result of a process—winning versus losing—rather than on the process itself. I'm telling you, folks, it is in the journey that you will find your day-to-day happiness, not in the thrill of victory that comes around once in a while. Furthermore, when you dictate to the universe that everything has to be your way and that losing is unacceptable, *you will make losing inevitable* when it shouldn't be.

Winning and losing are too often the states of being in which we choose to live. How limiting! In life we not only have black and white but several shades of gray as well. If there is a position posted where you work and you and the person in the next cubicle both apply for it, someone will win and someone will lose. Or will they?

The truth is, the outcome of such a situation is often based on purely subjective factors. Perhaps you would get the promotion if one particular person is the decider, while your colleague would get the job if someone else is rendering an opinion. None of this directly places value or lack of value on you unless you allow it to do so. Don't take it personally, and trust that everything happens for a reason.

When things are out of your control, there is not a lot you can do except to have faith in yourself, your abilities, and the fact that you did your best. Time and time again, I've heard people say that in the end, "This was the best thing that could have ever happened to me!" Perhaps something better will come along for you, or you will reevaluate the situation. We always learn more from our mistakes than from our victories. If you add it up, you are better off losing sometimes because of the important lessons you learn from any mistake you make. Losing and making changes puts you even farther ahead of yourself than if you had been winning everything right along.

Here are some questions to ask yourself: What are the lessons to be learned here? Would you do anything differently if you had to do it over again? Maybe not. When you seek to understand what has happened and look at it unemotionally, you will be less concerned that you did not get what you wanted and more concerned with how to take better action the next time. It is ironic that we sometimes find that the things we desired so much are not really what we wanted after all. They did not bring us the happiness and success we imagined they would.

It is not my intention to get too sticky and philosophical about it, but sometimes things really do work out for the best. Ever hear of the "Peter

Principle"? It's the theory that we all rise to our level of incompetence. For example, we take a great carpenter and because of his success, we promote him to construction supervisor. The truth is, the company is now minus its very best carpenter. Meanwhile, the carpenter may have no leadership or supervisory skills whatsoever.

It sometimes seems that there is a spiritual or karmic hand in our affairs. One mystical example is when we lose out on a job or an opportunity that, if we had gotten it, would have kept us from something far better. Let's return to the example above where both you and the person in the next cubicle apply for a higher position. Imagine that you don't get the job and therefore give notice and go elsewhere. Six months later, your old company folds. Meanwhile, you've hooked up with a far better company with a much higher salary, and you're far, far happier than you had been at the old place. Life is like that sometimes. "Winning" and "losing" are merely words we choose that may unreasonably dictate our feelings and our happiness or lack thereof.

Here's another example of how the universe knows what is best for us. Several years ago, when my husband and I were looking to move from New York City to New Jersey, we thought we had found the house of our dreams. The broker said we had the house 100 percent. Unfortunately at the time, but fortunately for us in the long run, we found out that someone else put in a higher bid. When we heard the news that we had lost the house, we were shattered. It didn't seem fair and it certainly didn't seem ethical. But a few months later, we found a house only five minutes away from the other house. This house was a thousand times better for us. The first house was bigger, but in every other respect, our new home sweet home seemed to have been built for us.

Whenever I drive by the other house, I am reminded of an important lesson. When you make an energetic intention to have faith in the universe, the universe will honor this trust by directing more blessings and good fortune your way. If you are not ready to make this conscious, energetic shift, just give things time to happen in the way that will benefit you most in the long run. Know that everything happens for a good reason and for your benefit. It may not occur in the time frame you were expecting, but if things move too quickly (according to your schedule), you may not be ready for the next step and it may not bring you the success and happiness you wanted.

Most people quote famed football coach Vince Lombardi for all the wrong reasons. ("Winning isn't everything. It's the only thing.") But he once said a very profound thing after his team lost a big game. "We didn't lose. We were just behind when the clock ran out." It is most important to acknowledge your opponent for his or her win and efforts, but it is also important to acknowledge and honor yourself. There is no shame in losing when you have tried your best. There is always something for which you can be grateful.

The point here is, during any competition or conflict in which the participants are fairly evenly matched, each side will likely be winning for a while, losing for a while, and so on. Both winning and losing are just temporary states of being anyway, so why attribute so much importance to them? If I lose a tennis match to someone over the course of three sets, who's to say that I might not have won had we played seven sets? This is the futility of being a slave to the score. Again, the Middle Path is the one leading to enlightenment and focus.

We all have our demons inside us. None of us is perfect, yet perfection (giving and being your best self) is something worth striving for—assuming you are not obsessed about it, of course. Unfortunately, winning a single victory or competition is not the definition of perfection.

Let's say you are competing for a contract of some sort. You and a representative from another company are squaring off, each trying to persuade the client that he or she should use your company. Maybe you're new to this, or maybe you only have one type of sales pitch, but it doesn't seem to be working with this client. You lose and the other person gets the big contract. Should you concentrate on the "winning or losing" aspect of this event? I wouldn't. I would try instead to analyze *why* you lost and how you might do better in the future. Maybe as a salesperson you are a one-trick pony, and that trick won't work with every client. Maybe you came off as too comical while your competitor was more serious and clinical. Your shtick didn't work on this particular client because he, too, was a dry, analytical type. You've got to get more tricks in your bag! You've got to learn different approaches for different audiences. In neuro-linguistic training, practitioners learn how important it is to size up people so that they can see where others are coming from and what they might respond to better. You can do this too, simply by training yourself to be more aware of other people's words and mannerisms.

Remember that the scoring isn't over until we visit that big umpire in the sky. One match is just one match on any one day. And, God willing, we will live to see another match on another day. Sure, we all hate to lose the big ones, but in the big picture, we tend to feel that far too many incidents are "the big one" when they're not. As Robert Louis Stevenson says, "Don't judge each day by the harvest you reap…but by the seeds you plant." Life is all about the journey. Work on improvement; don't focus only on winning today.

FAILURE: Everyone loses sometimes. But it's not just at competitions. A sense of failure is also at issue when we ask someone out on a date and are turned down. We've put ourselves out there and been rebuffed. We've failed. My husband said that in his college fraternity, they gave points to people who were turned down for dates. The person with the most points at the end of the month was rewarded for his efforts. This clever game allowed even shy people to know that it was okay to be rejected and that it was not the end of the world.

For everything in life, there is a positive and a negative. And, of course, for every negative there is a positive. Take a look at everything in your life, and you'll see that this gold principle applies. Here's one: I always say it is a sacrifice to have kids and a sacrifice not to have kids. Here's another: Most people like the idea of having a big house and a big yard, but with this luxury come the expense and energy costs of having to take care of them.

Now, let's get back to the subject of failure. Another common form of failure is to make a mistake in public. We're in a house of worship, perhaps shaking hands with the minister or rabbi as we are about to leave, and someone accidentally steps on the back of our foot with all of his body weight. The pain is excruciating and we shout out a four-letter expletive.

Look, it happens to everyone. But the biggest problem with failure or embarrassment is allowing it to control your life and put you on a path to more and more failure and embarrassment.

You've heard of losing streaks, haven't you? Here is why they happen: We fail once, and then we let it plague us. Instead of going about life with a positive attitude and expecting the best, we fear failure and begin to anticipate and expect it. Expect failure and you shall receive failure.

Here's another idea that has become clichéd but is so true that it bears repeating: The only people who never make mistakes are people who never do anything. The more you do, the more you will experience some failures. This is why the people who are most successful have undoubtedly made the most mistakes. It's fascinating when you think of it that way. The same is true of anything you do a lot of in life: The more you talk, the more likely it is that you will misspeak.

Should you allow a fear of failure to cause you to live like a hermit, afraid of embarrassment? That's crazy. I guarantee you, you have seen every person you know well say or do something embarrassing. Shall we name a few for fun? Wiping mustard from your hand onto your white pants, not realizing that your napkin fell to the floor. Blabbering the world's worst gaffe at a posh cocktail party. Walking around with your trouser zipper down or the button on your blouse popping off because it is too tight—the one that is right at your cleavage.

Here is one of my favorite public blunders: Several years ago a friend of mine was taking a flight from Minnesota to New York City. Unfortunately, he got on the wrong plane. During the flight, the flight attendant stopped by his seat and briefly chatted with him. My friend asked the woman if she was leaving home or going home. In a heavy southern drawl, the woman said she was going home. My friend was quite surprised that someone from NYC would have such a heavy southern accent and deduced that she most likely was not originally from New York. As the plane landed, the pilot announced over the intercom, "Welcome to Houston." My friend, still under the assumption that he was going to New York, thought to himself, *"Is this pilot nuts? We're in New York City!"* Well, when he got off the plane and looked around, he quickly realized he was in Houston and that he was the nutty one.

We all make these kinds of blunders and, yes, they make us all human. So in essence, you can curb your failures by practicing Right Concentration. But then, give yourself a break. To err is human, after all, and to laugh at your mistakes is a good way not to take them personally.

RECOVERY: What do we do when we "lose it"? It happens. I'm sure even Gandhi blew his stack at someone or something once or twice in his life. How do we recover from that? Sometimes the best thing is to find a way to think about something else or take the focus off ourselves. We need to find a way to remove ourselves from the situation and regain our objectivity.

Anger feeds into more anger. When we lose our temper, it is often at other human beings. And they are most likely to react defensively. That defensiveness may result in a knee-jerk reaction and equal anger, or it may be worse: They may come off as so calm and collected that we *really* feel embarrassed. Even if we were in the right in this hypothetical argument, losing our cool made us *appear* to be wrong.

In such situations, I say, "Thank God for bathrooms!" Excusing myself for any flimsy reason, such as "nature calling," removes me from the flames of my own anger and the person at whom I have directed them. It gives me a chance to take a deep breath or splash some cool water on my face and collect myself. Some people find an excuse to take a walk around the block; that works too. The idea is to disengage. When a person is really centered, they may be able to stay where they are and recollect their wits at the scene of the crime. Far more often, however, the mere sight of the person they are having a conflict with will make their brain whirl around at warp speed as they keep trying to "beat their argument" or win the point they were making.

It's all about Right Speech and Right Concentration. The best of us will still succumb to Wrong Speech from time to time, and the anger or embarrassment that result from this speech will affect our concentration. This is a clear sign that our ego has gotten the best of us. Either way, the walk around the block or the trip to the bathroom gives us a chance to reclaim our Right Concentration.

If an outburst was really out of line, the disengage/reengage tactic often makes it far easier to manage an apology than if we were to stay right where we are. So if you are faced with this predicament, wash your face and then return and *save* face.

TRASH TALK: Today, trash talking has moved beyond sports and seeped into everyday culture. This practice teaches every kid who plays anything that part of the game is to insult your opponent verbally. Unfortunately, lessons learned on the field of play often get carried into other aspects of life. Sure, there are some who trash talk with such wit that they are downright hilarious. But more often than not, this verbal volleying only creates bad feelings.

One particular form of trash talking is gloating over a victory. In tennis star Chris Evert-Lloyd's last big tournament appearance, she lost to Zina Garrison. For Zina, it was a big victory, but Zina is a class act who knew that even in defeat, this was still Chrissie's big day. She allowed herself a little involuntary fist pump but then stepped back and let Chris receive the adulation of the crowd in appreciation of her long and glorious career.

Bottom line? In any aspect of life, take responsibility for your words and actions and try to understand the effect they may have on others. Comments that seem like fun to you may be hurtful or incendiary to others.

"HOMER" CROWDS: Ever wonder why gamblers give a lot of consideration to whether a team is playing at home or away? The truth is, the level of audience participation can somewhat affect the performance on the field. If 10,000 people have shown up to cheer for one team and only 100 have traveled to cheer for the other, it can be a bit overwhelming and at times disheartening for the visiting team.

Is this Right? Is it fair? Well, what it is, really, is commonplace. However, I think there are ways in which we can make this situation more Zen-like.

Should we cheer a great play or a winning point scored by our "team"? Of course! But do we need to cheer simply when the opponent screws up? Let's say I am at a marketing meeting and "Ace Punchline" is facing off with one of my junior staffers. A major client contract is on the line. Yes, I am rooting for my protégé. But if Ace's proposed campaign lacks luster, should I openly show satisfaction? I say nay. What did my co-worker do to earn that point? Absolutely nothing. Ace simply beat himself, nothing more. So for me to smile, smirk, and cheer would be to grind it in Ace's face. Karma goes around. I don't want my own protégé facing that sort of rude behavior, so I make my karmic peace by saving my cheers for the times when he or she impresses the hell out of the client.

The best approach in these situations? Cheer for great play, not for blood. When the cards are reversed—and eventually they will be—payback will stink. Why play into that? The Golden Rule applies everywhere. If your friends, family, and colleagues are of the bloodthirsty sort, you'd better be thick-skinned and ready to survive the same sort of treatment in retaliation when you have a less-than-stellar performance yourself.

One last thought on this: I have seen players in some sports who have a coterie of friends and family who are into this over-the-top, bloodlust behavior. The players themselves usually hate it. It embarrasses them and estranges them from other players. Players of a sport have the opportunity to form bonds based on their mutual love of an activity. If your fellow players ostracize you, you will miss out on a major part of the competitive experience. The loss of that camaraderie is a shame. When former tennis students of mine had these "crazed fan" families, I would suggest that they have a long talk with them at the appropriate time and let them know how much their behavior was hurting them rather than helping them. How can players do their best when the behavior of their own fans in the stands causes them to cringe? It breaks their Right Concentration, and that's not Right.

WINNING: When I give motivational speeches on "The Essence of Being a Winner" in business and in life, I always emphasize that a winner is a person who has winning traits, not just a person who wins competitions, makes lots of money, or is high up in the company. A winner shows respect for others, has control of his or her emotions, and generally does the right thing, setting an example for others. In short, a winner is someone whom others like to be around.

Winners attract friends and acquaintances. The people they know speak well of them. No, they are not perfect, but they look upon each day as a positive opportunity for *something good to happen*. When winners are in the worst situation imaginable, they think, "How can I make this better?" Winners never feel stuck because they find difficult situations to be a challenge—they are opportunities to build up their own confidence and do things that even they thought were not possible. Try the same approach yourself. Even if you have a troubling day or challenging situation to deal with, get in the habit of not focusing on the negative and letting the ordeal mean so much to you. Achieving this mindset takes practice, of course, but it is well worth it.

Whether an activity is mundane or extraordinary, winners also look for a way to get enjoyment from the situation. These people tend to be the ones who whistle while they work. Some of the most successful people in the world swear that they *don't* work. They love their jobs so much that they can't stand to be away from their work—even on vacation! What a contrast to the person who complains about his or her job and life continuously. You know the ones: "Oh, poor me" (do you hear the violin music in the background?). Studies have shown that people with these winning traits are not only more successful at work but also are the happiest in life.

Anyway, who wants to be around a sourpuss? Not me. I want to inspire and be inspired!

ANYTHING TO WIN: One of the more frightening things happening in sports today is the big steroids controversy. Not only is the use of steroids cheating—on a moral and ethical level—but it also has the potential to shorten careers by helping to cause certain injuries. There are even fears about a link to premature death. There is an incredibly long list of pro wrestlers—a sport where steroid use is rampant—who have died mysteriously at a very young age. This stuff is dangerous.

But here is the real danger: A message is being sent out to young athletes that in order to compete, they must do something that may significantly harm their health.

The steroids issue has less to do with cheating, which will always be with us in one form or another, and more to do with workplace safety. Think about it: You are in a labor union. What is the single most important item on your union's agenda? Workplace safety. Don't believe me? Ask a coal miner.

Pro athletes are unionized. Where is their union leadership? If players entering or wishing to enter the field believe they must do something that is not in the best interest of their long-term health (in this case, use steroids), where is the outcry from those who are supposed to make their workplace a safer one? You may think that I am building the case that pro athletes are being *forced* to take steroids. In a sense, that is not far from the truth. If most of the players who take certain drugs experience, say, a 25 percent increase in their performance, that increase does, in a way, force all others to follow suit.

The harsh symptoms that occur while taking steroids are bad enough, but the real difficulty comes when players stop taking the substances. Injuries and problems become overwhelming, and the coaches and higher-ups in the league who turned a blind eye when the steroids were being used—after all, they wanted their team to win—don't want to be involved. Where you were once revered for your home runs, you are now pitied for the price you have to pay mentally, physically, emotionally, and monetarily.

Now, if the drugs were as safe as Flintstone vitamins, we wouldn't be having this conversation. We could all buy them over-the-counter at the local drugstore. That is not the case. The people getting busted are breaking federal laws concerning misuse of controlled substances. This should tell us everything we need to know for now. Once the FDA changes its tune on that, so will I.

Winning is never worth shortening or risking your life. If you feel you need to win at something that badly, there is something else sorely missing from your life. You need to examine that problem before you do further harm to yourself.

THE UNDEFEATED: Some people have been blessed. They were born with many natural gifts, they were taught right from wrong, and they learned to work hard, play hard, and do right by others. For their efforts, they have received much and they have earned whatever they have received.

And then comes the crash.

Richard Nixon once said, "It is only when you have been to the lowest valley that you can appreciate the highest mountaintop." Losing is something we all experience, but some people just never learn to lose. The truth is, if you do everything right—if you are a wonderful, marvelous, giving, loving, hardworking person—you will win far more often than you lose. The irony, however, is that people who excel so much will literally crack when they finally suffer a massive public failure.

If you are used to winning and a debilitating loss comes your way, you must learn to disengage and take personal inventory. It is important to first address the practical nature of the loss. You've just been diagnosed with a terrible disease. Okay, first off, what should you do? What can be done about it? Is time of the essence? If so, it is even more important that you not wallow for too long. Needless to say, it is natural to feel down and crestfallen when tragedy strikes. But the response you need is to make optimal choices and improve your situation. You need to spring right into action as quickly as possible.

Another example: You lose control of your car on a dark, rain-slicked highway. You have a case of wine in the backseat, and now the bottles are smashed and alcohol is splashed over everything. You haven't had a drop to drink, but at first blush it appears that you've gotten sloshed and imperiled yourself and others. They put your picture on the front page of the local newspaper. Your neighbor suddenly stops carpooling with you, and your daughter is called names at school. What do you do?

Again, you must first ask yourself: What can be done to fix the problem? Only after you have taken clearheaded action can you allow yourself time for emotional healing. People who have never failed miserably don't always understand this.

Next, you must look around at all the good things you've got and embrace them. Remember our earlier point that for every negative, somewhere there is a positive. It is when you are down that you learn who your real friends are. And what should you do when those good and true friends come to your aid? Allow them to help you! Too often, "undefeated" people have no idea of how to accept help. They are so "together" that they've never really needed help before.

Dale Carnegie once said that if you want to make a friend, ask for a favor. That's right. *Ask* for a favor! Most of us think we have to give a favor, but the psychology is this: People love to feel needed. It makes them feel special. It gives them an opportunity to feel good about themselves by helping *you*. If you've always been the "undefeated" one, the one thing your friends have been lacking is the opportunity to come to *your* aid. After all, you've probably been coming to *their* aid for years and years.

Far wiser people than I have said, "True character is not in whether or not you fall, but in whether or not you get back up." No one's life is perfection, even though for a scant few it may appear that way at times. Perfection is meant to be an unachievable goal. If we were able to attain perfection, what reason would we have to get up the next morning?

On the other hand, don't be a leech! Who, me? Once again, you know who you are. These are the people who live life as helpless victims. They expect everyone to jump when they call and somehow believe you should feel privileged that they even asked for your assistance. If you don't help them or jump to their aid (and these are *very* needy people), they lay a guilt trip on you—you're a bad friend, a bad sister, a bad boyfriend, a bad parent.

Always respect people's time, and don't take advantage of their good nature. In return, they will be there for you when you need them—really need them—the most.

POOR LOSERS: The gracious acceptance of loss is the Zen Game way. When I watch a sporting event, I think the greatest thing in the world is when both of the participants or teams leave the field of play and you cannot tell who won and who lost.

In tennis, the greatest players of all time often were great sportspeople as well. They embodied the ethics of being a good sport. When you watched Monica Seles and Steffi Graf exit the court together (or Roger Federer and Rafael Nadal), you knew you were seeing two consummate professionals who admired and respected each other. Each brought out the best in the other. Their rivalry was as pure as sports itself.

This is what we should all strive for in life. When a co-worker is promoted and we are not, we should give him or her respect and sincere congratulations. Sure, no one should enjoy losing, but the idea is not to look at life through such a narrow spectrum. We all have our strengths and our weaknesses.

Even the most casual music and film lover knows John Williams, the composer of the themes for *Star Wars*, *Jaws*, the *Indiana Jones* movies, and so many other Hollywood blockbusters. He is the best of the best; he has probably written more memorable music for movies than anyone in history.

Now, have you ever heard of Van Cliburn? Cliburn is arguably America's most heralded classical pianist of all time. As a young man, Cliburn won some of the world's most prestigious international piano competitions. Do you know who often came in second? Another young classical pianist by the name of…John Williams! Williams figured out that as long as Cliburn was alive, he would never be No. 1. Cliburn was simply a better classical pianist than he. Thus, Williams left classical performance and drifted into film scoring. The rest is history. Both men flourished at what they did best.

Williams could have pulled a Tanya Harding and hired some guys to whack Van Cliburn on the knuckles, but instead he applauded Cliburn's immense talent and then set off to find his own place to shine. Williams therefore provides us with a perfect example of good sportsmanship—and one very practical way to be a graceful loser.

EXCUSES: As much as I hate to admit it, we are a culture obsessed with winning and losing. Don't you just hate that cliché of telejournalism in which one reporter goes into the victor's locker room, where the champagne is flowing and everyone is elated, and a moment later, as if you have been transported to a funeral parlor, a somber sportscaster is speaking to the loser?

The best way for a gracious loser to respond is to say, "I just didn't have it today. The better player won." That's classy. It's also usually true. Lift your opponent up for the occasion, and maybe karma will pay you back and you'll be treated the same way the next time that you win.

No one wants to hear, "This was a travesty today. If it wasn't for that terrible call in the third quarter, things would have turned out a lot differently." That's weak and pathetic. It demeans you and it demeans your teammates and the other team. Yes, bad calls get made in every aspect of life, but they usually cut both ways over an infinite amount of time. Get over it. If you feel you were wronged, keep it to yourself. Make it a part of the healing process and silently get past it. But don't open your mouth and make a fool of yourself with excuses.

Remember, people win and lose to one another when they play the same game (and I use the word *game* euphemistically). That means you will certainly have to co-exist with one another over time. If you're the sous-chef and a rival is chosen to be executive chef, the two of you will still have to work together in the same kitchen. If you make excuses for not getting the top job, be aware that all of those excuses will be carried back to your new boss, and the kitchen will be a lousy place for both of you to work. Your boss will feel disrespected and you will feel bitter. How can that be good for the quality of the work?

When all is said and done, the only real explanation for losing is that someone did better or was perceived to have done better at some activity on a particular day. It's nothing more and nothing less than that. If you are asked about it, admit it out loud, act with dignity, and move forward with your life. It's the Zen Game way.

OBJECTIVE VERSUS SUBJECTIVE: Here's more food for thought on winning, losing, and being judged: You turn on the Olympics and see the graceful figure skaters. The judges post their scores and you, as a layperson, cannot understand why certain people score higher than others. Sure, sometimes you agree with the scoring, but you also see how much of it is based on personal opinion. It's subjective.

Next, you watch the speed skaters. The gun goes off and a few seconds later someone crosses the finish line ahead of the others. There's a high-speed camera to overrule any disputes and identify a clear-cut winner. This is *objective* judging. There is no space for second-guessing.

In life, we are judged subjectively more often than objectively. Two men ask the same pretty girl to dance. Whom will she pick? It's her choice and hers alone. Whatever fits her fancy. The same goes for job interviews, promotions, and so many other activities and areas of life. Painfully little that we do is judged with pure objectivity.

This reality is both good and bad in life. Imagine that both suitors of the pretty girl had to take some sort of written exam for her to decide which one she wanted to dance with that night. That would be preposterous! So subjectivity is more often the rule.

What does this mean for us? It means that some pretty girls will choose us to dance with, while others will pick the fellow with the neat tattoos, rocker hairstyle, and cool pose. We'll win some of the time and lose other times. In the dancing example, we must console ourselves with the knowledge that we were judged by only one person, and her determinants may have included looks, personality, sense of humor, or, heck, even the color of our socks or our failure to wear socks! Frankly, it doesn't matter, because it is *all subjective*. If the same two men were to ask another girl to dance, the result might be completely different. Many women have told me that initially they didn't like their man, then one day something changed. Life is often a matter of timing, and the subjective nature of things can be seen as a positive. Remember this, and deal with winning and losing accordingly.

MONEY ÜBER ALLES: Professional sports have become a barometer in our culture of the state of society. So let's take a look at what we can learn about society from what we're seeing these days in the world of professional sports and fandom.

I, like most fans, have a bone or two to pick with some professional athletes, starting with the mercenary attitude that seems to be on the rise. Yes, I know, the teams trade you like baseball cards. But still, is going to the highest bidder always the be-all and end-all of life? I equate this type of employment decision with the choices we all must make in the real world. Granted, we in the stands deal more in terms of thousands of dollars than in millions, but most of us—at least those I most respect—base their place-of-employment decisions upon, yes, salary, but also on issues such as loyalty, work environment, collegiality with co-workers, and a location that is preferable to the entire family, not just the employee.

When I see a player choose to stay with his team out of loyalty, despite being offered a bit more from another team, I respect that. When I hear of a player choosing a team based on where his family would prefer to live, I respect that as well.

LOVE OF MONEY: The fact is, money has become the gauge that many people—athletes and nonathletes alike—use to keep score of how they are doing in their lives. Hey, I don't know about you, but I look at the person, not at his or her tax return!

Too many people equate dollars earned with respect. But what do a few more dollars mean if you are not able to rise above the pettiness and focus on the real job?

In sports, premier athletes make more money than they will ever *rationally* (key word) be able to spend in a lifetime. If they feel "insulted" because some other player outearns them at any given moment, they should use that as a motivator the next time they step out onto the playing field, rather than as an excuse not to give their all because they feel "disrespected." This, too, is a lesson to impressionable fans. If you feel you are underappreciated at work, work that much harder to further prove your case to your boss. That is Right Livelihood.

DON'T PLAY; POSE: Here's another one of Nancy Pristine's pie-in-the-sky ideas: We should limit the endorsements that athletes can earn.

There are a handful of athletes who are so famous and so photogenic that they make far, far more money in endorsements than they do by playing the sport.

There are a number of other athletes, mostly in individual sports such as tennis, golf, and NASCAR, who can be satisfied with "just good enough" because their looks or personality are such that they can significantly augment their playing salaries with endorsement deals.

In my opinion, this is bad for sports. It creates a disincentive for athletes to "be the best" because all they have to do is be "just good enough" and then hope that someone thinks they are "hot" or "interesting."

I think companies should chase the No. 1 athlete for endorsements, or else go after players after they've retired. Hey, it's worked in some cases. Look at Mike Ditka and Bob Uecker. Or how about George Foreman—that guy is ubiquitous! All of them are retired, but they still get some pretty big endorsement money.

All I know is that it would be beneficial for everyone, fans and athletes alike, to live up to their true potential. They should not fall short of this goal simply because they received a ton of money for being "good" versus "great." They are cheating themselves, along with the fans, and they will never know how truly good they could have been until it's too late. They will have missed out on their chance at Right Livelihood.

ZEN GAME ON THE FIELD: In football, two opponents hit each other hard and one goes down. When the play ends, one extends his hand to the other to help him up. When pro wrestling mogul Vince McMahon Jr. started the XFL, he declared that such acts of sportsmanship would be cause for a penalty. I'm thinking about putting Mr. McMahon in the Sports Hall of Shame.

I am asked about this scenario a lot. Should players be "nice" on the field by helping each other up and the like? I say yes.

Granted, football is a violent sport. But if you cannot control your violence so that it exists during the play and ends after, then you have an issue with Right Concentration. After a play ends, there is nothing wrong and everything right with practicing good sportsmanship. Some of the most famous hard-hitting players did this too. Running back Jim Brown would get kicked and even bitten when in a pile of players after the whistle had sounded to end a play. His response would be to look his opponent in the eye and say, "Now Sam, you're a better man than that." Imagine the effect this response had on the opposition. You can bet it was a lot more effective than punching him in the nose and then having everyone get into the fight and be penalized for it.

The late Hall of Fame defensive tackle Reggie White, an ordained minister, would proselytize from those same human piles, saying to players who had blocked him well on the previous play, "Jesus has certainly blessed you today."

Jim Brown and Reggie White are two of the greatest football players to have ever lived. If Zen Game worked for them, why shouldn't you give it a try?

RUNNING UP THE SCORE: It happens in a lot of sports. A person or team is so far superior to the opponent that they start to make a joke of things, creating a margin of victory that is utterly preposterous and downright embarrassing to the other team.

Sometimes it is impossible to avoid. If I were to play tennis against Rafael Nadal, he would literally have to play without the use of one leg and one arm not to beat me 6-0, 6-0. But here is the subtlety of the situation: If in the last game, Nadal was still firing aces down my throat and at my face, that behavior would be unsportsmanlike.

Now let me give you another thought on this subject. If I am beating my opponent easily, why not turn this easy match into something that will be beneficial for my opponent, myself, and the fans? How, you ask? By changing my strategy. Let me explain. A few years ago I attended a football game at Lehigh University. Everyone knows Lehigh is an exceptional college. I know that because my brilliant husband went to school there. My husband and I were enjoying a football game on a beautiful, sunny day. Unfortunately, it wasn't a good day for the Lehigh football players, and halfway through the game, the other team, Holy Cross, respectfully stopped trying because they did not want to embarrass the Lehigh team. They stopped throwing and moving the ball.

Was the Holy Cross decision the best option? Back in the days when I was a tennis pro, I would teach my students to make the most of every situation. If they were winning a match easily, that would be a perfect time to use this competitive situation to their advantage and try another strategy. For example, if they were winning a match pounding the ball from the baseline, why not change their strategy and practice their serve and volley? With this strategy, they wouldn't exactly even out the match, but they would do something constructive for their own game. And they would make it more competitive for themselves, the opponent, and the spectators.

Bill Tilden, arguably one of the greatest tennis players ever, used this tactic with his opponents. He was so good that he often played to his opponents' strengths to make the match more challenging for him. He particularly liked getting behind in the match so that he really had to work hard in the end to beat his opponent and bring the crowd in the stands to their feet. For Bill Tilden, it was not all about winning for him; it was about giving his all even if he was outclassing his opponent. It was all about his love for the game, and he spread this love for the game to everyone who watched him play.

Back to the Lehigh game. While I applaud the Holy Cross football team for their sportsmanship that day, I do think that if they had brought in their third-string players and worked on some new plays, it could have been a more interesting game for everyone.

GRACE: Baseball Hall of Famer Mike Schmidt of the Philadelphia Phillies got off to a poor start during the 1989 baseball season. Despite this, he continued to start for his team and was so popular with the fans that he led in balloting for the All-Star team. However, Schmidt found his own performance so personally embarrassing that, nearing his fortieth birthday, he abruptly retired in a tearful, appreciative press conference. When the All-Star ballots were finally tabulated, Schmidt was still in first place for National League third basemen, and many people thought that he might make a ceremonial final appearance. But Schmidt thought this idea was unfair. He sincerely felt that he had not earned the honor but had won it only because of the popularity he'd gained from stellar performances in previous years. Rather than take a final bow he felt he did not deserve, he requested that Major League Baseball pick a more deserving player.

This, my friends, is the definition of grace. The world of sports provides us with many positive examples of how we should live our lives, and this is one of them. Exiting the stage is never easy for any of us, whether it involves retiring from work or backing off from "over parenting" children who have reached the age that they no longer require such attention. Grace in this case was Mike Schmidt's approach to Right Livelihood. He rightly was too proud to accept pity and nostalgia when an honor was designated for current performance only.

IT'S ONLY A GAME: Penn State football player John Cappelletti won the Heisman Trophy in 1973. Cappelletti's acceptance speech, in which he dedicated his award to his dying brother Joey, is one of the most memorable in the history of college sports. Cappelletti supported his young brother through his battle against cancer. "If I can dedicate this trophy to him tonight and give him a couple of days of happiness, that is worth everything," he said. In those few moments, which brought everyone in attendance, including Vice President Gerald Ford, to tears, John would totally redefine the meaning of the words *courage* and *inspiration* by looking to someone he knew very well—his eleven-year-old brother. "They say I've shown courage on the football field, but for me it's only on the field and only in the fall. Joey lives with pain all the time. His courage is round the clock. I want him to have this trophy. It's more his than mine because he has been such an inspiration to me." Joey died of childhood leukemia less than three years later.

I do believe we sometimes become so sports-obsessed and self-obsessed that we miss the heroism of the everyday. It is obvious but necessary to mention that we must always acknowledge the people who put their lives on the line for our safety and freedom: the firefighters, the police, and the men and women around the world who fight for our freedom.

It is of Right View when someone like John Cappelletti sees this need and brings it to our attention, much as Arthur Ashe did when he heroically battled AIDS not merely by trying to extend his own life but by becoming the "ambassador" of the disease. He was unafraid to speak about AIDS and to lobby for the acceptance of its victims and the furthering of research to combat it. He did not speak of AIDS purely in the context of himself but rather by universalizing it. In doing so, Arthur Ashe showed that heroism is not simply about what happens on the field. Those events are inconsequential when compared with what we are called upon to do off the field.

SUPERFANS: There's a cute movie called *Fever Pitch* in which Jimmy Fallon plays a Boston Red Sox "superfan." His entire life is Red Sox, Red Sox, Red Sox, and because of this obsession, he is incapable of sustaining a loving relationship with a person. The movie is a comedy, but it would be even funnier if it were not so disturbingly true to life.

People, you are not your favorite team. You are a person. If your team loses, you did not lose; they did. If they win, you are not No. 1; they are. You should not subjugate your entire being and your personality to your team. If you have to love something sports-related, love the sport itself, not just one team or player in it. Learn to appreciate the beauty that is sports. The best sports fans can cheer the other team (heaven forbid) if they make a great play. This is not just sportsmanlike Zen Game; it is good mental health. So take back your soul and your individual personality—you know, the one you gave to the Green Bay Packers. Go into sports fan detox if need be. Again, this is about Right Livelihood. Being a fan of a sports team should not be anyone's defining characteristic. Be all that you can be—which means you must stop being just a fan of someone else's efforts.

NATIONALISM: Hey, the Olympics are great. And yes, we all cheer for our country. But can't we also respect the performances of athletes from other countries?

Right now, professional sports in America are inundated with athletes from around the globe who have blessed us—yes, blessed us—by coming here to compete. And yet I find that some American fans don't appreciate it. Maria Sharapova. Yao Ming. Ichiro Suzuki. Tony Parker. Those are only a few of the athletes who have more or less taken up residence in America or are playing on American professional teams. In addition to that, there are many players in individual sports such as tennis and golf who may not have chosen to live here but do compete in all the major tournaments (such as Roger Federer and Rafael Nadal). They are splendid to watch.

I dislike it when sports fans or journalists make snarky comments that "there aren't enough great *American* players anymore." So what? There are still great *players*, period. And great sports are still being played. So get off your jingoistic bandwagon and come down and watch some great competition! That's my idea of a real fan.

HAPPY WARRIORS: I was watching a fabulous match between Nadal and Federer—well, *every* match between them is fabulous—when Nadal double-faulted in the tiebreaker for match point. This is major. This is the sort of thing that makes people bug out their eyes and gasp for air.

Nadal smiled impishly, almost laughing at himself.

That is a Happy Warrior. I believe this is the state of mind every one of us should achieve in life. It is the essence of Zen Game. Once you eliminate the obsessive focus on winning and losing, you can only win. Choose your occupation not only because you are good at it, but also because you love it. Don't be dissuaded from that feeling because you are not "winning" at it.

I never played in Wimbledon, I never won Wimbledon, and I never will. It doesn't matter; I still love to play tennis. Should I have quit the moment it dawned on me that Wimbledon wasn't in the cards? Quit and done what instead—something I liked to do less? Perhaps I could have worked hard and become the world's greatest chef, but could I really have taken the leap from fish sticks to beef bourguignonne? It sounds like a lot of hard work to me, so whatever I do, I do it for the love of it. You should too.

9
ROLE MODELS AND SUPERKIDS

Role models are found everywhere in life. The first ones we encounter usually are our parents or other family members. The power of their influence should never be underestimated. It can stay with us throughout the course of our existence, prodding us on and helping us to progress, or, on the flip side, slowly destroying us inside.

Then there are other role models—the celebrities—who have been granted a golden opportunity. Any celebrity who does not believe he or she is a role model, or can be viewed as such, is living in an imaginary world. The stars who shine on TV, the stage, and the playing field are viewed by others as awe inspiring. People look up to these performers and athletes as they would to a mentor or a parent. The stars' behavior is noted by many—particularly the malleable youth—as an example of actions to admire or follow.

As a result, entertainers and athletes who enjoy fame have a tremendous responsibility to their young fans. Their actions can affect the mindset of an entire generation of believers, who literally can be "programmed" by the myriad mixed (and perhaps not so positive) messages they receive from these sometimes unlikely or undeserving role models. A celebrity's way of speaking, behaving, or dressing is emulated because it is considered "cool."

In some cases, however, these stars are barely out of the schoolroom themselves and are struggling to find themselves and their place in this world. As young and inexperienced as they are, how can they be an example for others? They have to grow up, and they have to do it fast. It is a great burden indeed. But when they are able to recognize this responsibility and act on it with integrity, the principles of Right Action and Right Intention can help them to serve as good role models.

These same principles of the Zen Game should be applied by all adults—parents, teachers, coaches, and others—who are role models and mentors for children.

GRACIOUSNESS: Despite the prominence of celebrities, parents are still their children's primary role models. And yet, on many occasions, I have seen sourpuss parents at sports competitions literally booing and trash talking their child's opponent.

Plain and simple, that's not the Zen Game way. How disappointing when parents do it even once.

So here's a fundamental rule: You teach children graciousness by *being gracious*. Applaud the performance of another parent's child, and recognize the opportunity for social fraternity provided by your children's activities. These functions can be a good chance to meet other cool parents and expand your own circle of friends. This is great! Don't be the Parent from Hell who sits in the stands filled with bloodlust.

Parents who behave this way will not make friends themselves and will prevent their own child from making any as well. Do you think that after these parents have made fools of themselves at a children's hockey game the other parents will encourage their kids to hang around the devil's unfortunate spawn? No way!

Become known as the parent with graciousness, class, and Zen Game. Both you and your child will benefit as a result.

"I AM NOT A ROLE MODEL": This is the famous quote from "Sir" Charles Barkley, basketball player extraordinaire. It was actually a longer statement, which I'll paraphrase as something on the order of, "If I am your child's biggest influence, you're in trouble."

I agree with the second part of that statement. If your child looks up to some pro athlete more than anyone else, such as a parent, there is definitely something wrong. But that aside, Charles, you really don't have any choice in the role model issue.

Kids have always put athletes on a pedestal. They begin playing sports at a relatively early age, and so they do, in fact, want to emulate the best of the best. This includes a bit of personal idolatry, which occurs at a very impressionable age when they are trying not only to swing the bat like A-Rod but do everything else like him too. I've actually known kids who turned away from a sport because their hero did something unseemly that made the news. Or, on a smaller scale, the kids went to a game and tried to get an autograph, but Mr. Big Star brushed by them as if they weren't alive. Likewise, even adults can become disillusioned when one of our "adult" heroes turns out to be quite human, causing some of us to question our line of work or our political or religious affiliations.

The truth is, while athletes should not be surrogate parents to the children of strangers, they should still bear in mind that kids look up to them. (Hey, once those kids are older, they will move on and begin looking up to captains of industry, scientists, or great financial minds.) Athletes must acknowledge that they are an influence on our youth, whether they like it or not. Their best reaction to this reality would be to tread Zen's Eightfold Path. Be their best not only at their game, but also as a person who is being watched by impressionable young people. It's a burden that comes with the territory.

OTHER ROLE MODELS: So here you are, practicing your Zen Game, being a good world citizen and, in the situation I wish to discuss, a good parent as well. But then you send your child off to baseball lessons with…the baseball coach from hell! He spits after every other word, he curses, he screams, he throws vile insults. Now what happens to all that good work you put into your child?

Part of protecting children—and as a parent, that is your main job, particularly when they are underage—is to keep them away from bad influences. Therefore, you cannot judge a child's coaches and teachers based on their talent alone. Watch these mentors and teachers when you can, and listen to your child if he or she comes back to you telling tales. I would rather my child go with a mediocre instructor than with a fabulous one who turns her into a prima donna whose attitude is, "I will do what I want, when I want, where I want, at anyone's expense." The chances of your child becoming a pro athlete are slim. I hate to say it, but I know it to be true.

The same philosophy applies to schoolteachers. I would be more upset if my child's calculus teacher was rude and out of control than if he or she was merely mediocre in the field. What are the chances that my child is aiming to become a mathematician? And even if that were the goal, self-study and other options can mitigate the effects of a less-than-stellar academician. But on the other hand, how easy is it to undo validated bad behavior?

SCANDAL: Scandal has been very good for some celebrities, and I sometimes feel they purposefully court it. What's the phrase, "There's no such thing as bad publicity"? Everyone wants to talk about the latest episodes of Paris Hilton, Britney Spears, and Lindsey Lohan that are displayed in the tabloids. I say give them their privacy, but people are always interested in dirt. Unfortunately, good news never sells papers or magazines.

We have a different perspective on sports. We look to it for purity, not salaciousness and scandal. Sports, for better or worse, are held to a higher standard.

Wayne Gretzky was called The Great One, and he remains unarguably the finest ice hockey player to ever put on skates. Gretzky so valued his image that he would do almost anything to avoid even the possibility of scandal. It is said that if he was in an elevator alone and a single woman got on as well, he would step off and take another elevator. Why? He was afraid that within the confines of the elevator, with no other witnesses, the woman might think, "Wow, I could step off of here, claim he put his hands on me, and get a big payout since he's such a big star and has so much money."

These things happen. Basketball's Derrick Coleman once sued a woman who had falsely accused him of rape. This was one of the first cases of athletes fighting back against the scandalmongers.

It is a shame, but athletes and celebrities have to be careful and understand that they are targets. They are always in the public eye, much like politicians, and therefore must accept certain realities. These are the ground rules and traditions of their occupation. If they choose to enter it, they have to deal with it.

CONTROVERSY OVER SUBSTANCE: Who are the most widely read columnists in the media? The controversial ones. The most read bloggers? The same. Controversy, like sex, sells.

Anytime I have appeared on radio shows, I have been encouraged and goaded to "be more controversial." I hate that. What most readers don't know is that once I begin to promote this book, talent bookers will be thumbing through it not for news they can use, but rather for anything controversial. Did I dis someone famous? Did I dish some dirt? If not, they will still look for such openings. If they find any passages about impropriety, for example, I will be put on the spot to give my opinion about so-and-so, the wrongdoer who is in all the tabloids this week or month. Is that what I want to talk about here? No. This practice takes me out of *my* Zen Game. It makes me a hypocrite, doing the opposite of so many things that I write about in my books. But do the interviewers understand this? Unfortunately, no. They feel it's their job to focus on the controversy.

Here's the rub to that: Perhaps I could sell more copies of this book if I were to trash more people by name, giving out juicy gossip on famous people I know or giving my uncensored opinions of the infamous simply to drop names and make negative comments. But I won't do it. Yes, there are names of famous athletes and people in this book, but not for the sake of controversy or titillation. These people are mentioned merely to find common ground on which I can make a point and you can understand where I am coming from. I mean no harm to anyone.

Our culture's obsession with controversy can only survive if the monster is fed. If consumers turn it off and read or listen to something else, sponsors and advertisers may begin to get the picture, and things might change for the better. Just as we conduct ourselves in a Zen-like manner, we can spread that gospel by basing our decisions about consumption on the same high level of civility.

BABIES WITH RAZOR BLADES: Another troubling aspect of money in sports today is that athletes peak at such a young age. Just think of what you were like when you were in your early twenties. Less mature than you are today? Capable of poor decision-making? Now imagine that you'd had tens of millions of dollars at your disposal. Most of us would go utterly crazy, which is exactly what happens with a lot of pro athletes.

I once heard it suggested that maybe athletes should have to put some of their money into a trust so that they don't blow it all before their twenty-fifth birthday. It's all become too much, as exemplified in the MTV shows *Pimp My Ride*, *My Super Sweet Sixteen*, and *MTV Cribs*. These kinds of shows glorify the idea of being young and rich without a care in the world, but look at how the people profiled on the shows spend their money: on ridiculousness. It is their intention to be as wild, crazy, and over-the-top as possible.

These programs seem to be seeking justification of the "money is everything" attitude. The athletes and celebrities presented have very short careers and receive very high wages during a relatively brief period of their lives. If any of them were to receive really sound advice, it would be to capitalize on obtaining so much wealth so early in their lives and save it. True wealth is attained by saving *early*. If these young celebrities put more money in the bank than into a fleet of custom cars before the age of twenty-one, they'd never have to worry about money another day in their lives.

Parents, don't let your kids get taken by these TV shows and this message of excess. Give your children good financial grounding to go with their human grounding. If they come into money early in life, let them know what a blessing that is. A few thousand invested conservatively in your teens and twenties can grow into millions by retirement time. That's Right Mindfulness. That's just common sense!

THE GOLDEN CHILD: And speaking of giving razor blades to babies (bad idea), what about the way we place young celebrities and prodigies on a pedestal at such an early age? There are many things truly unhealthy about this practice, and I've seen them with my own two eyes.

These "special" people often are treated as such beginning at a very, very early age. Managers and parents see dollar signs. Even teachers and school principals envision being thanked from the podium when the kid wins the U.S. Open, an Oscar, a Grammy, or an international academic award. How can adults who are in such a state be expected to treat the child as they should and as they would any other child?

Youthful stars often don't have to go to class, do their homework, do chores, or do whatever else is typically asked of other kids their age. In return, they are given the opportunity to excel at something that we mere mortals view with awe.

For a while.

The fatal flaw in this scenario is that these stars, unlike most other people, make their mark almost exclusively with their bodies or their particular gift. And their bodies (or natural gifts) are tested to the limit every single day. If a surgeon tears up his knee, he goes to a surgeon (ironically) and gets it patched up. While that knee may never be 100 percent again, the injury has no effect whatsoever on his ability to perform surgery. But if you're an athlete and rip up an ACL, it's all over. Slipping and falling can have major consequences for a dancer. This moment can happen at age ten, age eighteen, age twenty-five, or whenever. It can happen before a career really takes off and any money is made, or it can happen just as the prodigy is on the precipice of making serious money, the kind of money that could put her on Easy Street for life.

So where are you then? What you have on your hands is a pampered child with one skill, and that one skill is no longer viable.

My advice? If I were in such a situation, I would take as much care in making sure my "little superstar" is emotionally and intellectually grounded as I would apply to her athletic or artistic talent. I would strive to make sure she is ready to handle both the success and the failure that comes from a highly competitive world. I would get her to understand humility and to appreciate what God has given her.

As a parent, I would preach education. If I thought her teachers and school administrators were allowing her to cruise, I would sit them down and explain that they are not doing anyone any favors. Again, remember the extreme chance of a career-ending injury. I would want my child to still have a bright future if that occurred, one that didn't necessarily rely on one particular talent alone.

Even aside from the issue of a career-ending injury or poor money management, there is the issue of Jerkdom. If you cater to and pamper children simply because they have a special talent, you are sending the message that because of this gift, they can live by another set of rules. This is wrong. This is why we have our fair share of tantrums in all professions. Some people call them divas; I call them talented people with a sense of entitlement. No one has ever said "no" to them. Everyone has coddled them throughout their lives.

Treat a budding star the way you would anyone else. They need proper grounding, a good human foundation, and inner values as much or more than any other person. If you want to do them a favor, put them on the Noble Eightfold Path and have them apply it to every aspect of their being.

THE SUPERKID SYNDROME: You can check me here if I'm wrong, but I believe that MIT still has the highest suicide rate of any American college. At Harvard, 80 percent of students reported that they have faced mental health problems while enrolled at the school, according to a 2004 article in the *Harvard Crimson*.

In sports, a young man was on all the news programs a number of years ago being hailed as the "bionic quarterback." From the moment he was born, his father geared and controlled every single thing in his life toward making him a football star. Every meal was monitored. He watched no TV. He did no activities that were not moving his father toward his *own* goal of making him a football star.

He was the nation's most highly recruited high school football player. Shortly after he arrived at college, awash for the first time in freedom, he was busted for drugs. He had a college football career that was good but did not live up to expectations, and was then drafted into the NFL, where he was a complete bust. Today, he leaves behind a trail of drug arrests, child-support warrants, and even a sexual assault charge. His father? He remarried a younger woman, they had a baby, and he's back at it again, trying for another NFL star by running his new kid through the same domineering program. That son has also just been arrested. Some people never learn.

It's called the Superkid Syndrome, and no, kids do not choose to be a part of it. The syndrome occurs when parents live out their dreams through their child. As you can see from the above examples, it can be dangerous and even fatal, although more often it simply makes the kid miserable.

Most of the kids I have taught in tennis wanted to be there. Some did not. They were simply pushed into the sport by their parents. This is sad. It's no fun for the kid and it was no fun for me. Look, kids should keep busy and do constructive things, but there are tons and tons of options out there. If children are cut out for MIT or Harvard and going to either school is their own personal dream, that's great. But if they're not, they may have another muse to follow, one not so narrowly focused on academia. They may be artistic or musical, they may be great at working with their hands, or they may be phenomenal in sales. It's all good as long as your child grows up to be a happy and productive member of society. Let me repeat the two most important words again: *happy* and *productive*. Notice that I did not say "star," or "genius," or "award winner," or any other such nonsense. I said "happy" and "productive."

Some children will drive themselves hard because they have a passion for a particular activity or field of study. In that case, by all means facilitate their dream. But let them have friends, let them play, let them be kids! If they become a Superkid, let it be their own choice, not yours.

LOVE, HATE, AND COACHING: A great coach inspires. A bad coach poisons the soul.

Sometimes as a parent, it is difficult to separate a child's attitude toward an activity from his or her attitude toward the leader of that activity. If you have a lousy biology teacher—a nasty person who fills the classroom with negativity—it can potentially turn a gifted future doctor toward a career in pastry making.

So is it the teacher or is it the subject? Again, it all comes back to observation and careful listening. If your child doesn't like biology and has no interest in it, a great teacher might, at best, make it tolerable for him or her. This is good. But if your child always liked a subject or an activity in the past but recently has turned away from it, as a caring, concerned parent, you need to find out why.

If the cause of the problem is a bad coach or teacher, face the situation and address it accordingly. Sometimes you are in a position to make changes. With a private teacher or coach, it may be time to bail on them and move on to someone who gets a more positive reaction from your child. If it is a teacher in school, the situation may be a little trickier. Still, children sometimes can be switched out of one class and into another. At the very least, parents should bolster their psyche at home, supporting them as they suffer through the experience and helping them find ways to augment what they are not learning in class. Remember, we have all had a few "duds" as teachers or coaches. Life is like that. The Mary Poppins type of mentor is a rather rare specimen, while every village (or school) has an instructor with a chip on his or her shoulder. In most cases, we survive and persevere, particularly with good parental support.

A PERSON OF INFLUENCE: No one influences a person more than his or her parents. Following shortly behind parents are teachers. Stepping right behind teachers in that line are coaches. Finally, there are the general mentors—those who enter people's lives at various points and have the ability to teach them, bolster them, and make their mark on them.

Think of the movie *Rudy,* everyone's inspirational favorite. Rudy himself was an underdog success story, but look at all the characters he came in contact with who believed in him, encouraged him, and gave him a hand up. Each one of us has the opportunity in life to be that sort of person for someone. It isn't even necessary that we become parents or teachers in the traditional sense. We can take new employees under our wing and let them know we see their potential, even though their inexperience is causing them to make a lot of rookie mistakes. We can set aside some time and give good advice to younger people who seek us out because they aspire to enter our field of endeavor. There are millions of ways in which we can be of Right Livelihood and be a positive influence on some "Rudy" out there.

10
BREAKING OLD MOLDS

Perhaps the biggest challenge introduced in this book is the need to make changes in our lives. Change is not easy. We follow routines and get comfortable in our motions, day in and day out. People come to expect certain behaviors and words from us, and that is just what we give them. But are we living life like zombies, half asleep, or are we open to change and being the best we can be? How about breaking the mold for a change? How about doing something different, something that is not expected of us at all? It doesn't take much really—only the readiness to do it.

The best place to start is by monitoring yourself. We all need to stop every once in a while and think about our recent actions and behaviors. A little time-out will allow us to see whether or not we've been acting with change in mind or instead acting mindlessly. It's up to each person to set a schedule for these evaluations: weekly, monthly, yearly.

Life does not boil down to good or bad, winning or losing, you have it or you don't. It is about changing flavors and tasting all the options that good, responsible living has to offer. For us to discover the Right way, we need to change paths many times as we progress in age and (we hope) wisdom throughout the years. There is not one clear-cut way to be a part of this world; there are several Right options that we have the duty to explore. Pilots change their flight plan many times before they reach their destination, and so will we.

When we embrace the Zen Game, we learn to change, learn how to deal with change, and even come to appreciate and enjoy change as we find ourselves growing in wonderful ways. Here are some positive changes that include all of the Buddha's guides to better living:

LET'S GET LOST: Do you want to break out of your same-old, same-old doldrums? Need help with finding your Right Concentration once more? Then try this: Hop in your car…and get lost. That's right. Pick a day when you have no work to do and nowhere to go and simply try to get lost. Don't worry, in this big, developed land of ours, you won't really find yourself in a place where you can't retrace your way home (and no cheating by using your GPS).

Act like a carefree nomad once in a while. Free your mind, allow it to wander, maybe take along a friend or a significant other and see what happens. You'd be surprised by how many wonderful places you can find that you never would have known about on your scripted travels. And since you won't be looking for specific turnoffs and such, if you find yourself curious about a particular unknown road, you can just go with it. You've got nothing to lose. You never know what exciting adventure lies ahead unless you are ready to go out on a limb.

GOOD SAMARITANS: Unless we are professional first responders, we don't choose emergencies; emergencies choose us. We don't go looking for trouble, but trouble finds its way to all of us at one time or another. When it does, we may see another person in need. How should we respond on those occasions? Perhaps this is an area of your life that calls for change.

First off, think of what you should *not* do. The most common mistake is to do nothing at all—to just drive away and expect someone else to call 911 or stop to give aid and comfort. The second most common problem is simply stopping and staring like a gaping ghoul, causing stress to others and impeding professional assistance. This is called "rubbernecking," and it is offensive on many levels. Once police, fire, or ambulance service has arrived on the scene, do your part for society and keep moving. Don't slow down and stare. If you were the victim, how would you like it if everyone stopped and stared at you?

Be a Good Samaritan. Don't ever be in such a hurry in life that you don't have time to help a fellow human being in need. Someday the person in need could be you.

FOUND MONEY: You see a dollar bill on the ground. What do you do? When I was a kid, I used to see such things and say, "Wow! This is my lucky day!" That money would go into my pocket and a big smile would spread across my face.

I'm older now (not *that* old, but older), so I know that the money on the sidewalk once belonged—and *still* belongs—to someone else. Today, my first reaction is to look around and see who is likely to have dropped it. The same goes for being undercharged for something I've bought. When I get a check in a restaurant, I look it over. If I've been overcharged, I mention it. But does everyone mention it to the waiter if they've been *under*charged? They should. Some hardworking, honest person made a mistake and is now going to lose money because I was less than honest. When we find errors that benefit us, but do nothing to correct the situation right away, it is even worse than if we stand by idly when we see other people break rules.

ANGER MANAGEMENT: Ever see a "person" hitting their child, pet, or spouse in public? I can think of few other things that are more apt to elicit a negative response, and rightly so.

But let's take a good look at this situation. We find ourselves focusing on the "in public" part. Does this mean it's okay to hit people or pets in private? No!

A person who does this, either publicly or privately, needs something, and it's not what you're thinking. You're imagining that they need a sock in the jaw, but what they really need is help. They have a problem: Violence. Rage.

To state the obvious, an inability to control violence and rage is a major, major problem. Responding in kind is not the answer. It is important to try to quell the situation as it stands before us, but just as importantly, we must do whatever we can to suggest or see to it that the person gets psychiatric, therapeutic medical attention. If an intervention does not occur as soon as possible, they will eventually do serious harm to someone.

Ask yourself, what sort of society do I want to live in? Do I want to be surrounded by people who hit each other, or maybe even me? Obviously not.

Don't turn a blind eye to violence. Take care of it, but also understand the need for follow-up intervention. Merely making it stop for the time being isn't even a decent Band-Aid. The problem still exists and needs to be addressed. Be of Right Mindfulness and try to see that it gets done. There are many organizations that help abused victims. When intervening in these situations, seek the help of the police or a professional in addressing the problem at hand.

COMPETITIVENESS: Although my competitive playing days are mostly a thing of the past, even today I often step onto a tennis court with a desire to win. It's not for money, a trophy, or a ranking. I just want to push my craft to the limit so that I can gauge my own talent and prowess. I am competing against myself more than anything else.

Now I am driving home and I am on a four-lane road (two lanes each way). I am in the slow lane. The car in front of me is going slowly and I want to pass him. There is a car behind me. I signal to pass the car ahead of me, but no sooner have I done so than the car behind me does the same and then rushes into the passing lane before I do. Okay, I can deal with this. He is in a big hurry so he wants to get ahead of both me and the car in front of me. That's okay.

But then he sits in that passing lane, matching my speed. Why does he do this? Or else he finally passes me, but then crosses back into my lane and goes right in front of me while decelerating. I go to pass him, but then he speeds up.

This is usually the guy who feels that everything in life is a competition. Every car on the highway must be passed. Every story he hears must be topped. If someone else gets or earns something, he must too. I have seen people drive themselves into bankruptcy simply because they not only had to "keep up with the Joneses" but *exceed* them.

This is terribly self-defeating behavior. No one can win at everything all the time. Furthermore, why would anyone want to? Yes, in our society, people are driven to succeed. This ambition is fine, but only if we approach success in a Zen Game fashion. Constant competitiveness shows a lack of self-confidence. If people were truly secure within themselves, they would not have to pass every car, own the biggest boat (even if they don't like boating), get the highest score at mini-golf, and so on. None of these things are life-and-death. Granted, we should strive to do and be our best at the things we consider most important to us. If I am a video game designer, I want to be the best there is. I want to create a game that will sell millions of copies and make a lot of people happy. But if my next-door neighbor beats me at beach volleyball, I don't have to morph into the Joker marching on a path of vengeance.

That Middle Path between winning and losing is the key to so much happiness in life. We all must face problems, real problems, as we travel this road—sickness, death, and financial or personal catastrophes. Those things inevitably will cause us many sleepless nights. But losing sleep because you lost at ping-pong? Think about the madness of that for a second. Time's up! Life is too short to waste any of it on such trivialities.

FREEDOM AND RESPONSIBILITY: Childhood is life's training wheels. During that period, we are all on a short leash and must toe the line in any number of ways, overseen by parents, teachers, and other adults in authority. When kids play Little League baseball and argue with the umpire, it gets back to their parents. So, too, if they misbehave in the classroom.

But then there's adulthood. We're free! Free…to act like as big a jerk as others will allow.

This becomes a problem for some otherwise well-raised "children." You're thirty years old and you cheat at golf. Nobody's really watching you. Or maybe they *are* watching you, but they don't want to start a ruckus by calling you out on it. Ah, freedom! Freedom to be a jerk.

The Zen Game way of life is not to think of existence as an opportunity to get away with things. That is not at all noble. Yes, we *can* get away with a lot here in Big Person World, but is that Right?

No, it isn't. I believe there are karmic prices to pay for such transgressions.

Don't cheat on your taxes. Don't cheat at golf. Don't cheat on your spouse. Don't do anything bad simply because you feel no one is watching closely enough and you might be able to get away with it. Imagine the shame if you *don't*. Imagine how you will feel if you do get caught. Is it really worth it? Is shaving a stroke off your golf score one afternoon worth losing the respect of everyone in the club? I say nay.

It is natural to make mistakes along the bumpy rode of life. I am guilty of them like everyone else. It's called being human. Let's also hope those errors in judgment become fewer and fewer as you get older and, hopefully, wiser. To be mature and to feel truly proud of yourself, live life as if you are always being watched. Even if no one else sees your actions, you see them. And of all people, why would you want to let yourself down? Be honorable and true to humanity itself. That approach is all eight "Rights" wrapped into one.

NEATNESS COUNTS: A person walks into a public place, says "What a dump!" and then proceeds to unwrap a stick of gum, stick it in her mouth, and toss the wrapper on the ground.

It's true! People act this way all the time. Sure, there are some public spaces where cleanliness is not enough of a priority—we've all experienced those gas station bathrooms in the middle of nowhere that haven't been cleaned since the Ford administration. But too many times it is we, the public, who make the places we inhabit uninhabitable.

I've also seen people get up from a table in a restaurant and leave their chairs in the middle of the room in a pell-mell fashion, where they can be an obstacle for other people or servers to get around. Gee, how much leg room does one need to get up from a table? Then again, I wonder how much energy it takes to replace the chair *at* the table. Perhaps after a high-calorie meal, common sense flies out the window. Who knows? The last time I visited a friend's child in preschool, I was impressed by how all the children pushed in their chairs when they got up from their desks. It's amazing the common-sense things we lose or forget as we get "older and wiser."

You should make yourself comfortable wherever you are, but only to the extent that it does not infringe on others. Set a high standard for yourself. Think of how you act when you invite your boss and his or her significant other over for a nice dinner, rather than how you act late at night in your family room, wearing old sweats and eating with your hands. You're on much better behavior when the boss is over, right? Even if you're not the world's neatest neat freak, I bet you try extra hard to clean things up and make the best appearance possible of both yourself and your home.

For optimal self-esteem, why not always take the time and effort to be your best self, even if no one is watching? Why should you be your best only when you are with someone else? Don't you count? By honoring yourself and continually embracing your best self, you will not just be going through the motions when you are with other people. Instead, you will always be living your highest vision of yourself. Now that's powerful!

A LITTLE HELPS A LOT: When I reflect upon the Noble Eightfold Path, I think to myself, What is more important, that which we do to make ourselves better or that which we do to make the world a better place? Some might say that the two are inextricable, that by improving ourselves we *are* improving the world. I can't argue with that.

What I find in talking with people, however, is that they are often filled with large and bold beliefs but feel inadequate about the "footprint" they have left upon the sands of time. "I didn't cure cancer, I didn't lead a nation, I didn't earn billions and then give it all away to the poor and oppressed."

The important thing is to do *something*. Open your newspaper. Check out the "public notices," "community calendar," or other sections of the paper that list various requests for community participation and volunteers. These may include "walks for hunger," "community cleanups," or "reading to lower-income preschoolers." I'll bet you've whizzed past that section of the newspaper a million times without even thinking about it. But here you are, thinking you're a failure because you've never done anything significant for your fellow man and woman.

So do something. Yes, yes, I know; none of those listings look very interesting. They don't have "Nobel Peace Prize" written all over them. So what? Instead of doing nothing, you'll be doing something positive. Give a little or a lot of your time. When you've helped clear the brush from a historic cemetery, you can look at your labors and say, "Hey, I did a good thing today." The same goes for making balloon animals for kids at a cancer center or raising money and awareness for clean oceans. In addition, you will find yourself surrounded by good people who appreciate you, and isn't that the greatest feeling in the world?

Don't get hung up on the enormity of the world and its problems. Do a little something and feel good about it. If everyone did that, things would improve a lot.

DONATE: I like to think of myself as a "green" person. "Reduce, reuse, recycle!" The "reduce" part applies to all the "junk" that collects in our homes. But as the saying goes, "One man's trash is another man's treasure." A friend of mine told me about cleaning out his mother-in-law's garage. Decades' worth of pure, unadulterated junk! They dragged it out to the street to await the garbage man. Do you know what happened during the twelve overnight hours that passed before the garbage man came? Half of it was gone! People drove by, saw what was there, and went rummaging through it, finding things they valued.

I'll bet there is very little you have that is not of some use to somebody. If you're not using it and you want to unburden yourself of clutter, consider that there are people in this world who might find value in what you have. Thrift shops, often run by charities, are a great place to unload. I've even heard of towns that have reclamation centers where fix-it men repair old, broken appliances and other items and sell them cheaply. Instead of tossing that old microwave, perhaps you can give it to a place where someone who cannot afford a new one will appreciate being able to pick one up for pennies. Shoppers at these places may include college students, fixed-income people, the working poor. Don't incinerate or put into the local landfill things that someone else could put to use.

When it comes to being philanthropic, some of us are wealthy enough to write out big checks. Others have time on their hands and donate that. Both of these are wonderful, wonderful things. But there is this third option—donating unused household items—that we rarely think of, and it is perfect for the person who is working long hours just trying to make ends meet. Donate items that are no longer of use to you, and notice how good you will feel about it.

SHARED RESPONSIBILITIES: In a sense, shared responsibility is what life is all about on this earth. We are all global neighbors who have a role to play. Society itself is about how we share duties so that we can spread out responsibility and avoid total chaos.

Roommates, families, and couples all must share responsibilities. I could write an entire book about being a good spouse, family member, or roommate when it comes to the division of labor. I am also sure that everyone has at least one horror story about having to share space with some selfish dingbat who felt he or she had no responsibility except to breathe and make messes for the other person to clean up.

I once read an interesting article in the paper about shared responsibility. It was so long ago that I don't know where I saw it, but here is what I remember about it: The article was encouraging men to put more effort into working around the house. By doing so, they would be the one to reap the greatest reward from their effort—not their partner, as one would initially suppose. The author's point was that when household work is divided up evenly, everyone is happier. Wives and girlfriends are much happier, there is more sex and better sex, and there is less arguing. The conclusion was that housework is not just about women; it's also about men.

Now, what do you do with the person who does not want to meet you halfway with the household chores? First and foremost, it requires diplomacy and a calm but direct confrontation. As I've mentioned in discussions of other issues, it is important to focus *solely* on the topic at hand and nothing more. You will have a greater chance of finding a solution if you avoid bringing up every annoyance you've had with this person from the day you met him or her. For the highest good of all, you need to focus on one problem at a time.

I have found that the best way to confront people is with the sandwich method—which, unfortunately, does not involve pastrami or any actual food. I don't know who invented it, but believe me, it is simple and it works. Here is the process: First you give the person a compliment. There is always something good you can say about a person. It is important for good rapport that you always try to be sincere with your comments and compliments. Next, you must tell them in a constructive way what bothers you (the list may be a mile long, but try to rein yourself in a bit). Don't speak in generalities, such as "You are so messy." People will understand you better if you give them an actual example of their messiness. Finally, leave the person with some positive words. For example, if your daughter forgets to clean up after dinner, you can say, "Sweetie, I'm so proud of your progress at school, but just because you are very busy, let's not forget to clean up after you eat—and that includes putting your dish, glass, and silverware in the dishwasher. When you finish cleaning up, let's watch some television together."

As I mentioned before, it is so common for people to tolerate, tolerate, tolerate and then finally explode, spewing out every annoying thing the other person has done to them over the past month or so. This always degenerates into total negativity. The person feels attacked and so attacks back. Pretty soon, you have two people doing nothing more than acting and sounding silly as a conversation that should have been about doing the dishes degenerates into one about bathroom habits, eating habits, general hygiene, fashion sense, musical taste, etc.

AND IN CONCLUSION...

RIGHT VIEW
RIGHT INTENTION
RIGHT SPEECH
RIGHT ACTION
RIGHT LIVELIHOOD
RIGHT EFFORT
RIGHT MINDFULNESS
RIGHT CONCENTRATION

In this book we've identified numerous ways to be "cordial," "respectful," and "civil." Should you discard these methods if they sometimes fail to work? I say no. We've also discussed what to do when confronted with rudeness and other affronts. Will these tactics always be successful? No, they will not. There is no panacea for all that is difficult. But the beauty of life is that you are the captain of your own adventure, and with the Zen Game, you learn to be a better navigator through the challenges that life presents.

Still, I do have to warn you: The Zen Game is addictive. The more you use it, the more you will see positive results. And the more positive results you see, the more you will want to use it. With the Zen Game, you will always look and feel like a winner because of the personal pride and satisfaction it will bring to you in almost every situation.

The Zen Game is for the person who wants to take control of his or her life. When you become a practitioner of the Zen Game, you will instantly notice other people's lack of Zen Game and feel compassion for them. The people you think of as "troublemakers," the ones who treat you with disrespect, are not bad people. They just lack understanding. They do not appreciate that we are all connected and that what one person does has a concatenating effect on everyone. Accepting all people for who they are, where they are on their journey through life, and where they want to go is the kindest thing you can do for both them and yourself. The Zen Game reminds you that being positive and proactive is the route to happiness and success.

I know people who focus every day on the idea that life is a struggle. They whine and complain. They tear down friends, family, and all of mankind. They point their finger at specific people and say, "This man has it easy in life. Why does he have it all and I have nothing!" But when you focus on struggle, you will always see struggle. If you are critical and envious of others, you will always find something to criticize and envy with everyone you meet. These are the people who see life as a game with "winners" and "losers." They become so focused on "winning," within their limited understanding of the word, that they are willing to sell their souls to do so. They think this is the only way to get ahead in life.

It's not what happens to you in life that's important, but rather how you deal with it. If you think life is good and feel grateful and blessed for what you have (as little or as much as it may be), then I would say, "Congratulations!" You are living your life with the Zen Game perspective. If you *don't* feel that life is good and you see it as a constant uphill struggle, don't fret. You have the power to change that situation right now. Just by reading this book, you have shifted your energy and consciousness for the better.

Aristotle said, "We are what we repeatedly do. Excellence, then, is not an act, but a habit." By cultivating the art of the Zen Game, you lift your own spirits *and* the spirits of other people. This cultivation enriches relationships and allows you to have a powerful impact on others. The more you do it, as Aristotle would imply, the more it becomes a habit and the less you actually have to think about it. When you adopt these behaviors, the Zen Game becomes who you are. It builds on itself.

This book is not about "the big things." There is no grand plan or call to action to solve the problems of peace, energy, or disease. I cannot speak to those things, but what I can speak to are the smaller issues that collectively impact upon your happiness and fulfillment. When you reciprocate social invitations or dress properly, you are placing yourself in a better position to be taken more seriously. When you give up gossiping or making others feel bad about themselves, you will have more civilized dialogues about any number of larger issues.

Think of it this way: Scientists have proven that all human bodies are made up of the same elements and that everything in the universe, at a subatomic level, is made up of energy. But even though we all consist of the same chemical elements, we all radiate at different frequencies of light and energy through the "Law of Attraction." According to this law, what you send out through your thoughts, words, and actions invariably will reflect back to you. Basically, this means that a positive person will attract more positive people and positive experiences. For example, you never see positive people hanging out with the gossipers or the people who like to belittle others to build themselves up. These negative folks usually mix with other negative-minded people. They are usually the ones who walk around looking miserable, and that's because of the misery they are perpetuating.

In the end, your life's worth will not be measured by your bank account, the size of your yacht, or the number of plaques you have acquired. Have you ever been at a funeral service and heard the clergywoman say, "This man had the biggest yacht in the harbor" or "This woman was so rich that she never wore the same dress twice"? Absolutely not. Why? Because these things obviously are not important, but often this does not appear obvious until it is too late. When you hear of someone who worked eighty hours a week and died of a heart attack, you think to yourself, "What a waste of time!" This man never got to spend time with his loved ones or to enjoy life.

You see, the Zen Game is not an in-your-face power; there is no ego. It's all about positive energy, and nothing is more attractive and infectious than positive energy. What really matters is the many simple kindnesses we show to others. Holding open a door for someone, petting a dog, making a baby smile, or letting a car merge in front of you on a busy road. All the little smiles, thank-yous, and acknowledgments that we exchange with others. These are the things that make ordinary days more meaningful and that will bring you more happiness and success in the long run. Know that each time you use your Zen Game, I and the rest of the world will share the joy of your success!